Cast of Characters

Lais Karaides. She's the tyrannical owner of the House of Lais, a very expensive and exclusive Manhattan beauty salon. Called simply the Kyria (Greek for Madame), she's a striking figure with her long white hair.

M. Maurice. He's pallid yet elegant with a skullcap of shiny black hair. He has the misfortune to be the Kyria's son.

Toni Ney. Director of the Lais exercise program, she's a slender, striking, green-eyed former dancer who still loves the ballet.

Eric Skeets. An advertising copywriter at Lais and a veteran of the Spanish Civil War, he's a handsome young man with a gleaming smile and flyaway eyebrows who likes the ballet and Toni Ney.

Lili Michaud. The "French Lana Turner," she's come to Lais as part of a publicity stunt. Her beauty is matched only by her temper.

Henri Barrat. A young Frenchman, much abused by Lili. He's her impresario. He's also something else.

Alicia Howe. A gossip columnist with an acid tongue whose recurring acne has made her a regular at the House of Lais.

Doctor Winogradow. He's a cadaverous tower of a man with a beautiful beard and a horrible secret. He's the chief chemist at Lais and is on a quest to discover the Perfect Perfume.

Hortense. She's a facial operator at Lais with a talent for gossip and being in the wrong place at the right time.

Doctor Rudoph Berchtold. With that romantic Teutonic scar, he's almost as irresistible to the ladies as he thinks he is. Toni might disagree.

Jeanne. The receptionist at Lais. She's a slim, pretty little blonde with doe-like eyes and a slight Viennese accent.

Mrs. Sterling. Her husband is a dollar-a-year man in Washington. If she can, she'll spend every penny of that dollar.

Mlle. Illona. The salon's manager. Toni is usually late for her Wednesday morning pep talk to the employees.

Captain Andrew ("Limey") Torrent. A detective in the Homicide Squad, he's of English extraction, loves the ballet, and thinks the world of Toni.

Moran. Torrent's right-hand man, he's as amused by the denizens of the House of Lais as he is impressed by his captain.

Mysteries by Lucy Cores

Featuring
Toni Ney-Eric Skeets-Captain Torrent

Painted for the Kill (1943)
Corpse de Ballet (1944)

Non-Series

Let's Kill George (1946)

Painted for the Kill

by Lucy Cores

Introduction by
Tom & Enid Schantz

The Rue Morgue
Boulder / Lyons

For E.K.

Meet Lucy Cores

ONE OF THE MYTHS that refuses to die among modern mystery schol-
ars is the notion that strong independent female sleuths didn't begin to
appear in American crime fiction until the 1970s and 1980s. Nothing, of
course, could be further from the truth. Female authors writing about strong
female sleuths were quite prominent in the genre until the post-World War
II and Korean War era, when male action thrillers, particular in paperback
originals aimed at returning veterans, drove many of them from publish-
ers' lists. Reading tastes, then as now, reflected the general mood of the
country. After years of war, America was ready for a time out. Rosie the
riveter went back home to become Rosie the housewife. It was the abso-
lute nadir of feminism, a time when you could put a television show on the
air called *Father Knows Best* and not risk daily pickets by women's groups.
Mickey Spillane could bed his women and blow 'em away in the same
paragraph, while John D. MacDonald took misogyny and turned into an
art form that most men—and many women—accepted with relish.

But it was an entirely different time for women writers between the
two world wars. Having won the right to vote in 1920, women—and women
writers—were embracing new lifestyles. Women voters may have been
largely responsible for forcing prohibition on the country, but ironically that
doomed "noble experiment" also led to increased public drinking by women,
albeit in the speakeasies that flourished in most major cities. If women
were getting out more, they were also going to college and entering the
labor force. The crash of 1929 didn't halt that movement but rather further fueled it. Times were tough and a paycheck was a paycheck, whoever earned it. And when the war came along and took most of the young
men with it, women assumed even larger roles in society. Detective fiction reflected those changing conditions.

Lucy Cores' inspired creation, Toni Ney, a dancer turned exercise maven, is a prime example of the kind of strong-willed female sleuth that graced the pages of American detective fiction from suffrage to the bomb. She's smart, self-assured, independent, and not afraid to speak her mind. She likes men but doesn't require one to put food on the table. Work means a career, not something to do while waiting for Mr. Right to come along. Still, she's a bit of a romantic. Like many young girls, Toni dreamed of being a ballet dancer, and, like most young girls, she soon realized that while many are called, only a few are chosen. Instead of being devastated, she became an exercise director (today we would probably say aerobics instructor) at a fancy beauty salon (*Painted for the Kill*), before embarking on a second career as an exercise columnist and dance critic for a major Manhattan newspaper (*Corpse de Ballet*). Her powers of observation are especially keen, which is why ballet aficionado Captain Anthony Torrent of New York's Homicide Bureau seeks her out when he needs a fresh perspective on a case. But Toni doesn't look for crimes to solve. She's on the scene in her work capacity when murder strikes in both of her recorded cases. For the most part, she and boyfriend Eric Skeets earn high marks from Captain Torrent for staying in the background, offering insights instead of digging for clues on their own. Of course, you can't always be good (otherwise we'd have nothing but police procedurals and private eye novels) but Toni is usually joined in her ill-advised clue-gathering by the stalwart Eric Skeets, whose heart is in the right place even if his punches don't always land where they should.

If Lucy Cores' books differ any from other mysteries of the day, it's in their playful attitude toward sex. There's nothing particularly salacious—it's more what used to be called slightly "naughty"—in the narrative but the talk is frank, and the sexual peccadillos of the characters and just the right amount of bitchy asides provide much of the books' humor. There are gay characters, as you might expect in books set in the world of the theater and the beauty industry. Cores doesn't dwell on their sexuality, but this was a period in which gays were seldom identified as such in detective fiction, even in passing, and if they were, it was usually as villains, such as the "gunsels" in Dashiell Hammett's *The Maltese Falcon*. In Cores' books some gay characters are bad, some are good, some are just indifferent, but none are pitied, despised or played for laughs—at least no more than any of the other characters are. Much the same spirit can be found in another contemporaneous two-book ballet mystery series (*A Bullet in the Ballet* and *Murder a la Stroganoff*) written in 1938 by Caryl Brahms and S.J. Simon..

Cores dedicates her second Toni Ney book, *Corpse de Ballet*, to Olga Ley, "who knows all about ballet." But we suspect that Olga Ley was also the inspiration for Toni Ney. Aside from the rhyming similarity in their names, Ley was not only a dancer, like Toni, specializing in ballroom as well as ballet, but she was an expert on exercising, eventually writing two major books on the subject. Her own lean, athletic figure matched Toni's. Like Cores, Ley was born in Russia (St. Petersburg) in 1912 and emigrated to the United States after the Russian Revolution and Civil War. In addition to dancing and exercise, she worked as an illustrator (as did Cores) and a costumer designer. She married Willy Ley, a German-born rocket scientist who once tutored Wernher von Braun. Willy Ley fled Germany in 1935 when he learned that Hitler wanted rockets for weapons, not space exploration. Unfortunately, the U.S. government wasn't interested in rocketry and Ley changed careers, becoming one of the foremost science writers of his day. He also dabbled in science fiction, a passion he shared with Olga, a frequent attendee at science fiction conventions, where she dazzled everybody when she appeared in the costume pageants. They passed their interest in science fiction on to their daughter Sandra, who in 1976 edited *Beyond Time*, an anthology of alternate history stories. Olga contributed a story, as did Lucy Cores, whose "Hail to the Chief" speculates that if the Watergate burglars had not been caught, Nixon would not only have served out his second term but would have found a way around the constitutional two-term presidential limit to stay in the White House until 1994.

Lucy Cores was a very versatile writer. In addition to the two Toni Ney mysteries, she published a third comic mystery, *Let's Kill George*, this time a stand-alone, in 1946, before abandoning the form, at least as a writer. She was an avid mystery reader, according to her son Michael, and in her later years particularly admired P.D. James, Ruth Rendell, and Martha Grimes. Among earlier writers, Ngaio Marsh was obviously a favorite. There is a reference to Marsh's Inspector Roderick Alleyn (misspelled, however) in *Painted for the Kill*. Cores was also fond of the classics and once wrote the book and lyrics for an unproduced musical version of Wilkie Collins' *The Moonstone*.

Romance featured in many of her other books, including *Women in Love* (1951), which was based on one of her own early love affairs. The 1952 paperback edition bore the lurid subtitle "She substituted sex for passion." Most of her other romance novels were historicals, including *Destiny's Passion* (1978) and *Fatal Passion* (1989), set in the Regency period. *The Year of December* (1974) chronicles the adventures of Claire

Clairmonte, the onetime mistress of Lord Byron, in Russia. *Katya* (1988) was another novel of romantic suspense set in imperial Russia. There are also elements of mystery in *The Misty Curtain* (1964) in which a young girl attempts to reconnect with her mother, now a princess, who abandoned her as a baby. *The Mermaid Summer* (1971) was set on Martha's Vineyard, where Cores lived for many years, and contained characters easily recognized by her friends there. A short story in *The Saturday Evening Post* was turned into a television series, *The New Loretta Young Show*, which ran during the 1962-63 season. It featured a New York magazine editor who was trying to raise seven children. In addition to her writing, Cores also worked as a book illustrator and graphic designer, notably for Walter J. Black's Classics Club in the early 1940s.

Lucy Cores was born to a middle-class family in Moscow in 1912. For most of her life she thought she had been born in 1914 and only toward the end of her life did she discover the mistake. Since that meant her ninetieth birthday party would be held that much sooner, she was overjoyed. Her family fled Russia after the Communist revolution and she hid out with her mother in Poland and lived for a while in Paris before arriving in the United States in 1921. It's a period of her life that she did not like to remember and refused to discuss. Although her father, Michael Cores, had been a lawyer in Russia, it was not a career he could follow in the United States and he eventually became a professional musician, playing the viola in the NBC Philharmonic under Arturo Toscanini. Her uncle, Alexander Cores, was one of the most celebrated violinists of the twentieth century. Isaac Stern played at his funeral. He was also responsible for teaching comedian Jack Benny how to play the violin badly (Benny could already play it competently). The family musical ability was passed on in full measure to Lucy's younger son, Danny Kortchmar, one of the country's foremost guitarists and a songwriter as well who has played with Jackson Browne, James Taylor, Linda Ronstadt and Carole King (and just about every other legend in the music business) and who today is primarily on the production end of the recording industry.

After learning English, Lucy Cores attended the Ethical Culture School in Manhattan and was graduated from Barnard College. She met and married Emil Kortchmar, the son of Russian Jewish émigrés, in 1942. Although Emil did not go to college first, he attended New York University Law School before he went to work in his father's business, manufacturing screw-machine parts. He eventually took over the business and then sold it in the 1960s, although he continued to run it for the new owners for a time. Until the last year of his life he helped a nephew operate a similar business in New Rochelle. He loved sailing and the family owned several boats over the years. He taught his elder son Michael, who today specializes in restoring old wooden boats, to sail, but Lucy made it clear that sailing was not an activity in which she was interested.

The Kortchmars moved to Larchmont, New York, in 1940s, where Lucy met Frederic Dannay, the half of the Ellery Queen writing team who founded and edited *Ellery Queen's Mystery Magazine*. In 1950, they rented a summer home on Martha's Vineyard, fell in love with the island, and eventually bought a house on North Road where they spent every summer for the rest of their lives. In the 1970s and 1980s they also spent a month or two every winter in Grenada in the West Indies. During those years Lucy made her mark as a formidable poker player and enticed any number of people into joining her in hard-fought Scrabble games. She loved word games and was giving to making puns. She was asked once if she wanted to surf and replied, "They also surf who only stand and wade."

Following Emil's death in 1990, Lucy moved back to Manhattan. She frequently entertained friends and grandchildren in her living room, the focal point of which was a large bowl of M&Ms on the coffee table. She continued to spend her summers on Martha's Vineyard where she swam every day and was a regular at the local library. She died there in her sleep on August 6, 2003, at the age of 91. At the time of her death, she was learning how to use a computer and working on a novel about the Russian poet Alexander Pushkin.

Lucy Cores' sophisticated and charming mysteries are little known today, if only because she survived them by six decades, but they are well worth revisiting. Toni Ney isn't a relic of a forgotten era, trapped forever in the conventions of her time. A few superficial trappings aside, she seems as modern in her outlook as any of today's current female sleuths. The times may change but well-realized characters are never dated.

Tom & Enid Schantz
April 2004
Lyons, Colorado

The editors are grateful to Michael Kortchmar for his very helpful assistance in putting together the biographical portions of this introduction.

Note on the text

This edition contains every word found in the 1943 Duell, Sloan and Pearce hardcover. The Dell Mapback edition published during World War II was severely abridged, although those cuts were not acknowledged. Samples of those cuts are to be found starting on page 188 of this edition.

CHAPTER 1

"HOW ABOUT LUNCH with me? After all, you've just had breakfast with me. After a girl has had breakfast with a man, it's more or less indicated that she should have lunch with him."

Toni Ney quickened her steps, smiling at the speaker. His name was Eric Skeets and he was a slight dark young man with a humorous quirk in his mouth and flyaway eyebrows.

"I'd love to, but I don't really see how I can, today. What with the glamorous Lili coming around and all, the order has been to stand by and make no lunch appointments."

"Worse luck. I've forgotten about today. See, one breakfast with you—and a chancy little one in Childs at that—and I forget our dazzling French visitor. And that in spite of the fact that she's my baby, in a manner of speaking."

"Really?"

"Yes, really. It was my idea to get her to come in for a day at Lais, right off the boat. Neat, eh? We refresh her, style her hair, make a new woman out of her, with photographers watching every inch of the way, and then she flies on to the coast."

"Very neat. Talking about flying, we'd better do that ourselves. I think we're going to be late for the pep talk and I still have to get my work clothes on."

They had come abreast the House of Lais before which paced the brawny doorman dressed like an evzone, his white skirt billowing snowily above his muscular legs, his embroidered red sheepskin-lined jacket bursting on his manly chest. Most people's first thought as they ran into him usually was Greek war relief. But as a matter of fact, long before Hitler's inva-

11

sion had made New York Greece-conscious, the majestic Greek had come to stand for Lais to Fifth Avenue.

"See you later." Toni left her companion, flashed through the door leading to the employees' entrance and was soon running down the stairs to the locker room as fast as her long legs could carry her.

Being late to one of the pep talks which Mlle. Illona, the manager of the salon, inflicted on her helpless employees the first Wednesday of every month was no laughing matter. They were scheduled for 8:30 on the dot—before the salon was actually opened to the clients—and lateness was tantamount to a crime.

No fellow criminal lingered in the lockers. In a moment Toni had thrown on her work clothes: white rayon jersey trunks and bra-top, against which her legs, arms, and midriff, thoughtfully tanned by Lais' sunlamps, seemed browner than ever. She zipped on a white silk pleated skirt with a deep Greek border around its hem, pushed her small feet into sandals, and ran upstairs into the salon.

Lais (the vowels are pronounced to rhyme with *naive* although the vulgar have been known to pronounce the name to rhyme with *pays*) is New York's foremost beauty salon. It pursues a cult that takes a lot out of you and still more out of your pocketbook. But the promise of exclusiveness extended by the lovely show window, where three Greek alabaster horses gallop motionlessly over a miniature beach speckled with jars of Lais' famous Lotos facial, is certainly carried out in its lush interior.

The salon on the main floor, which Toni had entered and was traversing in a hurry, was deserted. Silence—a sacred holy hush—pervaded the tremendous room, carpeted in white, with mirrors gleaming among soft blue draperies that looped gracefully at the ceiling and fell down in column-like folds to the floor. The silence was not only due to the salon's comparatively deserted state. Even in the busiest hours, it was so still at Lais that you could hear a hundred-dollar bill drop—and often did. It was a policy stringently enforced. The slim nymphs who skimmed noiselessly over the white carpet, or, like blessed damozels, bent down from the counters to douse the customers with magic perfume and to heft jars of precious ointments in scarlet-tipped hands, never raised their voices. Sometimes an uninitiated customer would stand for ten minutes before one of the nymphs, watching her rosy lips move in what seemed a silent incantation, while what she had been saying with angelic patience all that time was, "Does madame wish to have her package wrapped up in our special scented gift paper?"

All the nymphs were in the theater in back of the salon listening to

Mlle. Illona's talk. Only Miss Gorham at the appointment desk was at her post. She flashed a significant look at hurrying Toni and raised her eyes heavenward to a clock, whose hands stood implacably at 8:34.

Toni sidled into the theater, where Mlle. Illona was holding forth. She was a statuesque blonde with polished hair becomingly disposed around a face like a beautiful egg, completely smooth and devoid of any expression. Her musical voice droned on in a familiar monotone to which most of the listeners attended in a spirit of hopeless resignation, except for some of the toadies in front, who determinedly kept on an expression of rapturous attention. Toni noticed that the authorities had turned out in full force. From where she stood she could notice M. Maurice and by the subdued and slightly harassed expression on his face she guessed that he was seated next to his redoubtable mother.

M. Maurice's special misfortune was being the boss's son. That served to sour his character considerably. He spent most of his time running around the establishment doing odd things in various departments, looking somewhat like the White Rabbit, when he wasn't being browbeaten by his parent. In common with everybody else at Lais, he shared a nasty liking for gossip and backbiting and would often be found in the midst of a squabble, casting aspersions with both hands just like the rest of the girls. Tony often ran into him in his natty artist's smock, staggering under a load of new products which he would take up to his studio on the sixth floor to photograph or paint. Apparently he used to be a pretty good artist, though not good enough to avoid being submerged at Lais. The fact that he was the heir apparent to Lais and all the wonders thereof made little impression, probably because by no stretch of imagination could you think of Kyria needing an heir. There was something discouragingly indestructible about her. Periodically he would appear behind his mother at some cocktail party given for the press or the clients, looking as though he were being drawn in her wake by some mighty undertow, pallid and elegant, with an extravagant buttonhole and a faintly satiric smile on his face.

Next to him towered the cadaverous figure of Dr. Winogradow, the chemist responsible for most of Lais' boons to womankind. He looked somewhat like Boris Karloff masquerading as Paul Muni—that is, over his corpse-like makeup he had apparently glued a beautiful beard. His tall figure with its bent back and scooped-out chest was bent into a dollar sign.

Farther back she spotted Eric Skeets, who was trying to catch her eye. He had apparently saved a seat for her. Toni smiled her thanks but declined to join him, not wishing to draw Illona's attention. The latter, who was blind as a bat, at that moment put on her harlequin glasses to consult her notes and saw Toni.

"Good *afternoon,* Toni," she remarked pointedly, drawing thereby a snicker from the sycophants in the second row.

Toni, who was thinking of something else, started and replied politely, "Good afternoon, Miss Illona."

The snicker this time came from the last row.

"As I was saying," Miss Illona went on, "it's up to us to make our clients feel as if they were at home. We must not be remiss about all the little points of courtesy that mean so much. You are expected to meet the client at the door when she comes in and to accompany her to the door when she leaves."

Toni suppressed a smile. As a result of this much repeated edict, every client who entered Lais was startled by the pack of salesgirls who rushed spasmodically toward her in a sort of a race, with the winner gasping triumphantly, "Good morning, madame."

"But at the same time you must remember that relationship to the customer is not a personal one. Thus," said Mlle. Illona, peering hard in Toni's direction with her beautiful myopic eyes, "under no circumstances must you call a client by her first name. Such a situation simply mustn't arise. Nor must you discuss your personal affairs with the client, although you are expected to respectfully listen if she condescends to tell you about hers. It has been brought to my attention that a client gave one of the girls on the fourth floor a present for her baby. We, of course, don't mind your receiving presents from clients. What I would like to know is how did that client know that the operator had a baby? That is precisely the sort of thing we want to avoid.

"Today is an important day for Lais. Mlle. Lili Michaud, the celebrated French star, will do us the honor to visit our establishment. There will be press photographers and reporters. We must, therefore, put our best foot forward. I want each of you to undergo mental inspection before going to your posts today, asking yourself, 'Am I in every way a fit representative of Lais?' I noticed yesterday one of the salesgirls wearing a nail polish that, firstly, did not match the lipstick and, secondly, was not a Lais product! The girl confessed to me that the nail polish was purchased at Woolworth. Now really, girls—outside of the rank disloyalty, suppose a customer liked the nail polish and wanted to know its name! Can you imagine the horrible situation in which this would place all of us?"

Mlle. Illona looked at her notes for a second. "And now we are coming to a very important question. It has been reported to me that many of you have been heard discussing the war with the clients. One of the young ladies on the third floor remarked to a client about her sympathy with General de Gaulle and the Free French. And while walking through the second floor yesterday I saw that one of the employees actually had a map on the wall of her dressing room." Toni grinned a little as a few eyes again turned her way. "Needless to say, I expect that map to be taken down immediately. We must keep war away from Lais!"

The words died away in an awed silence. Then a hand shot up. Mlle. Illona nodded indulgently and a girl from the third floor wanted to know what to do if a client persisted in talking war.

"That," answered Miss Illona, "is of course a problem. Your task in that case is to turn her thoughts in another direction, by mentioning one of our beautiful new products, such as our wrinkle-erasing cream, for example. Your point of view must be that in this time of emergency, a woman can best contribute to the war effort by keeping up her morale and being as beautiful as she can be."

Another hand went up in front. Decked with flashing diamonds, it beckoned imperiously. Illona ran down the stairs like a startled doe and bent down obsequiously before a white-haired, statuesque woman in the front row.

Lais Karaides, known to the trade and to her employees and clients as the Kyria, was still a beautiful woman, although everybody had long ago stopped guessing at her age. The profile she presented to Toni's eyes had the startling regularity of a cameo. Yet the smoothness of her skin was not young, not natural; at close quarters you had the impression that her skin had been pulled taut, the slackness tucked away somewhere behind her ears. The pure white strands of her hair were artfully coiled and held in place in true Greek fashion with just one pin of green malachite, and a thick rope of pearls was wound in the coil.

Illona came back to the platform to continue her talk now on the crass materialistic plane. The laundry bill this month, she confided, was much too large. The girls did not take proper care of their uniforms. The product advertised this month, and to which the customers' attention was to be constantly called, was the herbal bath cream. The price was merely twenty dollars for a half-pound jar and it was to be pointed out to the customers that terribly expensive ingredients went into it and that the bottle was designed by a famous artist and was definitely an ornament for madame's bathroom. The treatment of the month was, of course, still the Winogradow pack. The monthly prize for the best salesmanship went to Hortense, who had sold twenty jars of the Attic Paste. It was not a terribly good record and they were only awarding a prize to Hortense because nobody had done better. All around the salesmanship could be better. . .

Here the Kyria's deep, queerly accentless voice filled the theater. "It's easy enough to get the customer to buy the products we advertise in newspapers, after my advertising department has done the selling for you. You people are supposed to dispose of the stuff that isn't so well known." The complaining note deepened. "Sometimes I wonder what is the matter with you people. You are part of the best salon on Fifth Avenue and you are handling the most salable products in the world to the best customers in the world. You just don't make the most of your opportunity. That to me shows an appalling lack of appreciation and loyalty. You must see every client that comes in as—yes, as a gold mine—and it's your duty to get the most out of it. In these days when taxes strain all our resources. . ."

Toni listened to the sorrowing voice and fought an overpowering desire to yawn. The Kyria's monetary difficulties were vast indeed. She had paid a million dollars' worth of income tax last year, after unsuccessfully asking for a sizable exemption on account of labor troubles.

Publicity releases from the advertising department always pictured the Kyria as a woman not moved by any worldly considerations but merely engaged on a lofty quest for beauty. They neglected to add that she found a special sort of beauty in large amounts of money.

The Kyria having come to the end of her speech, Illona said in hushed tones, "You will now return to your posts," as if nothing more could be added now that the Kyria had spoken. There was a sound of scraping chairs and a subdued hum of conversation. The pep talk was over at exactly 9:00.

The haggard Dr. Winogradow shambled past Toni, lost in thought. On his way to the door he stumbled over Toni's foot and stopped for a moment to regard it with such cold malevolence that the limb in question felt momentarily chilled.

"My God," said Eric Skeets behind her, "a gloomy sort of Joe, isn't he? What's he doing here? I've never seen him at any of these meetings before."

"Picking a victim, I daresay," said Toni. "He's experimenting with a hair dye."

She grinned, remembering the anguished wails of the victims who were occasionally sent up to Dr. Winogradow's laboratory to be experimented with. The forty Athenian maidens sent into the Minotaur's maze had nothing on them. There was some justification for their alarm, outside of Dr. Winogradow's unprepossessing appearance. Two or three of the victims had the products tried out on them while still in an uncertain stage. One of them had been subjected to a lip bleach which promptly suffered a sea change, leaving her temporarily with bright green whiskers. Later, and in an improved stage, this preparation reaped vast success under the name of lemon verbena.

"Incidentally," Toni inquired as they made their way through the crowd that surged over the salon and stopped to wait near the elevator, "what's all this strange harping on loyalty? I've noticed lately that every time you breathe the wrong way somebody talks to you darkly about loyalty."

"I think I know why, though I shouldn't tell you this." Eric Skeets lowered his voice. "Point is that all during the fall season our competitors have been scooping us. Every time we had a campaign all worked out, it appeared elsewhere. The Kyria seems to think it's an inside job and she's fit to be tied."

Toni nodded. "I thought it was funny how all these creams came in sort of quietly. Do they know . . . ?"

"Nope. We all held our breaths about that disgusting Winogradow treatment and the herbal bath cream last month. There was no trouble, however, so whatever it was must be over now. But the old lady is still stewing about it." Eric Skeets grinned irreverently. "These, by the way, are state secrets. I'm just telling them to you in order to impress you and to show my devotion. And that reminds me. I'd better prepare to impress la belle Michaud. I'm on a reception committee of sorts. So long."

Young Mr. Skeets made for the back elevator which was supposed to be used by those working on the fifth and sixth floors. Toni got into the front elevator with a little smile on her wide mouth. This friendship between her and Eric Skeets had caused many comments in the salon. As in every organization there were rigid caste distinctions in Lais. Usually the advertising department, which was on the fifth floor, considered the lower floors beneath it in every possible sense of the word, and even if Toni, as physical director and the head of a department, rated infinitely higher than the plain or garden variety of the salon employee, snagging a copywriter was still an achievement.

Her first acquaintance with Skeets came during one of her demonstrations for the clients, when he had taken the place of Illona, who had come down with laryngitis. His running commentary to her exercises, although of necessity impromptu, was fairly serious. At the end, however, he lost his head. As she lay on the floor pedaling madly while a hundred overweight matrons watched her every move, she felt her instep grasped by a firm hand. "Hold it, Mlle. Toni." He turned to the audience. "I can think of no better time to show you exactly what I mean. You have all, Mesdames, read Plato." Toni, lying in a particularly cramped position, grinned cynically. "You know his theory of ideas—all things having an ideal prototype on which they model themselves. Well, ladies, this is an ideal leg." He ran his hand down it impersonally. "This is what we all must work for."

The stylishly bonneted, coiffed heads dipped in approval, and young Mr. Skeets released the ideal leg, his dark eyes alight with mischief and mirth. Toni, retaining her impassive mask with some difficulty, decided then and there that she liked him even if he worked at Lais.

The second floor was quiet. Odette, the receptionist who, with three others, doubled as Toni's assistant in the gym, was doing her morning telephoning. She was saying with tremendous dignity, "This is *not* a personal call, operator. Of course it's a business call," and a moment later, "Hello, sweetie." Toni looked over the mail and the schedule of appointments. There was a note to be posted, requiring everybody on the floor who as yet hadn't taken the Winogradow pack to do so at their first convenience and report the results to the manager of the salon.

The schedule for the day was a pretty heavy one. Outside of Lili Michaud, there were at least three "difficult" clients.

Miss Gwendolyn Browne, who came at 1:30, was one. Miss Gwendolyn Browne was a buxom young heiress of eighteen. Her mental age was that of a child of eight, and she liked to play with her doll, Maria, which she brought with her to the salon. These handicaps notwithstanding, she was to be married in a month to a bright and ambitious young man in her father's office. Toni's task was to see what she could do in the way of teaching Miss Browne some sort of physical coordination so that the bride's journey to the altar would not be attended by any minor misfortunes. It was a strenuous and heartbreaking job, made only a little easier by the fact that Miss Browne was really fond of Toni and tried hard to please her.

Miss Alicia Howe, on the other hand, was in full possession of her mental faculties, as could be easily verified by reading her syndicated column, "Howe's Tricks." The trouble with her was simply that she was a neurotic woman with a nasty temper, and she was not fond of Toni.

Although cordially hated by the salon employees who had the misfortune to come in contact with her, Alicia Howe was admittedly the best customer Lais had. Her spare figure in fabulous tweeds, surmounted by a severe John Frederick bonnet, strode through the hushed halls of Lais every day. She acted as if she owned the place and even had a room all her own. Although preferring steam baths and face treatments, she occasionally took exercise. In the skintight bathing suit she wore for the occasion, she looked painfully thin, with attenuated legs and a flat, meager chest—and she knew it and resented it bitterly. Nevertheless she did little about it, but went through her exercises in a perfunctory and halfhearted manner. Toni knew better than to urge her to further efforts by word or touch. Alicia Howe could not bear to be touched. Toni had found that out the first time she came in.

"Take your hands off me, damn you!" The columnist had snarled and pushed her away viciously. Toni still remembered how shocked she had been. They had looked at each other for a moment and then she had said dryly, "This will be all for today." Howe had scrambled to her feet, her eyes narrowed in fury, and Toni had thought, "This is where I lose my job. She's going to slap my face and I am going to punch her in the jaw." But nothing happened and the exercise lessons continued. It was mind over matter or something. Only Toni was careful never to touch her again.

Then of course there was Mrs. Chester Sterling III, a rather pretty, feather-headed woman in her forties, who chattered like a magpie, sometimes uttering such incredible nonsense as to stagger even Toni, and who drenched money in perfume before giving it to the girl she wanted to tip.

The others were the usual brand of clients, whose hips or thighs or derrieres were running away with them. Toni ticked them off, one by one, and went to her room, where she took the offending map off the wall and stuck it into one of the drawers of the toilette table in which she kept her exercise forms. She also decided to forestall further criticism from the reproachful Mlle. Illona by fixing up her face.

Toni surveyed her reflection gravely. Once the Kyria had remarked to her irritably, "*Ma foi,* child, why can't you have a face like everybody else here? You could look pretty if you really wanted to." Toni wasn't sure that she wanted to. There certainly was nothing pretty about the dark, impassive face, with the high, slightly bulging forehead, perversely accentuated by the pompadour of black hair. The lifted eyebrows and wide, faintly sullen mouth gave her a somewhat arrogant expression, relieved by the green eyes in which there seemed to smolder a spark of obscure amusement. She could see how people might find it an irritating face with its look of reserve and cool, secret mockery. Well, let us say provoking, thought Toni, smiling.

While applying a bit of the Nile-green eye shadow to the edges of her eyelids—a device that helped to enhance that Egyptian look—she listened to the noises outside. A cheery baritone—that was Dr. Berchtold coming in—was accompanied by a chorus of feminine sopranos cooing a rapturous good morning. Toni, applying Lais' Fury-Red lipstick to her rather wide mouth, frowned. Why was it that bounders like Dr. Rudi, as he was affectionately called (Toni herself called him, less affectionately, Rudi the Rat), invariably appealed to women, even decent little girls like Jeanne?

Hortense, a facial operator from the third floor, poked her thin, fox-like face around the door.

"May I come in?" She whisked in without waiting for permission. Her sharp eyes darted around the room and she grinned. "Ah, I see—you have taken the map down. Listen, I'm going to smoke a cigarette. I need one." She sat down and lit a cigarette swiftly. "You won't squawk on me, will you, Toni? I know you aren't the sort."

"I'm sorry that I can't truthfully return the compliment," Toni remarked coolly.

"What do you mean?"

Toni bent forward to repair an eyebrow, "Strange how Mlle. Illona knows all about people calling clients by their first names. One would think she was there."

"Listen, I never–"

"Skip it, my pet. What brings you down here?"

The employees of Lais were discouraged from leaving their floors except when sent down by a customer. In order to prevent infractions, the doors leading to the exit stairs had special locks put on them so that people could get out and go downstairs but could not come out on any floor from the stairs. They had to take the front elevator, which was run by one of the "trusties," a term Toni coined, and everybody gleefully used, for people who were encouraged by the management to spy on the other girls. If anyone used the elevator too much for interfloor travel, a little talk with the management followed.

"I want to borrow some cream from down here. We're all out of it."

"You've been visiting us a lot lately," Toni remarked idly. "Aren't you afraid that Marthe will report you?" Marthe being the current trusty on the elevator.

Hortense laughed and inhaled the smoke deeply. "Nope. I've got some-thing on her, but good!" She met Toni's quizzical eye and had the grace to look a little embarrassed. She changed the subject quickly. "I am so nervous my hands are shaking. I'm supposed to give the facial to Lili Michaud. It's a responsibility. I don't know why all the other girls are so peeved at me for getting her. I'm sure I didn't ask for her."

"That's right," said Toni. "Always be sweet to the right people and have plenty of nice stories to tell Mlle. Illona and you'll be sure to get what you want without having to ask for it."

Hortense changed the subject again. "Here comes your friend Jeanne. Sneaking down to see Dr. Rudi again." She waited for comment. Toni made none. "She's going to get herself fired if she doesn't look out. You better tell her if you're so fond of her. Howe saw her making calf's eyes at the doctor, and she didn't like it a bit. 'Common little thing, isn't she?' she says to me later." Hortense was obviously making an attempt to imitate someone's Boston accent. Toni ignored her, turning with an affectionate smile to hail a slim little blonde with doe-like eyes who had paused diffidently in the doorway.

"Good morning, Toni," she responded. There was a faint slur of accent in her speech.

"Sorry you couldn't make it last night," Toni said. "We missed you. It was sort of a nice brawl." Her quick eyes noticed the irresistible childish blush staining the transparent skin. "What can we do for you?"

"Not a thing," Jeanne said quickly. "I—I'm just bringing down Mrs. Caldwell's exercise chart, that Dr. Rudi left upstairs yesterday."

Toni extended her hand. "That really belongs in my files," she said casually. "I want a look at it myself."

"But the doctor wants to look—"

"I'll give it to him myself later."

Jeanne surrendered the chart with the utmost reluctance. Her lower lip pushed out a little like a stubborn child's. Before she had a chance to say anything Hortense broke in.

"You haven't come down to make another date with Dr. Rudi, have you, dearie? Look out and don't get in trouble with his girlfriend. She'll scratch your eyes out."

Another date, Toni thought. That's bad.

"That hag," said Jeanne with the withering scorn of extreme youth. Her blue eyes dilated and darkened. "And Alicia Howe is *not* his girlfriend. Why, I've heard him laugh at her. Besides, what can she do to me?"

"She can take your job away from you, and he can take something else from you."

Toni got up, took the cigarette out of Hortense's mouth and crushed it in an empty cream jar. "Supposing we all mind our business. Jeanne is old enough and smart enough not to make a fool out of herself over a man twice her age with the reputation of a petticoat chaser." She smiled a little at the uncertain look, half-dismay, half-anger, on Jeanne's face. "And

Hortense—don't you think they are going to miss you upstairs, or do you have something on everybody there?"

"I know when I am not wanted," said Hortense, getting up. "But it's no use talking to her, Toni. She's got it bad."

"I am coming with you," said Jeanne in her soft breathless voice, avoiding Toni's eyes. "I think I have something to do."

It's bad, Toni thought again after they had gone. Apparently having Jeanne transferred upstairs hadn't helped much. Jeanne was only a year younger than Toni, but there was a naive helplessness about the little Viennese that aroused a feeling of maternal protectiveness in Toni. Poor little Jeanne, with her childishly sun-streaked blond hair and too-slender neck—she *would* seem a tasty dish to a wolf like Dr. Berchtold. And since she herself had gotten her the job of receptionist at Lais, Toni had felt responsible for her.

Accordingly there was a touch of grimness in her manner when she knocked at Dr. Berchtold's door.

"Come in," said a magnetic baritone. Its owner, seated at the desk, smiled at her charmingly. He was a tall, fair man whose jovial expression somehow failed to reach his cold blue eyes. The strong virile line of his jaw was only slightly blurred by a suspicion of a jowl, and a scar ran down his cheek. Toni was accustomed to hearing her clients raving about Dr. Rudi's romantic scar. "He must have gotten it in one of those student duels at Heidelberg." She herself thought a street brawl in Munich more likely.

"Ah, Toni. I can do something for you, I hope." Some people, thought Toni, had a knack of making everything they said sound as if there was another meaning behind it.

She laid Mrs. Caldwell's chart down on his desk. "You wanted to see this," she said. But after he took it, she lingered until he looked up. A smug gleam came to his eyes. "You have something else to tell me, eh?" At her reluctant nod he got up and closed the door. On his way back to the desk, his arm slid around her expertly. Toni slipped out of his embrace.

"This isn't what I meant at all," she said, like Alfred Prufrock, rapidly moving behind the desk. "Frankly, Doctor, I don't feel like running around tables right now."

"So early in the morning and already tired? Perhaps a metabolism test is in order . . ."

"Dr. Berchtold, I want to talk to you about Jeanne."

"Oh, yes?" He sat down at his desk again and smiled at her good-naturedly. "What about little Jeanne?"

"Well, to put it vulgarly, you've been trying to make her, haven't you, Doctor? It's been bad enough when it was right here where nothing much could happen, but I have an impression that you have been taking her out."

"And is that any of your business, Toni?" He still smiled, but his eyes had grown colder.

"I'm pretty fond of Jeanne and I don't like to think of her getting hurt."

"Come, Toni, you sound like a little old maid. I've always thought you were a sophisticated girl. A little—shall we say—experience is good for a young girl."

"You are speaking as a doctor, I presume?" Toni inquired cynically. "Seriously, I want you to leave Jeanne alone. I mean it. I'd like to have your promise that you won't make any more dates with her."

"Ultimatums, eh?" Dr. Berchtold said softly. "And how are you going to make me do all those things?"

"Well," Toni hesitated. "I was appealing to your better nature. If you haven't any, why I really don't know what I can do except," she laughed prettily, "maybe give all the circumstances to Miss Howe to put in her column."

This broadside delivered, Toni turned around and walked out of the office. Once outside she shook her head at herself ruefully. It certainly was far from wise to make an enemy of Dr. Berchtold. He was quite a power at Lais and very close to the Kyria herself. Besides, Toni had no illusions on the score. If Jeanne wanted badly enough to act like a lovesick little fool she certainly couldn't stop her. At least, said Toni to herself, I have done all I could.

At that point Odette came over to announce that "your ten o'clock is here." Toni's ten o'clock, a large but hopeful lady wearing a monogrammed cape over her exercise outfit, followed close upon her heels.

"Good morning, Miss Toni," she said brightly. "I'm getting measured today, aren't I? I bet I'll surprise you!"

Like hell you will, thought Toni eyeing her rotund contours grimly. Aloud she said, "That will be nice, Mrs. Glendenning. Let's see how well we can do today."

The day at Lais had begun.

CHAPTER 2

LILI MICHAUD came to Lais at 10:30 with the joyous impunity of a spring breeze. Her yellow curls flying from beneath a small mink toque, she walked through the sacred hush of the outer salon with the swinging, lilting stride of a woman accustomed to being followed by a retinue. Her retinue this time consisted of her impresario, a slim, pallid young man with black hair and the longest sootiest eyelashes, and a small crowd of reporters and photographers with notebooks and cameras poised. She was greeted by the Kyria herself in the manner of an elder deity greeting a young and giddy Venus. And she gave a dazzling smile to young Mr. Skeets, who had put himself in charge of the proceedings, and a slightly more restrained one to M. Maurice, who was also vaguely hovering in the Kyria's train.

The first impression of the "French Lana Turner" was that of undiluted youth and radiance. A more careful analysis showed that her face with its somewhat sharp features had the petulant charm of a gamine. Her eyes were the innocent limpid blue of a convent novice, or a Persian kitten, but her body was that of a practiced little courtesan. You sensed immediately that that was the commodity on the market and that it was currently on display. She threw off her mink coat with the air of discarding the last veil, and one of the photographers whistled involuntarily. Her black dress had apparently been simonized on to her; the décolleté was distractingly low but discreetly veiled by a yoke of smoke-thin chiffon. Her slim wrists were weighed down by exotic heavy bracelets; her beautiful legs were clad in cobweb cancan stockings, and she wore shoes with mad, mad heels. Cameras clicked and clicked.

After the brief ceremony of greeting, Lili Michaud was duly turned over to Illona, who made cooing noises over her and took her to the "Analyzium." The photographers crowded in under her indulgent eye.

Lili Michaud sat down a bit apprehensively. She dropped her bag and the young man with the eyelashes dashed to pick it up. He got between her and the cameras and Mlle. Michaud spat a bit of guttersnipe French at him. The young man, still crouched, responded briefly and in a low voice, and for a moment the two of them were like nothing so much as two alleycats.

Mlle. Illona, tactfully overlooking this display of French temperament, kept up a running stream of explanations. She plunged the room into darkness and focused a blinding white ray of light on Lili Michaud's face, at which she peered long and earnestly through a gigantic magnifying glass.

"You see, gentlemen," Mlle. Illona burbled happily. "This way the analyst sees the client's face in enlarged form and can discuss it intelligently with the client. Now Mlle. Michaud's skin is definitely the creamy type."

"*Non!*" Lili Michaud shook her head emphatically. "My face—not cream. *Je ne suis pas jaune, par exemple.*"

One of the photographers remarked *sotto voce*, "Get together on this, ladies," and there was suppressed laughter. Mlle. Illona, still looking like Sherlock Holmes with her magnifying glass, pinned her smile on more tightly and went on suavely discussing "those lovely warm nuances in Mademoiselle's skin . . ." with no further mention of cream.

Precisely at 10:45 the procession arrived on the second floor, where Toni awaited Mlle. Michaud. The Frenchwoman scrutinized her with the narrowed eyes of a professional meeting a professional and said baldly, "'Oo is she?"

Illona and Skeets explained together. Lili remarked graciously, "She too 'as a pretty figure. As pretty as mine, you think?" she appealed to her audience. There was a polite murmur.

"We thought," said Skeets, "that it would be nice if Mlle. Michaud were to pose for some exercise pictures with Miss Toni."

Mlle. Michaud did, in a rather startling bathing suit designed for her by Lanvin. While getting into it, she chattered gaily in French with Toni, to whom she had taken a fancy. She thought the little charm bracelet on Toni's ankle was cute—*trés chic, ça*—wanted to know the name of the perfume she was using and where to buy things she needed before leaving for the coast, for she intended to do *du* shopping on the grand scale.

In the gym she pounced happily on the white leather ball.

"I am going to pose with that," she told Toni. "That is effective, no?"

"For the picture, yes," Toni agreed.

"I hate exercises," Lili confided. "Massage is sufficient for me. Besides, what could your exercises do for me?"

Toni said diplomatically, "Mademoiselle's figure is so perfect that the only exercises she would need would be ones calculated to keep up that perfection. Perhaps something for—"

She indicated that voluptuous curve in the small of Lili's back. The star twisted around to look at herself in the mirror and widened her eyes at Toni with mock horror.

"And you wish to correct that, *petite*? Never." She smiled a little. *"Mais voyons, les hommes adorent ça!"*

Mlle. Michaud then proceeded to make hash of her schedule by refusing to take massage or to stay in the sunroom longer than was necessary for pictures. She was chiefly interested in the Hermes hairdo (designed by Dimitri of Lais especially for her) and in the Winogradow pack. The other things she was skipping because she wanted to be through in time to get to a cocktail party given in her honor at the Ritz Plaza.

In a very short time she had sampled all that the second floor had to offer. A streamlined naiad, she lolled coyly in a bubble bath blowing iridescent bubbles at the delighted photographers who invaded the sacred confines of the *baigne*. She posed in the sunroom lying on her stomach in a sand bed, clad chiefly in sun glasses, with a towel flung carelessly over her pretty rump. This was after a brief discussion about the exact amount of bosom to be exhibited. Mlle. Michaud was fairly generous about this but willing to listen to advice, as she didn't know how much breast it was permissible to show in the United States. After the photographers withdrew reluctantly, she sprang up to put on her robe, which her young man with the eyelashes (addressed as Henri) had whipped out of a dressing case he carried around.

This young man fascinated Toni, mostly by the matter-of-fact way he made himself useful. He handed her things with deftness that bespoke long practice and as a matter of fact would even have remained in the room to help Lili with her toilette if he hadn't been thrown out by the scandalized Illona.

The photographers repaired downstairs to wait for Lili to emerge with her new coiffure. Of course, she was not to be photographed in the less glamorous stages of her "Day at Lais," as for example, under a dryer or under the Winogradow pack. Mlle. Michaud also made preparations to depart to the fourth floor for the Hermes coiffure. Before going she turned the charm full blast on Skeets, that is to say, she regarded him from under lowered lids, bent toward him lithely so that he had a glimpse of the dazzling breasts beneath her wrapper (Lili was obviously a sweater girl from way back), patted him delicately on the cheek and said, "You 'ave been so sweet." Then she slanted her eyes at Toni and said, *"Mais je ne dois pas faire ça, vous êtes* zat way, no?"

Young Mr. Skeets and Toni both grew scarlet as if dipped in boiling water, and Mlle. Michaud was wafted away in the elevator, laughing like a hyena.

"Mademoiselle is some babe, no?" offered Skeets, tugging at his collar.

"Obviously," Toni replied. "You like her, yes?"

"Never cared for blondes," said Skeets. "Brunettes are my dish." He leered feebly.

Mrs. Sterling, Toni's next client, arrived as usual one hour late and of the blissful conviction that she was precisely on time. It was apparent in the gymnasium that her mind was not on exercise. She sketched a few halfhearted nip-ups and sat down abruptly on the mat.

She said, "I know, I know, one must carry on, no matter what happens, but sometimes it's so difficult. You know, I was certain this would be a trying day—the horoscope, you know, plain as plain. I suppose the thing to do was to stay home and not stir out, but after all one does have a sort of responsibility to the world, in my position…"

"Of course," said Toni brightly. "Now let's see what we can do with this ball."

The medicine ball rolled out of Mrs. Sterling's inert hands. "Still," she said, in deep thought, "I don't see how staying home would have helped about Chester. And I do always read the *Globe*… What is she like?"

"Who?" asked Toni, bewildered.

"What's her name—this Mimi or Lili or what have you? She is pretty, of course, but has she got that certain—"

Mrs. Sterling gesticulated.

"Frankly, Mrs. Sterling," said Toni. "I don't know what she's got but she's certainly got something."

Mrs. Sterling sighed. "I knew it." She walked out of the gymnasium and Toni, who followed her, mystified, found her near the telephone about to put a call through to Washington.

"If you can't find Chester there immediately, keep on trying. And I'll take my Winogradow pack today after all." Odette, with an imperceptible sigh of resignation, called the appointments desk to see if a room could be found on the third floor and Mrs. Sterling turned to Toni. "You understand, don't you, dear? I just had to have it settled after what you told me."

"It's quite all right," said Toni, completely at sea.

Odette put down the receiver. "I can get you a room for the Winogradow pack at eleven-thirty."

"Who'll take care of me? I insist upon Hortense. She knows all my little ways."

"I'll try to, Madame. But I think Hortense has Mlle. Michaud at about that time."

Two high pink spots suddenly blossomed on Mrs. Sterling's cheek-bones. "Then we'll share her. Mlle. Michaud and I seem to have a lot in common, anyway. I should think I ought to get some consideration around here."

She stalked back to the gym and a few minutes later was telling Toni another of her involved stories. This one dealt with her habit of creaming her face every night.

"Angus—my husband, you know—would say, 'darling, do you have to do this, after all, you've got me now,' and I'd say 'you never can tell.' And what do you think, Miss Toni, he died and I married again.

"And Philip kept on saying the same thing. 'Darling, why do you have to put this stuff on every night?' and I'd say the same thing, 'You never can tell.' Well, *he* died, too, and I am married to Chester now, and do you know, Miss Toni," she finished triumphantly, "I am still creaming my face every night!"

At twelve o'clock Toni descended to the first floor to get a bite to eat. Since she couldn't give this necessary function more than ten minutes, she had to eat in Lais at the Ambrosial Bar. This exotically named commissary in the back of the theater was not overmuch loved by the Lais employees. They felt that something was put over on them whenever they sipped *chalice de pomme d'amour* (tomato juice to hoi polloi), or poked halfheartedly at *Potpourri Epirote* (raw turnips, olives and shredded cabbage). In the first place they could only get vegetables and fruits— a fitting fodder for voluntarily starving clients but not for the employees who really worked. In the second place they had to pay fifty cents a throw and their indignation at that was not soothed by their knowledge that it cost the customers about five times that. But the Kyria was adamant in refusing to allow packages with vulgar but sustaining corned beef sandwiches to come in from the drugstore around the corner, and the unfortunates who weren't able to get out for lunch had to eat bunny food and like it.

It was funny, Toni thought, how in some mysterious way the uneasiness about Lili Michaud had spread through the salon, from the Kyria up in her office to the elevator operator who told Toni in a worried way, "That Lili Michaud is pretty temperamental, isn't she? They tell me on the fourth that she won't let Dimitri give her his Hermes coiffure, after all that advertising."

Illona, who swooped noiselessly around the salon looking like some glamorous species of blond bat in her fluttering draperies, also showed signs of strain on her beautiful egg of a face. When the telephone at the appointments desk rang and Miss Gorham beckoned to her with a hushed, "The Kyria!" she actually sprang at it and stood quivering.

"Yes, Kyria...Well, she still thinks it will make her face look too long. Well, we sent Mr. Skeets up to cope, and Dimitri has done it so that it can be combed either up or down. She will decide"—she looked at her watch—"at twelve-fifteen, after she has had her lunch. Yes, I told them to call you up immediately."

She turned to Toni with a wan smile.

"This has been a horrible day. Mlle. Michaud's refusal to take massage disarranged the whole schedule, and Mrs. Parmalee has again become wedged in a chair, and Mrs. Sterling is being difficult on the third floor, and"—Illona sighed—"Miss Howe has come in and *she* is being rather—nervous, because her acne has begun bothering her again. Ah, Madame," she smiled enchantingly at a petulant woman with a bored-looking poodle, "but certainly we will take care of the little darling. Madame wishes to see for herself? Certainly."

Illona floated off again. Before becoming the manager of the salon she had given a course in graceful movement. She still practiced its principles of "beauty in motion," which Toni irreverently paraphrased as "fanny in motion."

M. Maurice was puttering around the long crystal shelves that lined the walls of the salon, getting together various bottles of preparations. With his white little basket on his arm he made one think of a somewhat affected middle-aged woman picking flowers in a garden. There was a peaceful look of absorption on his face. Illona swooped down on him.

"Monsieur Maurice, would it perhaps be possible for you to write out the requisition for these things instead of picking them up off the shelves? We don't want those empty spaces..."

M. Maurice transfixed her with a coldly loathing eye as he plucked a bottle of lemon verbena lotion from the shelf, leaving another regrettable blank space.

"It would be possible but could I perhaps leave this task to you, my sweet? It would be such a change for you to be something more than ornamental around here."

Temper, thought Toni, passing on like Pippa. Tempers were certainly being worn thin this season at Lais, almost as if all the nasty little intrigues were finally coming to a boil.

In the theater, the photographers were slouching wearily on the stairs leading to the platform, a sort of disreputable Greek chorus, with the dull resignation characteristic of press photographers the world over. They

watched her stonily as she ate her salad, and one of them muttered something indignant about bars without drinks.

When she came back into the salon M. Maurice had almost finished
denuding the shelves, but Illona wore a look of boundless relief. In the
fullness of her heart she shared it with Toni.

"She's going to have the Hermes after all. Mr. Skeets has been able
to swing it. Isn't that splendid?"

Toni looked at her watch and decided that she still had time to bring
Mrs. Sterling the therapeutic sandals she had been ordering and forgetting
to take along for days. It was 12:30, which meant that this vague lady
would be having her Winogradow pack on the third floor. Toni took the
elevator up to that floor and walked into a scene.

Alicia Howe was standing in front of her room. The cords of her
somewhat scrawny neck stood out and she was screaming like a fish-
wife. "Get out of my room or I'll kill you!" Toni looked inside the afore-
mentioned room and was enlightened. Lili Michaud was apparently pretty
firmly entrenched in what had always been considered Howe's private
den. Her peignoir, half concealing, emphasized her pretty figure. Her beautiful blond curls were up on top of her head in the Hermes coiffure, but
she was by no means ready to face her public. A stream of pointed comment in emphatic French was pouring from her red lips.

Among the small audience who watched this scene speechlessly was
Dr. Berchtold and he was taking in an eyeful of Lili in *deshabille* with an
enjoyment that no amount of professional dismay could lessen.

"I want that little French tart out of my room!" Alicia screamed. "Is
anybody going to do it or do I have to do it myself?"

The little French tart, her red-tipped claws curved invitingly, invited
her to come and get her. Dr. Berchtold, with an apprehensive look around
the corridor, moved toward Alicia and whispered conciliatingly in her ear.

"Don't tell me to be quiet," Alicia Howe grated at him. "What does
this little tramp think this is, that she's making herself so comfortable? I'm
going to throw her out of here."

She made a step into the room. Her opponent picked up a small jar of
cream and threw it. It whizzed by Alicia and spattered squashily on the
opposite wall. Miss Howe looked at the spot it made and deciding against
further advance began to totter and close her eyes, apparently getting
ready to faint.

"Aha," said Michaud with satisfaction, flashing the doctor a gamin-
like smile. She looked devilishly pretty at that moment. Toni was to remember her like that, a pretty little hussy, flushed with her silly victory.

Then she turned away and motioned to Hortense, who crept speechlessly into the room.

"Ohé, toi, assez de cette bagarre-là. Fermes la porte."

The door shut. The extraordinary scene was over.

Toni helped the doctor to bring Alicia Howe to the couch. He waved ammonia salts in front of her nose and went through all the motions of reviving a woman who had fainted. The columnist moaned and clutched at her heart. There was a peculiar pinched expression on her face. Toni was vainly ringing for the elevator.

"Take it easy, my dear," Dr. Berchtold was purring soothingly. His big, well-tended hand moved from Alicia Howe's wrist and stroked her arm. Toni heard a funny sound near her, a hiss of indrawn breath, and turning saw Jeanne watching that hand as if fascinated. There was a strange, sick expression on her face. "How about that elevator?" said Berchtold, impatiently. "We want to get her down, don't we?"

Jeanne explained, nervously, "They just called up from downstairs that the elevator has got stuck. Monsieur Maurice took it up without the operator and stalled it between second and third. We must keep all the stair doors open until it's fixed." Dr. Berchtold grunted with contempt, presumably for the stupidity of M. Maurice, picked up the inert form of Alicia Howe and bore it to the exit doors, stopping only to inquire, "Are the doors to the second floor going to be open?"

"Oh, yes," Jeanne assured him. She had turned her head away and her voice was strangled. "They are telling all the floors to open the stair doors."

Berchtold disappeared with his burden. Toni, about to follow, was stopped by the grimace of fury and jealousy that distorted Jeanne's pretty face.

"I hate her," the girl muttered. "And she hasn't fainted. She's just shamming. There's nothing wrong with her."

"Never mind that," said Toni severely. She shook the girl lightly. "Don't be a fool, Jeanne." The telephone was ringing again. Jeanne sniffed, gulped and went to answer it, while Toni followed the doctor and his still inanimate burden downstairs.

The doctor laid Miss Howe down on the cot in his room, crooning, "You'll be all right now," in a soothing monotone. His patient moaned a little and subsided, her eyes closed. In a little while she was able to sit up, supported by the doctor's tenderly encircling arm, and gulp down some water brought by Toni, pausing only to tell the latter in a matter-of-fact voice, "Get out."

Toni did so, with alacrity. She heard Alicia's voice rise in fury behind the door. In the austere privacy of her gymnasium she sank down feebly on the mat and began to laugh. There was something exquisitely funny about these elemental passions coming to life in Lais' perfumed rooms, with nature suddenly surging to the fore, wild of eye and red of claw. She was still laughing when she was called to the phone. It was Illona and there was a quiver in her voice.

"Toni, the Kyria is prostrated. Did this terrible thing really happen? You were there, weren't you? How is Miss Howe?"

Toni answered the last question. "Resting. She had a heart attack as a result of all the excitement, but Dr. Berchtold is taking care of her."

"How dreadful. How simply and utterly horrible."

"It could have been worse. Miss Howe could have been hit by the cream jar Mademoiselle Michaud threw."

There was a brief silence and Illona asked brokenly, "Did Mademoiselle Michaud throw a cream jar?"

"Just a little one," Toni reassured her. There was silence again while the wires hummed with horror.

"It's incredible," Illona said in hushed tones. "This is an accursed day, Toni. We'll long remember it. By the way, Mrs. Carstairs has canceled her appointment for one-thirty, because of the elevator. It's still stuck. The repair men have gone out to lunch. Why Monsieur Maurice insists on running that elevator—" she broke off. "But we must just carry on. The Kyria is going to speak to Jeanne. She might want to hear from you also about this—this unfortunate business."

Toni put down the receiver, grinning, and picked it up immediately when the telephone rang again.

"Hello." The voice that answered hers bubbled with amusement. "I understand you've been having a little trouble."

"A little, Mr. Skeets," Toni admitted.

"Don't call me Mr. Skeets. It makes me feel like a comic strip. Well, I suppose it's just as well to have some outlet here. It's probably healthy little quarrels like this that prevent a murder. Listen—did Michaud know at whom she was throwing things?"

"I don't know. Why?"

"Well, if she knew, her aim might have been better. I've just been reading Howe's column in the *Globe*. Very interesting. Say, if I stay much longer in this harem, I'll get as catty as any of the girls. What I really called up about was this—how about dinner and ballet with me?"

"It would be nice."

"Good! You're making me so happy, dear."

"Let's not be sentimental about it."

"You're right. How's Lili doing? I'm supposed to come around for her unveiling."

"I should imagine at this point she's happily slumbering under the loathsome Winogradow pack. By the way, I'm curious—how did you manage to get her to agree to the Hermes hairdo?"

"Simple, my dear. I just told her that she certainly should not have a coiffure that she feels is unbecoming, that everybody will understand, because not many people can look well in the Hermes style, which is a very special one." Mr. Skeets' voice grew perceptibly smug. "There are ways to make people do what you want them to do, particularly women. I'll be seeing you."

There was a copy of the *Globe* on Toni's dressing table and she turned to Alicia Howe's column. She found the thing about midway through Howe's cactus bed.

"A Cinderella story, for you sophisticated children. It seems there was a little French movie star, who likes great big strong tycoons, and a great big strong American tycoon, who likes his blondes fresh. They met in France before the German invasion at a dear friend's chateau and were immediately given adjoining suites by the perspicacious hostess. And that's why a certain pretty blonde French *vedette* had absolutely no trouble getting through the customs. Also it is whispered that her first picture will be financed by Mr. S.—but there I—we must be discreet. But the cream of the jest will come when Mr. S.'s blonde will meet Mr. S.'s wife today in a famous beauty salon."

"Wow!" said Toni. "If anybody ever translates this to Lili she'll come back and really take care of dear sweet Alicia. It's a surprise that nobody has done that yet."

With this sage reflection Toni went to take care of her 1:15-1:40 appointment. She had barely finished her and stepped into her own room when there was a sound of mild commotion on the floor, and Odette poked her head through the door.

"They are letting down the elevator." Odette was frankly giggling. "I can hear Monsieur Maurice inside, he's swearing like mad."

Quite a little crowd, among whom Toni was surprised to see Jeanne, had gathered to see M. Maurice emerge from the elevator. The spectacle was an edifying one. There was M. Maurice, crouching in the back of the elevator like a caged beast, in a cloud of mingled perfumes, dominated by the powerful whiff of the lemon verbena lotion. M. Maurice, shaking with nerves and rage, stepped over the broken bottles as daintily as a cat across a puddle, and made his speechless way out. His small white hands fluttered in agitation. He still had his little basket on his arm, with most of the bottles and jars still intact.

M. Maurice proceeded to curse out the elevator. He used all the profanity at his command. Toni's private opinion was that it was pitifully inadequate. The little group listened respectfully until M. Maurice grew hoarse.

Then he took a breath and said icily, "If somebody would clean out the elevator and get some of that *stink* out of it, I'll consider taking it up to my office. You can tell Illona that I am too *upset* to do anything today. I am going *straight* home."

When M. Maurice got excited he had a knack of underlining words like a debutante. The people around him burst into activity. Two of the masseuses, a class generally noted for good practical common sense, rushed into the elevator to pick up pieces of glass. Odette called downstairs to report on the elevator and to get hold of the operator. As for M. Maurice, he refused pettishly a timid offer to brush him off and flung himself on the couch, arising with a yelp of annoyance upon finding that he had sat down on the therapeutic sandals that Toni had brought for Mrs. Sterling and neglected to deliver because of the Howe-Michaud fracas. Toni rescued them with a murmured apology and wondered if she still could get rid of them. Mrs. Sterling's treatment was over at 12:30 and it was now 1:40, but Mrs. Sterling was a confirmed dawdler.

The doors were still open while the elevator was being cleaned, and Toni used the stairs to go up to the third floor. She bumped into the doctor coming down. He had a preoccupied expression on his face, and though she dodged him through sheer force of habit, for once he made no pass at her. She heard the door of the second floor shut behind him at the same time as she stepped into the vestibule of the third. Apparently they were the last to make the trip via the stairs. On the second floor M. Maurice, holding his handkerchief delicately to his nose, stepped into the elevator, which was now run by the operator. This was a sort of signal, like pushing the button that lighted the Chicago World's Fair. Telephones rang from the first to the fourth floors. Doors were shut firmly and the employees who had profited by the hour's interlude to pay visits to each other settled back to ordinary modes of communication via the elevator.

Hortense was sitting at the telephone desk, smoking, with the ashtray hidden in the drawer of the desk so that she could put away her cigarette quickly if anybody came in. She drew her hand out of the drawer where it had darted swiftly upon Toni's entrance and resumed her smoking. Her grin was relieved and impudent.

"It's only you...Scared me for a minute."

"Is Mrs. Sterling here?" Toni inquired. "I've got those sandals for her."

"No, she's gone just a little while ago. Just before I came back."

"Came back?" Toni's voice held a mild inflection of surprise. Hortense looked suddenly apprehensive.

"Yeah, I had to leave the floor for a while."

"What about Michaud?"

"Oh, she's sleeping. She threw me out after I put on the Winogradow pack. It made her sleepy right away. I looked in when I came back and she's not moved, just snoozing. I'm going to wake her up"—Hortense looked at her watch—"let's see, it's one-forty-five now—at two o'clock. It's a little late but it won't do her any harm, and Dimitri has just called that he's busy combing out the Princess Lubescu and could I stall Michaud for the next half an hour?"

"I see. I suppose you're sure that Sterling is gone?"

"Yes, thank God. I couldn't stand that screwy dame any more today. Listen, she got a call from Washington in the middle of the Winogradow pack, and she insisted on washing the goop off before she would take it. Says she, 'I always want to look my best when talking to Chester, particularly now.' What can you say to a dame like that?"

"Oh, did her husband call her from Washington?"

"Yes, Mr. S. himself."

"Mr. S..." Toni's eyebrows went up. She remembered Mrs. Sterling's vague complaints and the fact that she, too, read the *Globe*. "That's very interesting," she breathed. "I suppose you know what the call was about?"

Hortense shook her head regretfully. "I was being paged elsewhere. My Gawd, what a day."

Jeanne slipped into the loggia and took Hortense's place at the desk. Her heart-shaped face wore a subdued, pinched expression that made Toni obscurely uneasy.

"You certainly took your time about it," said Hortense nastily. "I suppose you stopped downstairs to see if you could get another date out of the doctor."

"I didn't. I was called down by the Kyria," Jeanne said indignantly, with another one of her devastating blushes. She got a fleeting glance at Toni's concerned face and dropped her eyes. "Be quiet," she finished in a low voice.

"Listen, dearie," said Hortense, with even more concentrated venom. "I know your type. I bet one date was all the doctor needed."

Toni said, "Why don't you go and see how Michaud is getting along, Hortense, and give your nasty tongue a rest."

"She gives me a pain," Hortense said, preparing nevertheless to move on. "Every time Howe comes around, she suffers. Listen, baby, if you're going to have fits every time Dr. Rudi looks at anybody, it'll be just too bad. Why, even Michaud gave him the eye today."

"Whom did she give the eye?" said Eric Skeets cheerfully. He had materialized out of the elevator, looking extraordinarily perky, and had flung his gangling length against the yellow corduroy of the loggia circular bench. "I would have you know that Mademoiselle Michaud is my particular cookie, and if anybody gets the eye from her it's me. Or is it I?"

"It's you," Toni conceded urbanely. Skeets grinned at her.

"Don't I look beautiful against that yellow?" he demanded. "I want to look my best when Lili comes out. And that reminds me, when *is* she coming out? With that Hermes coiffure," he added smugly.

"Hortense is just going to wake her up," Toni said. "See if you can contain that youthful ardor."

"Good!" Skeets sat up and rubbed his hands elaborately. "Go ahead and wake her up, Hortense, thou handmaiden of beauty. Put a wiggle on."

Hortense sauntered off, and Skeets collapsed against the couch.

"What a day," he mumbled. "Rife with emotion, packed with suspense…Did you notice how jittery everybody is today? I'm getting the willies myself. After all, it's my publicity stunt, you know."

"There, there," Toni patted his dark pate. "Everything will be all right."

"Well, so far Lili has thrown Alicia Howe into hysterics and has disrupted the hair department by having a fight with her young man. Did you know that?"

"You mean the sulky young gigolo with the eyelashes?"

"Yes, he went out like a bat out of hell with pineapple in his hair after she threw the salad at him."

"Maybe she didn't like the salad."

"Maybe. All I hope is the boys downstairs don't hear about this. That is not the publicity we crave. Then there was that damned elevator. There was the hideous uncertainty about Lili's hair. All that we need is that something should happen to the hairdo—"

At this precise moment a shriek split the suave stillness of the third floor. Its shrillness and unexpectedness jerked Skeets to his feet. He and Toni looked at each other a moment stupidly, as if trying to find the answer in each other's faces, then they pivoted in the direction of the sound.

Alicia Howe's room was again the center of horrid commotion. As they watched, Hortense came backing out of it, still screaming like a calliope. She stumbled on the threshold, fell down and was up again with enviable agility. She continued backing away, still screaming and pointing with a shaking finger, until she reached the opposite wall and could go no farther. There her voice gave out and she stood gasping and whimpering.

It was Toni who moved first. Closely followed by Eric Skeets she pushed by the gibbering Hortense and looked into the room. Lili Michaud was there all right, swathed in a monogrammed white cape as per regulations, with the Winogradow pack obliterating her features in its usual loathsome way. Now that celebrated new slumber mask, while it was supposed to be the last thing in repose and relaxation, was not quite as restful as all that. Mlle. Michaud was slumbering far too profoundly. Hortense's bloodcurdling shriek failed to arouse her. She had, moreover, slumped so far down in the chair that the very discomfort of her position should have been sufficient to awaken her.

Automatically Toni's hand went to Lili's wrist. The hand she touched was smooth and chilly and lifeless, not a flutter of pulse in it. Toni dropped it and stepped back. Her bare shoulder came in contact with the rough texture of Eric Skeets' coat and she shivered involuntarily as if her skin had become too sensitive. Eric's hand closed reassuringly on her shoulder.

"Steady," he said, "steady." She turned to him and saw that he was the delicate pale green of the first primrose buds in spring. He smiled weakly as he saw her calm face. "My mistake," he said wryly. He nodded toward the stiff figure before him. "Is she…?"

"I think so. There's no pulse I can notice."

Behind them Hortense broke into frantic whimpering. Her narrow face seemed to shrink into a dime's edge. There was horror in it, and— yes, something more personal than horror. Fear.

"She's dead! She's dead. And I'm going to get blamed for this. I left her alone with— Oh my God, I feel like I'm going to faint." She clutched hysterically at Skeets' arm.

"You'll oblige me by doing nothing of the sort, Hortense. Come on, buck up, there's a good girl." He patted her on the shoulder and his eyes sought Toni's. "I'm going to get Berchtold up to take a look at her."

"And we'd better let the Kyria know the glad news."

"Hell! Yes." He dashed to the telephone, leaving Toni to answer the questions of the girls whom Hortense's shrieks brought out of the facial rooms. Toni slipped out of the room, closing the door on the inanimate figure slumped in the chair.

"What happened? Another fight?" said one of the girls hopefully.

"My God, they're bringing the house down every hour," another complained. "It's making me so nervous—"

"Everybody is," Toni said smoothly. "Hortense here just had an attack of nerves. Jeanne, you had better take her into one of the unoccupied rooms. The doctor will be up directly. The rest of you get back to your clients, like good girls."

Toni had found before that a calm and authoritative voice had a good effect on people. They dispersed, disappointed but docile. She heard one of them grumbling as she disappeared into a facial room.

"People shouldn't scream like that. My God, I thought somebody was being murdered."

But apparently Lili Michaud had not made much noise when she died, Toni thought. Nobody had noticed. The dreadful metamorphosis from a breathing, living, pretty woman to a limp rag doll had somehow taken place without anybody knowing. She ran lightly to the telephone desk, where Skeets was talking into the receiver, his voice tight and razor-edged.

"If Dr. Berchtold is not in his room, locate him and send him here immediately. It's an emergency."

He replaced the receiver and stared at Toni. "Baby," he said softly. "That's a fine publicity stunt—see Lais and die. Oh boy!"

They both turned automatically to look at the closed door to the first room off the loggia. The luminous L that indicated an occupant in a room glowed softly as if not caring that there was no longer anyone there—only something.

CHAPTER 3

HALF AN HOUR after Mlle. Michaud had been found dead, Fifth Avenue was startled by the spectacle of a police car pulling up to the curb and its occupants disappearing into Lais, using the side entrance. About fifteen minutes later a few more cars drew up, this time with sound effects, and their occupants piled out and also walked into the salon. This time they used the front entrance, creating a minor sensation.

Captain Andrew Torrent of the homicide squad headed the invaders. A quiet, ruddy-complexioned gentleman of middle age and English extraction, with cold bright blue eyes and a reddish pompadour with a wave in it, he believed in getting down to business as soon as possible. He walked up to Collette, who was in charge of the first floor, Illona being absent, and asked her in a low matter-of-fact voice, "Where is it?"

Collette backed away.

"Who are you and where is what?"

Torrent sighed and let his eye wander over the crowd of befurred and perfumed women and their attendant nymphs, until one of the policemen who had already been summoned came down in the elevator and approached him. Trent listened to his brief report attentively, seemingly unaware of the looks of wild surmise bestowed upon him from all sides. But when a client, a befurred and perfumed dowager, started for the door, he motioned with his head, and one of his men promptly stationed himself at the door, intercepting her. His voice boomed with an unaccustomed volume in the sacred stillness of the salon as he explained to her.

"Begging your pardon, madam, but the captain wants to talk to you before you leave."

The third floor was a quiet pandemonium. Even the neoclassic Picassos on the wall seemed to have acquired a slightly befuddled look. In the loggia, Captain Torrent came upon a group frozen in an attitude absurdly reminiscent of family photographs of 1910 vintage. The Kyria sat immobile, flanked by Illona and Skeets, the doctor bending solicitously over her, with Hortense and Jeanne huddled on the left. On the right, to complete the symmetrical arrangement, sat Toni, idly glancing through the latest *Harper's Bazaar.* The Kyria rose and made a step toward Torrent. Torrent bowed slightly. To himself he thought, "Here's a peculiar old party. Sick as a dog, too, from the looks of her."

The Kyria said, "I'd like to speak to you alone, Captain. This terrible thing—"

"I'll be at your service, madam," said Torrent cheerfully, "right after I've had a look at the body." The Kyria gazed at him icily, her look saying plainly, "Why be uncouth?" and Torrent proceeded to the room to look at what remained of Lili Michaud.

The doll-like figure still sprawled awkwardly in its chair, looking rather terrible with its mud-plastered face below the precise yellow curls.

"The stuff that women put on themselves nowadays," Torrent sighed. He carefully lifted the cape and surveyed the slender body with a hard impersonal glance.

"No visible marks. Of course, the M.E.—" he leaned forward looking closely. Along the throat of the corpse there was a faint bluish tinge that showed only in contrast to the waxy whiteness of the rest of the body. Torrent straightened up. "Moran told me that their own doctor examined her. Get him."

Dr. Berchtold appeared promptly, his manner a correct mixture of dignified sorrow and a lively readiness to cooperate. Torrent said, "I believe you examined the body."

Dr. Berchtold inclined his head gravely.

"And?"

Berchtold shrugged his shoulders. "No apparent cause of death, Inspector."

"Captain."

"Captain. I am sorry. No visible injuries, that is, none visible now. The deceased might have been suffering from some ailment which would not be disclosed in a superficial examination—"

"Heart?"

The doctor shook his head regretfully. "No. I examined her before the treatment." Torrent raised his eyebrows. "It's customary to examine a client before she takes a new treatment like the Winogradow pack."

"Is that," Torrent asked, pointing to her face, "the Winogradow pack?"

"Yes, it is. Usually a call to the family physician is sufficient, but of course in the case of Mademoiselle Michaud, who had just arrived..."

"And her heart was sound?"

"As a bell."

"Can you place the time of her death?"

"From an hour to an hour and a half ago."

"I see. That makes it somewhere between one and one-thirty." Torrent nodded to his crew. "O.K., Mac, you can get busy on it. Photograph all you need and print the room and then you can turn the body over to M.E. And now, Doctor," Torrent's white teeth flashed briefly in an ingratiating smile, "I'd like to get some dope from you. Merely routine, don't you know."

Berchtold obliged readily. Torrent rapidly learned about his functions at Lais, but there was very little he could tell Torrent beyond the fact that he saw Lili when she came down to the facial floor, at which time he gave her an examination and found her in blooming health.

"Did you discuss anything outside of her health?"

"Nothing serious. Paris in the spring, that sort of thing..." Berchtold again showed his teeth in a deprecating smile.

"Did she say anything that might throw a light on this business?" Berchtold shook his head. "I'll talk to you again," said Torrent and left the room. In the loggia the Kyria pounced on him.

"I understand that our clients are being detained. This is an outrage. I insist—"

"It's a customary procedure," Torrent told her with his courteous smile. "We shall let them go as soon as we get their names and their business here."

"Their business here! Really, Captain, I should think it's obvious. These ladies come here to relax and to absorb beauty and serenity that we try to provide for them. You are making it impossible for us to—"

"Madam," said Torrent, "there's a body in that little room, and it's our business to find out why. I am afraid that must take precedence over beauty and serenity. Now, how can I get the names of all the people who were in the building when Miss Michaud was taking her treatment?"

"The appointment desk will answer any inquiries," the Kyria said automatically. "But I don't see—"

Torrent interrupted her smoothly, "Just one other thing. Is there anybody connected with Mlle. Michaud here in the building?"

The Kyria looked around helplessly, and Illona chimed in, "There was a young man with her, her impresario, a Monsieur Henri Barrat."

"Well, where is he?"

Eric Skeets spoke up, "We don't know. He walked out of the salon."

"Walked out?"

"Yes, you see, he had a little quarrel with Mlle. Michaud. So he left."

"At what time was that?"

"At about twelve-fifteen, while Mlle. Michaud was having her lunch on the fourth floor. That was before she came down to this floor."

"That's interesting," said Torrent. He turned to the Kyria. "Who were the first people to discover the body?"

"Hortense here and Toni." The Kyria indicated them with a bejeweled hand. "Mr. Skeets was also on the floor when it happened."

"Then I'd like to see them separately. Moran here will talk to the rest of the people on the floor. Is there a room where we can talk? This one, for example?" Torrent nodded toward the little pantry opposite the room where the body lay. "I think that'll be a bit better than your other rooms. They're much too elegant for me. I'd like Miss—Hortense, is it?—first."

The Kyria's white draperies floated with the swiftness of her movement as she darted after Torrent. Her fingers bit into his sleeve like white claws.

"Just one moment." Her resonant voice dropped to a confiding whisper. "Captain, this dreadful accident—it's not the sort of thing that should happen here. The publicity will be of the worst kind."

Torrent shrugged his shoulders and a courteous indulgent smile tugged at the corner of his mouth underneath the reddish mustache. "You have my sympathy, madam."

Apparently the Kyria heard what she wished to hear in this remark, for her voice grew subtly imperious. "I want you to get the—the body out as quickly and quietly as you can. And call your men off. There's no need to question any of the clients. Surely you can't suppose that any of them could have anything to do with this. They come from the highest circles of society. Neither they nor I want any publicity." She lowered her voice again. "You will find me grateful for cooperation, Captain. My clients must be protected from scandal and I am willing to pay for it."

Torrent stared at her incredulously and decided that she wasn't joking. But before he had a chance to answer, the elevator door burst open, disgorging photographers. The Kyria recoiled with a gasp and Torrent went to deal with the invasion.

The boys of the press were visibly cheered by the prospect of covering tragedy instead of plain cheesecake. They wanted pictures. One of them hopped up and down in front of a burly policeman, vainly trying to get a glimpse of the fatal room with the body, until the latter pinned him down with a paternal hand on his shoulder.

"Now boys," Torrent was saying gently, while his assistants were steadily pushing the disappointed newshounds back to the elevator that gaped behind them, "there's nothing that we can tell you right now. We've just arrived ourselves. The press will be told all there is to know when we'll be in a position to tell you."

They went sulkily, intoning the usual chant of the frustrated reporter.

"Have a heart, Captain. How about letting us in on it?"

Torrent frowned slightly. Among the familiar pandemonium of voices there was a discordant and alien sound. It came from a slight young man with wild hair who was desperately trying to scramble out of the elevator under the implacable arm of a policeman. It took a second for Torrent to realize that the man wasn't just griping, he was griping in French. At that very moment his arm was grabbed and young Mr. Skeets was gabbling excitedly in his ear.

"Henri Barrat, Michaud's impresario, the guy I told you about—that little Latin in the striped suit—that's him!"

"I thought he was out of the building."

"Well," said Skeets unnecessarily, "he's back again."

"So I see," said Torrent, dryly. "Mahoney, let go of that little guy, will you?"

The huge officer did, and the young Frenchman catapulted out of the elevator, a torrent of distracted French pouring from his lips.

"Steady," said Torrent. "What is he saying?"

Skeets sighed. "He wants to know what happened. He knows that something has happened to Michaud but not exactly what."

"Do you speak French?"

"Passably."

"Then," said Torrent reasonably, "you had better tell him."

Skeets shuddered. "All I can think of at this time of stress is about the daughter of my gardener who had a red umbrella. However..." He turned to young Barrat. There was a sudden hush. After the first few words the young Frenchman simply said, in a conversational tone of voice, "*Mais c'est pas possible. Pas possible, alors.*" He even looked around with a sick little smile, as if inviting people to laugh at the impossibility of it. Apparently what he saw in the faces around him crushed him because he suddenly threw his arm over his face and burst into tears.

Torrent hurriedly left the tableau with instructions to Mahoney to keep the weeping Frenchman there until he was ready for him and strode to the room he had reserved for questioning, scooping up Hortense on the way.

The foxy-faced young woman before him proved to be a twisty and nervous witness. Torrent questioned her at length, referring constantly to the appointment book which one of the men brought to him. Her answer as to the time Lili Michaud came down to the third floor coincided to the minute with the time indicated in the book: 12:17. She admitted, not too enthusiastically, that she was Michaud's sole attendant.

Torrent wanted to know if she was constantly in attendance on Michaud.

After a cautious little pause Hortense said, "Well, I went out of the room while the doctor was examining her."

"That was?"

"About five minutes after she came. He stayed with her until the scrap," she caught herself with a feline grimace, "until twelve-thirty, I guess."

"What scrap?"

Hortense told him, at first reluctantly then with the graphic enthusiasm of a professional gossip. Torrent listened impassively. When she was through he asked one of his men to locate Miss Howe, who was presumably still on the second floor. He turned back to Hortense.

"Did she seem very much upset or excited by the incident?"

Hortense shrugged her shoulders expressively. "Why should she? My feeling was she enjoyed it. She laughed about it all the time I put the pack on her."

"Now at what time did you leave her alone again?" There was a furtive movement of uneasiness and another hesitation. He explained patiently, "I am taking it for granted that you did. Because if you didn't, sister, you must have been there when she died and know all about it, and I'd be much obliged if you told me just how it happened so I can call it a day."

This accelerated the examination. Hortense admitted that at 1:00 she went to get a hair atomizer for Mrs. Sterling from Marthe on the fourth floor. Torrent jotted down, "Check with M. on 4th," and glanced at the appointment book. Then he wanted to know how come Hortense was running errands for Mrs. Sterling at 1:00 if she had gotten through with her at 12:30 as marked. Hortense replied merely that Mrs. Sterling was a slow dresser and wanted a lot of attention while she was dressing. At any rate she, Hortense, was back at 1:15. At that time she had looked in at Michaud, and she was still sleeping.

"How do you know she was still sleeping?"

"I asked her if she wanted something, and she didn't answer—Oh my God!" Hortense clapped her hand across her mouth and fear showed in her shrewd narrow face. "Do you think maybe she…"

"Did it occur to you at the time that she might be dead?"

"My Gawd, no! Lots of clients go to sleep under the Winogradow pack. Why, Alice was passing by and I let her peek in on account of I thought she was sleeping and she wouldn't mind."

"Very good. What did you do then?"

"I sat down near the telephone." Hortense pointed toward the desk with a movement of her sharp chin. "That's where I sat until I went to wake her up."

"And nobody outside of yourself had entered her room?"

"Not while I was there. I would have seen them."

"And until what time did you sit there?"

Torrent listened to the rest of the story closely. He was quite sure that somewhere during the interview Hortense had lied. He couldn't say when or how. But as he dismissed her, the impression that he had stored away was as tangible in his mind as if he had set a check on the margin of neatly typed notes.

Sallying out of his den for more victims, Torrent noticed that the young

Frenchman had recovered somewhat from his grief. He was talking to Illona in emotional rapid French. There were still marks of tears on his face. Torrent looked at the pair thoughtfully and fished Illona out.

Before he had a chance to ask anything outside of the preliminary questions, Moran came in to make a report. The people on the first floor had been questioned. Most of the clients had just come in to look at one of the art exhibitions on the first floor that were periodically given by the Kyria as cultural bait for customers. Moran had taken their names and addresses. Torrent jerked his thumb outward, indicating that they could now be let go. "What about the girls?" he asked and was told that they had all stayed downstairs under the unsleeping eye of Miss Gorham at the appointments desk.

The same held for the second floor. The movements of all the masseuses were accounted for and by the same token those of their clients, with whom they had been closeted. The physical director, Mlle. Toni, however, was not among them, having gone to the third floor at 1:40. "That was the babe who found the body." There had been only four clients on the third floor during Lili's treatment. One of them had gone home before the body was discovered—that was Mrs. Sterling. Three others had been questioned and had nothing useful to say.

"They just been sitting in their rooms with goo over their pusses," remarked Moran inelegantly, "and they didn't hear anything. No, they never even came out of their rooms. That's all, except that one old battle-ax by the name of Glendenning tells me that she knows the D.A. very well, and we better watch our step."

"You can let them go," Torrent told him. "What about the girls? The operators, I mean."

"There are six of them, not counting Hortense, on this floor. Two of them are out for lunch. You said you wanted to talk to the receptionist yourself. The other three kids were sticking close to their clients. When they did go out for a minute they didn't see a thing. One of them, Pauline, says that she went out once when there was nobody at all in the hall. Another one, Alice, says that she was in the hall when Hortense looked in Michaud's room and she peeked too. That was, she says, at one-thirty. They all give you the time to the minute."

"And what did she see?"

"Same thing as Hortense—nothing."

"What about that Howe woman? Did you locate her?"

"She ain't in the building, chief."

"Anybody see her go?"

"Yeah, one of the girls on the first floor. It seems the elevator broke down, and the customers had to use the stairs. So this babe, Brigitte, was stationed at the foot of the stairs."

"What for?"

"I don't know. To see that some of the customers don't sneak out without paying. That's what this lady told me." Moran winked ponderously at Illona.

"This is preposterous." Illona leaped to her feet. "I never told this— this person anything of the sort. I said merely that with the elevator out of commission, all the doors between floors must be opened and anybody can come downstairs and go out of the building without stopping at the first floor. As for our clients, none of whom would dream of leaving without paying, the girl was merely there to express the apologies of the house for their being inconvenienced and being forced to leave by the employees' entrance." Illona shuddered delicately at the implied outrage to the clients' feelings.

"Please don't apologize," said Torrent smoothly. "As a matter of fact it's a break for us because we can check on who had left the building when." Illona subsided and Torrent turned back to Moran. "What did the girl say?"

"Miss Howe left at about one-fifteen or thereabouts. We're getting from her the list of everybody who went up or down stairs after the elevator stalled."

"O.K., Moran. Carry on, will you?" Torrent still occasionally mixed the British expletives with his otherwise completely American way of speaking. That and his occasionally dropped g's and his "don't you know" which somehow inevitably found itself at the end of a sentence were the only leftovers of his British antecedents. But they were enough to gain for him the affectionate sobriquet of "Limey" among his subordinates.

"Right, chief." Moran turned to go and stopped. "By the way, this elevator stopping is going to be an awful nuisance to us. It seems they opened all the doors from the first to the fourth floors that they usually keep closed. Anybody coulda come in."

"Well, whoever came in from outside would have had to pass that girl."

"Yeah. What about people going from floor to floor? We gotta do some fancy checking."

"Well, get going. Wait. You said all the doors from the first to the fourth floors. There are—how many floors? Perhaps you could explain to us, Miss—uh—" Torrent, who was a rather formal soul, balked at the idea of addressing strange females by their first names.

Illona did, looking faintly harassed. Her face still held its expressionless beauty, as if the emotions could not break through the lacquered surface. Only a tiny smear of lipstick over her upper lip served to reveal her distracted feelings better than any overt expression of dismay or terror. The doors *were* usually closed, to prevent too much interfloor traffic among the girls. However, when the elevator broke down, "due to interference by people who ought to know better," she remarked acidly, it was necessary to open the doors to the floors.

"But not all the floors?"

"No, Inspector."

"Captain."

"So sorry. The fifth and sixth floors are taken care of by the back elevator. You see, these two floors are occupied by the executive staff and the advertising and publicity departments, so that in a way they are completely detached from the rest of the building, which is completely devoted to ministering to the clients, as it were. As a matter of fact it was not even necessary to acquaint these departments with the elevator's defection, and anyhow most of them were out for lunch."

"What about this other elevator? Why didn't you use it for your clients when the other one broke down?"

"It isn't at all suitable," Illona said with dignity. "The clients would have to go to the back of the salon and get off near unsuitable places like the washrooms and linen closets. That would not do."

"I see." Torrent fingered his chin. "Moran, you had better check up on that back elevator and see if anybody had come in that way. That will be all for the time being, Miss—uh—thank you so much. Could you send in the young lady who found Miss Michaud?"

Illona swept out, disregarding another prodigious wink from Moran who followed her.

Toni stood aside to let by the stretcher carrying Lili Michaud's body. It was slight and arrowy beneath the great sheet with the heraldic L embroidered on it.

"The corpse," Toni remarked *sotto voce* to Eric Skeets, standing next to her, "wore a becoming winding sheet, courtesy of Lais."

"I hope they took that damned stuff off her face," said Skeets inconsequently. "Well, go on in, dear, and be grilled."

Torrent did not grill Toni. The questions he threw at her were brief and matter-of-fact and he jotted down her answers without comment. He showed interest when she mentioned coming up to the third floor to bring Mrs. Sterling her sandals.

"Everybody," he observed, "seems to fetch and carry for that woman. Now you say this was at one-forty approximately, wasn't it? Then what made you think that she would be there?"

"I just had that impression. I thought she might still be in her room"— Toni caught herself just in time and finished her sentence— "dressing."

Torrent pricked up his ears at the slight hesitation. "What were you going to say?"

"Nothing. Oh, it's awfully silly." Amusement gleamed in Toni's dark eyes.

"May I hear it, nevertheless?"

"It's nothing ominous."

"Come on, now, Miss—Ney, is it? You look like a sensible girl to me. Don't stall."

"Well, I just remembered that Mrs. Sterling likes to sit in her room with nothing on and throw talcum powder around her." And enjoying the captain's foolish look, she added, "It reminds her of the Versailles fountains. I'm sorry, Captain Torrent, but you asked for it."

Captain Torrent grinned unwillingly. "So I did. To tell you the truth, this Mrs. Sterling bothers me, Miss Ney. I see here that she was through with the treatment about an hour before she actually left. I can't understand why the woman was staying here with nothing to do. Hasn't she anything better to do with her time?"

"Most of our clients," said Toni, "spend most of their lives killing time. This is as good a place to do it as any."

Torrent looked at her with closer attention. His cold blue eyes met her green ones in a level appraising stare. What he saw was an unusually slim, dark young woman, sitting in her chair with her hands folded in her lap as docilely as a schoolgirl. Smart, thought Torrent. Quiet but smart. Aloud he said, "Does she always hang around as long as that?"

"Well, perhaps not quite. But Mrs. Sterling hasn't the slightest conception of time." Toni's slender brows lifted a little. She wondered at this strange interest in Mrs. Sterling.

Torrent was wondering at himself too. He had been asking these questions at random, idly, yet moved by a certain compulsion. And he recognized the reason for it. Hortense's strange little hint of reserve was somehow connected with Mrs. Sterling. And his ear, attuned by many years' practice to catch the slightest nuances of evasion in his witnesses' testimony, seemed to detect that same almost imperceptible tightening up in

Toni at the mention of that name. Torrent stored the fleeting impression away for further reference and passed on to other subjects. He was still at it when Moran leaned against the door. Torrent looked at him inquiringly.

"The inspector and the D.A. have arrived," Moran announced. "They're having their pictures took downstairs."

"Good," said Torrent. "That ought to keep the press happy."

"Yeah, while we do the dirty work. I asked the girl on the fourth floor about Hortense and the kid says yes she saw her upstairs and gave her some damn doodad for downstairs."

"Happen to know the time?"

"Yes. One-twenty-six exactly."

Torrent said, "Funny how everybody gives you the time to the minute." He glanced at Toni.

"Well, we're all pretty time-conscious around here," she explained. "Somebody is always coming to an appointment and so one keeps on glancing at the clock."

"I see. Could you perhaps also tell me, since you are all so time-conscious, why that girl Hortense was a quarter of an hour off about the time when she came back? Was she deliberately lying?"

"I should imagine Hortense would instinctively make the time of her absence from the floor less than it really was. You really are not supposed to leave the floor when you have a client like Mlle. Michaud. But those open doors between floors were a temptation."

"Apparently you don't get much freedom here," Torrent said. "These open doors seem to have driven everybody delirious."

"Just a lot of boids in a golden cage," said Moran sentimentally, and subsided under his superior's severe eye.

"Are the boys through with the room now?" Torrent inquired.

"Yeah. Didn't find nothing interesting. I checked with the girls. There was nothing in the room that didn't belong, except Michaud's things and a newspaper."

"Not very exciting." Torrent shot a quick look at Toni. "You disagree?"

Toni's eyebrows rose faintly. She didn't think that Torrent had been watching her. "It's not that," she said. "I was just wondering whose newspaper it could be."

"Why?" Torrent asked. "I suppose you mean it couldn't be Michaud's who didn't know English well enough to read a paper, but it could be one of the girls..."

Toni shook her head. "Girls are not permitted to bring newspapers upstairs. War is bad for the clients' nerves.".

"Oh, really? We'll have to look into that, then. Miss Ney, you speak French, don't you?"

"Yes."

"I thought you did. You seemed to be amused by that Frenchman's remarks to Miss Illona. What were they, by the way?"

Toni smiled a little. "Nothing out of the way. Monsieur Barrat was speculating on how much money he could squeeze out of Lais as compensation for his Lili."

"The little jerk," remarked Moran. "After that crying act he put on..."

"Both reactions were genuine," Toni said. "This was a great blow to his heart and his pocketbook. Do you know what?" she added. "I bet he's her husband."

"What makes you think so?"

"Oh, the way he handed her dressing gowns and things. What I mean is you could see he's been around her bedroom a lot, yet she wasn't interested in him in the way she would be in a current lover. So he must be her husband."

"Q.E.D." Torrent agreed. "Interesting if true. But we'll soon know if you'll be kind enough to act as my interpreter."

The Frenchman's dark young face was still puffy with tears when he was shown in. Toni scored almost immediately, for upon being questioned about his relationship to Lili, he readily admitted that he was her husband.

"It was not generally known while Lili was alive, for professional reasons," Toni told Torrent.

"I can imagine," Torrent remarked dryly. "You might ask him whether his wife ever suffered from any illness that could carry her off this suddenly."

The Frenchman made a small gesture of disdain and replied volubly.

"He says, in effect, that she was as healthy as an ox."

By dint of minute and careful questioning M. Barrat's activities were somewhat clarified. At 12:00 he brought some fruit on a tray together with some flowers to Mlle. Michaud and was duly photographed proffering this dainty fare to the actress. After the photographers left there was a little argument ("Michaud thought apparently that he was mugging at the camera too much and after all it was her show," Toni explained), and he left with hunks of pineapple in his hair. Yes, he was quite furious, and in that frame of mind he rushed out of the building. After a brief walk along our beautiful Fifth Avenue ("*votre belle Cinquième Avenue*") he cooled down somewhat and went back because he thought Lili needed him ("*elle avait besoin de moi, vous comprenez*"). He waited downstairs until the reporters, who had somehow got wind of the tragedy, stampeded the elevator. He came along, not understanding until the very last the nature of the misfortune that had befallen him. M. Barrat was understandably vague about the times of his departure and return.

After yielding this meager information, M. Barrat was dismissed.

Torrent glanced over his notes and thought again that in spite of everybody's readiness to supply him with information and uncannily exact statements of time, he had very little to show. "It'll have to do for the time being," he told Moran. "We'll know better where we stand after we have heard the M.E.'s report. There's still that little receptionist to talk to. Do you mind sending her in, Miss Ney? Thanks for helping us."

Before departing to the second floor Toni sent Jeanne, who was waiting drearily in the loggia, to see Torrent. She wondered a little at the eagerness with which the little Viennese answered the summons. Her small chin was set in lines of unwonted grim determination as she almost ran to Torrent's office.

"What can she possibly have to tell him that I don't know?" Toni thought, and added soothingly, "I'll find out."

CHAPTER 4

THE ENORMITY of the catastrophe was brought home to the employees when they were dismissed an hour earlier than usual. Making a day at Lais shorter was a phenomenon comparable to Joshua's stopping the sun in heaven. It could only come as a result of flood, fire, or similar act of God. So they filed out with many a grateful and awestricken glance at the blue uniforms posted in strategic places.

It was with a guilty little start that Toni on her way out found Eric Skeets waiting for her in the downstairs passage. He looked at her reproachfully.

"You forgot," he told her, sadly. "You forgot all about our date, you wretch."

"I didn't," Toni said with complete disregard for truth. "I thought you'd call me at my house."

"Where are you bound for?" Eric asked.

"I'm going shopping. There's a sale at Bontemps-Saxe," Toni said. As they walked down Fifth Avenue, she remembered uneasily that somebody else had also been intending to "*faire du* shopping." And now no more shopping for her, no more expensive, frivolous perfumes and graces that made up a good part of what was once Lili Michaud.

"Lady, I am hitching my wagon to your star. Lead on, into the goriest of shambles."

"Brave man. Well, if you think you can take it…"

They swerved into Bontemps' entrance. "Did you have a pleasant chat with Captain Torrent?" Skeets asked, as he followed Toni through a maze of counters to the elevators.

"Quite. He seems to be pretty smart. And you—did he finally break you down?"

"Yes. I told all. I did it with an obscure South American poison— excuse me, madam," he interposed, skirting a large and horrified lady, who had obviously caught his remark. "Seriously, Toni, what do you suppose happened?"

Toni shrugged her shoulders. "I don't know, Mr. Skeets. After all, it's your publicity stunt."

"God!" Young Mr. Skeets made as if to tear at his dark thatch. "I know it too well. Believe it or not, I feel responsible. But you also think that everything wasn't kosher? I overheard Torrent saying that there were no wounds or marks."

"Well, people in perfect health don't just pop off for no reason."

"Maybe she was allergic to that damnable Winogradow pack. How anybody can put on that stuff and wallow in it—and women are supposed to be more fastidious than men. What's in it anyhow?"

"Don't you ever read your own copy? It's a special sort of clay and a lot of beneficial herbs. Just good clean dirt, you know."

"Maybe her food was poisoned."

"If it came from the Ambrosial Bar, certainly. It's a wonder to me that nobody has been poisoned by it before. I think it's because they immunized us by giving us such small doses. But Lili, with her healthy young appetite—" she broke off and added in a lower voice, "This is not precisely the sort of thing that should be discussed in an elevator. People are beginning to give us funny looks."

"Never mind that. I just thought—"

"We get off at the eighth."

Skeets stumbled after her abstractedly. "It was Barrat who brought her lunch."

"Yes. Maybe that's why she didn't like it. Remember? She promptly threw it at him, justly incensed at being served arsenic with her salad."

She stopped before a rack of dresses and surveyed them dispassionately. "I saw this at Klein's for four bucks," she said darkly.

"There should be a law," said Skeets dutifully. "Look, I would have sworn that the act he put on was the real McCoy. Besides, she was his meal ticket. Why should he kill her?"

"For each man kills the thing he loves," Toni intoned melodramatically. "Excuse me for a minute, will you? I think I see a dress."

She insinuated her slender form into the melee of women milling around a rack of dresses. Eric looked about him helplessly and was immediately accosted by a salesgirl who wanted to know whether he saw anything he liked. He pointed vaguely to a vivid red spot and was feebly gratified by seeing her dash off after it.

Toni, emerging empty-handed from a crowd that had proved too much for her, saw him standing with a red velvet dress draped on his arm.

"Oh." She surveyed it, head cocked to one side. "For me?"

"Just a little thing I threw together. Red, isn't it?"

"Yes, quite. I'll try it on, if I may."

Toni's reflection in the mirror twirled, and it was like a red tongue of flame leaping.

"And it fits me like a glove." There was respect in her voice. Eric cleared his throat.

"I like that effect around your hips."

"The peplum? Yes, it's a fine dress. Thanks for picking it for me, Eric." She smiled at him and Skeets suddenly felt absurdly exhilarated. "Do you know what? I'm going to wear it tonight. It's so pretty."

"That," said Skeets solemnly, "is a very pretty gesture. I feel as if I'd been knighted or something. Now where do we go from here? Is there anything else I can pick out for you? Or will you just take that price tag off and let me take you to dinner?"

"Not so fast. I've got to go home and feed my cat first. He is a very temperamental animal and he likes his dinner on time."

Toni lived in a brownstone house within walking distance of Lais. There were two rooms. The larger one boasted an outsize window that took up a whole wall, a fireplace, and a tiny kitchenette skillfully camouflaged with a screen, the rest of the wall space given to bookshelves and prints, among which Skeets happily recognized some of his own favorites. The bedroom consisted of a couch and a bursting closet. Toni installed Skeets comfortably in a chair with a drink and went to the bedroom to look for accessories to her new dress. First, however, she introduced him to Tom Jones, a gray Persian who had greeted her with a cordiality that froze when he caught sight of Skeets.

Skeets sipped at his cocktail and listened to Toni talking in the other room, while Tom Jones sat in front of him holding him, like the ancient mariner, with a cold amber eye, his plume-like tail curled around his front legs.

"What seems so peculiar to me," Toni was saying, "is that here's a perfect stranger killed at Lais with so many candidates of our own. Why, everybody is after everybody else's scalp in that place. There's the fascinating Dr. Berchtold, with all those females after him, in the midst of half a dozen intrigues, and Illona and Maurice hate each other like poison, and of course, everybody hates Howe. But what happens? An outsider off the boat without any associations or connections—"

"Lili struck me as the type that made connections easily," Skeets remarked. "Berchtold went after her in a big way."

"All the males in this highly feminine establishment did."

"Count one out. I guess I haven't told you this, but I had a bright idea of taking some pictures in the laboratory—cheesecake in science, you know, or is it vice versa? So I took her up to the sixth floor with a bunch of photographers."

"When was that?"

"Just before she came down to you. Anyhow, we battered on Winogradow's door and he turned us down flat. Got sore as a coot. Yelled his head off, with Lili standing there fluttering eyelashes."

"No soap, eh?"

"No effect whatsoever. I haven't told this to the Kyria, figuring I'd put my foot in it that time."

"Incidentally, there's another instance. Howe can't stand Winogradow. He gives her the creeps. I've heard her telling the Kyria that he shouldn't be allowed on the premises. So there's another potential murder, a much more sensible business than the Michaud one."

"You sound downright petulant about it."

"Well, I am disappointed," said Toni. She came into the room in her red dress with red sandals on her small feet. Tiny golden earrings glittered in her ears. "I have always thought that one day I'd find Alicia Howe with her throat slit from ear to ear. I feel that a hideous mistake has been made."

"Never mind that," said Skeets, getting up hastily. "Gosh, you look pretty."

"Thanks. If you'll pick out the dresses of young ladies you go out with you'll be sure to be satisfied. Stay out of my nylon stockings, will you, angel puss. How do you like my cat?"

"He's a beautiful hunk of cat," said Eric. "I don't think he likes me, though. I hope you don't belong to the 'There-Must-Be-Something-Wrong-With-You-If-My-Cat-Doesn't-Like-You' school."

"My cat," said Toni, smiling, "is entitled to his opinion as I am to mine."

"Good," said Skeets, relieved. He grinned at her and bent down to pat the cat. "Nice pussy. You and I are going to be great friends, ha, ha."

Tom Jones buried his chin in his enormous gray ruff and looked at Skeets broodingly. A white-lined ear flattened down distrustfully at the approach of Skeets' hand, and a tiny hiss issued from a suddenly cavernous pink mouth.

Skeets straightened up and looked at him coldly. "Do you know," he said thoughtfully, "I've always wanted to kick a cat. They've got such nice furry behinds. Come on, let's get out of here."

"Yes, let's. All these emotions have given me a healthy appetite."

"Besides," said Skeets, "we'll have to find out all about each other at dinner. All I know about you is that you like ballet, don't like the place where you are working, and have enough wit and charm to endow an army. True, somehow I feel very close to you. But I want to know why."

"Murder is supposed to bring people close," Toni remarked.

"Always provided," Skeets said helping her into her coat, "that it's somebody else's murder."

Captain Torrent looked over his notes and lifted the receiver. "No news from the M.E. yet? Hurry him up, will you? I particularly want to know about the contents of her stomach, and oh, yes, tell him to take a look at her throat. No, I don't know. It's just an idea."

He returned to his notes. It was a peculiar case all right. He felt that familiar tremor of excitement, the same feeling that a photographer has when the first faint outline of his picture begins to take shape on the wet paper, or that a scientist feels when he sees a hardly perceptible pattern forming on the slide. Perhaps the second simile was a more appropriate one. There was no shape as yet, just a few disconnected facts showing a tendency to cluster together, like cells around the nucleus of an as yet unknown organism.

Lili Michaud had died sometime between 1:00 and 1:30. That was the time that the floor was left unwatched. And that fitted into a larger time-unit, the time during which the elevator was out of commission and the doors were open between floors, allowing people to circulate. Soon, he knew, it was going to narrow down to minutes and everybody would have to avail himself of the terrific time-consciousness that seemed to prevail at Lais to give account of the way these minutes were spent. There would be something else to clear up: the reticences, the unspoken things that he had felt during the interviews. Torrent set a tiny but decisive mark next to the name of Hortense. She had been ready enough with her answers, but there was something odd about the way she had stayed away from the floor and lied about the time she came in.

Then there was Toni Ney. His feeling about her was different. It was not that she had withheld anything from him; he felt rather that he had failed to ask her something. She would probably tell him if he knew what to ask. Torrent had a feeling about her. She affected him as a well-designed tool does a good worker; with a little practice he would be able to make good use of her. He saw again her enigmatic, triangular face, with that disconcerting flash of amusement in the green eyes, when she told him about Mrs. Sterling's peculiar habit of strewing powder about. (Mrs. Sterling—that was another strange thing, her staying around so long after the treatment was over. Probably didn't mean anything.) But she had been helpful and quick, about the newspaper, for instance.

He looked at the paper in question again, more closely. It was folded, he noticed, at Alicia Howe's column. That might mean something. He read the thing through carefully. His eyebrows lifted. The woman wielded a nasty pen. He read on more carefully, trying to get the feel of her personality from the vicious little double entendres and brickbats couched in elegantly trenchant prose and thrown impartially at senators and debutantes. What was it he knew about Alicia Howe? She had a nasty tongue and a dreadful temper. She had fought with Lili Michaud over the room. People disliked her at the salon, particularly that little receptionist, the honey-blonde Viennese. There was an unmistakable trembling hatred in her voice when she told him what she did about Alicia Howe, about the fight and the other thing. He thought, smiling, that she sounded like a little girl going to the teacher with a story. Was it any less true because of that? A talk with Alicia Howe would tell him. At any rate she was going to have his special attention. He went on reading and pretty soon stopped at the poisonous item which, earlier in the day, Eric Skeets had brought to Toni's attention.

Another thing to add to Alicia Howe's record. He reread the whole column again, trying to decide whether there was a note of personal animosity in that item or whether the venom was purely professional. Could it be that she had known Michaud before their skirmish at Lais? That was something else he had to ask her.

One thing was a comfort. He didn't have to worry about crowds of possible murderers invading the third floor during the time when it was unguarded. Many people had gone out to lunch and so could be eliminated. Also it stood to reason that women blinded by those hideous masks or attached to electric machines were for the time being immobilized and also immobilized their attendants. The custom of not allowing the client to move a step without a Lais employee at her heels helped considerably. Practically all the clients and operators on the four floors could vouch for each other. Fifth and sixth were, as Illona explained, not connected with the others. Torrent had spoken to the man who operated the back elevator and got from him the names of people who used it. They all went down to the salon on the first floor, and it would have been impossible for them to use the stairs to get to the third floor without passing the sentinel below—all except the Kyria, and she got off at the second floor.

Torrent supposed that his task would eventually narrow down to the exhaustive examination of the people whose movements between 1:00 and 1:30 were unaccounted for. That is, if the autopsy showed what he rather suspected it would show. Tomorrow—Torrent rubbed his eyes and pushed his notes away. The facts were arranged in his head in an orderly mental folder, with space left over to accommodate unknown factors. He could forget about the whole affair for the time being.

Torrent fumbled in his top drawer and with an eye on the door brought out a long strip of paper—a handbill headed by the words *The Program of the Ballet of Monte Carlo*. Tonight's program, he noted with satisfaction, contained *Aurora's Wedding*.

The court of Princess Aurore, all rose pink with a tinge of scarlet, had just glissé-ed and chassé-ed through a typical finale and was bowing gratefully, when Toni grasped her escort's arm with an exclamation of amazement.

"Look," she said. "There, two rows in front of us!"

Skeets gaped at a ruddy trim man at whom she was pointing.

Toni said, "I've been looking at him for ages and wondering vaguely why he looked so familiar. What do you suppose he's doing here? Is he—what do you call it—tailing us?"

Skeets looked hard at Captain Andrew Torrent, who was apparently engrossed in reading those involved program notes whose sole purpose seems to be the complete and utter confusion of the reader.

"I don't think he's tailing us. I mean, after all, it's we who are behind him, not he behind us."

"It's funny, though, his being here, I mean."

It was long before Toni and Skeets could watch the ballet with the rapt attention it deserved. Their eyes kept straying from the stage to Captain Torrent. He seemed to be unconscious of their scrutiny. They forgot about him, however, when the prima ballerina, radiant in swan's-down and rhinestones, bounced onto the stage within the tender embrace of her partner. It was only when the ballet was over and they were applauding furiously that they remembered him again. His seat was empty.

"Maybe we just dreamed him," Toni remarked.

"Must have been that lobster we ate."

They drifted backstage under a barrage of excited chatter in French and Russian, interspersed with enthusiastic comments in English on Danilova's elevation and Gorin's precision. It was to the latter's dressing room that they made their way through Degas-like groups of wilted ballerinas.

"Gorin's name is really Mike Gordon," Toni explained to Skeets. "He's a nice Irish lad who by some miraculous freak decided he wanted to be a ballet dancer. He used to be my partner during my meteoric career as a dancer."

"Irish, eh? I thought all ballet dancers were Russian."

"It's a tradition. Mike's even developed a nice Russian accent now."

Gorin, a sandy-haired, slim man in his thirties, stopped creaming his face to greet Toni warmly. Toni introduced Skeets, and Gorin acknowledged the introduction graciously. He waved an airy hand toward the corner.

"I want you to meet a friend of mine, Captain Andy Torrent of the New York police."

Captain Torrent who, tastefully framed by a Spanish bolero and a *Spectre de la Rose* costume, had been quietly smoking his pipe in the corner, rose to his feet.

"Well," said Skeets inanely. "Fancy meeting you here!"

"Andy is an old friend," said Gorin. "First cop I've met who had the brains to appreciate ballet. Why, he even took a few lessons from me, didn't you, Andy? It certainly built you up."

The captain's naturally ruddy complexion became painfully heightened. He was the most embarrassed man they had ever seen. He even sweated faintly under his curly red hair. A pall of embarrassment descended on everybody except Gorin, who had addressed himself to the mirror again.

Toni said, wide-eyed, "So that's why you walk and move so well, Captain. I noticed that the minute I saw you. It even surprised me, because, if you'll forgive me, men in your profession as a rule don't move lightly."

"Flatfeets," said Gorin, going Slavic, and laughed. But miraculously Toni had said the right thing. The red tide subsided from Torrent's face. He said a little sheepishly, "Mike here blarneyed me into a few lessons at the bar, that's all. Just like setting up exercises, they were."

"I always told Andy he'd make a good dancer," Gorin said. "He's strong and wiry and flexible."

"I prefer my present position," said Torrent grinning. "This way I don't have to talk with a phony Russian accent."

"Oh yeah?" said Michel Gorin, né Mike Gordon, in perfect Brooklynese, "In that case, how about scramming out of here while I finish dressing. So long, Andy, nice to see you. Goodbye, Toni me darling. Glad to have met you, Mr. Skeets."

The three balletomanes left the theater talking amiably. Finding that neither Toni nor Skeets found his fatal secret excruciatingly amusing, Torrent let down his reserves and listened respectfully while Toni and Eric wrangled over the respective merits of their favorite ballerinas.

At that point Skeets suggested a drink at the Astor Bar, and Torrent, to Toni's secret surprise, agreed.

They settled down in a dimly lighted booth. Toni and Skeets faced Torrent, feeling somewhat like high-school children who have invited their teacher for a soda. Determinedly they talked ballet. Inevitably Nijinski's name came up.

"Oh, yes," said Torrent. "The daddy of them all. You think Mike's elevation is anything like his?" he inquired, in the tones of an anxious father worrying about the prowess of his offspring. "Not that I expect you to remember anything about Nijinski, Miss Ney."

"I remember a terrific publicity stunt built around him," said Skeets. "Another guy danced *Spectre de la Rose* for him and old Nijinski came out of his daze and electrified everybody by doing a famous Nijinski leap or something. Somebody even took a picture of it and it appeared in some picture magazine."

"If you ask me, a fake, if there ever was one," said Toni uncompromisingly, fishing an olive out of her martini.

"How's that? I remember the photograph and his feet were off the ground, all right."

"Yes, parallel with the ground and out at right angles, like a duck's. Look, Captain Torrent. When you jump up, your feet automatically point down even if you've never made a ballet step in your life. That's what pushes you up in the air. Nijinski is a dancer who has been trained to point down. He could no more hold his feet in that position when leaping than I could walk a tightrope. What they did was put him on a chair and then paint out the chair."

Skeets applauded and Torrent looked at Toni with renewed attention.

"You have pretty good eyes, don't you? Not very much gets by you."

"Why, thank you," Toni smiled at him. "Praise from Sir Hubert is great praise indeed."

"Bright, isn't she?" said Skeets, like a proud animal trainer with a pet seal.

"She is," Torrent replied, gravely. "I thought so when I was questioning her this morning. That's what made it so annoying, that I couldn't get more out of her."

Toni's eyes widened with surprise. "I told you all you asked me."

"I know. That's why I keep asking myself: what is it that I didn't ask her?"

"For heaven's sake." Toni batted her dark eyelashes rapidly. "I don't know whether to be flattered or alarmed."

"So far," said Torrent, "you can be flattered. You *are* rather quick, you know. For example, that newspaper—that was smart."

"Did you find anything of interest there?" Toni inquired.

"Yes," Torrent said. "That was a nasty little paragraph about Lili Michaud."

"Wasn't it, though?" Skeets interposed. "If Michaud had seen it, her aim with the cream jar might have been much better, don't you think?"

Toni giggled. "Personally, I like the idea of dear Alicia having to duck cream jars, for a change."

"Why, does she usually throw them?"

"When they are handy. She threw one at a facial operator the other day because the towels she put on her face were too hot."

"And what happened?"

"Naturally," said Toni, "the girl got fired. Oh, we all love Alicia."

"To get back to her column. Why should she have written such a vicious squib? It must have been meant to embarrass Michaud."

"And other people," Skeets pointed out. "What about the gentleman known as S.?"

"Dear Chester," said Toni.

"Do you happen to know who…?"

"Well, yes. Mrs. Sterling was completely and utterly derailed by this squib. Called Washington—that's where Mr. S. is, you know. You know how she is…" Toni stopped again and laughed apologetically. "Of course, you don't know. Lucky man."

"Would you mind telling me about her?"

"It's just that she was awfully upset by the column and by Lili's presence. When I read the column—that bit about Mr. S.'s blondes meeting in a salon—I just put two and two together."

"Tell me everything that happened, please."

Toni did. Her look of amused bafflement was slowly wearing off. She had gotten the connection at last.

When she was through Torrent said softly, "I knew there was something to be gotten out of you." His cold blue eyes rested on her with approval, then they shifted to the clock. He rose. "Will you excuse me? I have to make a call to my office."

"On our case?" Skeets grinned. Torrent strode away with a faint answering grin. Toni said to Skeets, "I seem to have given him an idea."

"Well, of course, you have. It's so obvious. The newspaper in that room, and Sterling being in a room near Lili when everybody else was out, and now this new factor about Mr. S. Simple. Torrent is practically as bright as I am."

"Both of you dazzle me. But do you really think that giddy little dope…?" She thought and shrugged her shoulders. "Maybe," she added and addressed herself thoughtfully to her drink.

Torrent came back. An indefinable change had come over him. "Policeman ousting the balletomane," Toni thought. His next question, however, was not about Mrs. Sterling but about Alicia Howe. He wanted to know whether she, personally, had anything much to do with the columnist.

"I give her exercises occasionally. Building up ones—she's so shockingly skinny. Outside of that I, like everybody else, try to avoid contact with her. She's a difficult client."

"Because of her temper?"

"Yes, and because of her peculiar mania. She can't bear to be touched, you know. People seem unclean to her. She's constantly spraying the air around her. That's why she spends more time at Lais than anywhere else—it's kind of hygienic there in a lush way. But she insists on using her own mattress for the exercises and she has fits if I touch her."

"I can see how it would be difficult for you. Incidentally, Miss Ney, you seem to be an all around expert on exercises there. I understand you've been teaching exercises for defense jujitsu, etc. Have you taught it to many people?"

Toni stared at him puzzled. "Jujitsu? Oh, that stuff. I'm afraid not. I'm sorry to say our clients are far more interested in multiplying their charms than in defending their virtue."

Torrent chortled appreciatively, "That's clear enough. How much do you know, yourself, incidentally?"

Toni said, "Well—this is confidential, I hope. Practically nothing. You see, this is the way it works. Mr. Skeets here gets a bright idea about teaching jujitsu to our clients. Being a persuasive young man he persuades the Kyria to try it out. A booklet is made up with me photographed in convincing poses. Then if the idea goes across and people start signing up for lessons, I study up as fast as I can."

Captain Torrent pulled a booklet out of his pocket and scanned it thoughtfully. "It says here," he observed, "expert instructor."

"That's me," Toni acknowledged modestly. "I'm a fast learner. At any rate, Mr. Skeets' brilliant scheme flopped and I didn't have to learn jujitsu."

"In a way, I'm glad you didn't," said Eric. "I feel much safer with you this way."

"It was your idea in the first place," Toni pointed out.

"Are you going, Captain Torrent?" The latter was motioning to a waiter.

"Yes, I think so." He beamed on them paternally. "This is on me. Come on, no nonsense. You've been very helpful to me, don't you know."

"How nice," Toni said politely if a little blankly.

"In that case," Skeets chimed in, "I think you owe us a little inside dope in return. How about it, Captain Torrent? How did Lili Michaud die?"

"I suppose there's no harm in telling you," said Torrent. "The Michaud girl died of strangulation as a result of fractured larynx. Well, it was nice seeing you. Incidentally"—he hesitated and his cheerful face flushed faintly—"I'd be obliged if you'd keep my—well, my interest in ballet to yourself, don't you know."

"Naturally, Captain. We understand. Goodbye."

Toni watched him striding lightly out of the restaurant and laughed in soft amusement. "I can see him in tights, holding on to a bar. He's a dear, isn't he?"

"Yes," said Eric sourly. He was in deep thought.

"You look bleak, Mr. Skeets. It is rather sickening about Lili Michaud, isn't it? How do you figure out that broken larynx business?"

"Don't call me Mr. Skeets," said Eric automatically. "Well, I've heard of a fighter who died because somebody smashed him in the throat and broke his Adam's apple."

"My God, how awful," Toni, staring at Skeets, felt her eyes growing big, like a cat's. "Eric, I can see it so clearly. Somebody came in while she was lying there, all covered up, with the mask on her face so that she couldn't see and her throat—such a pretty throat, too. One blow on that exposed throat..."

"Yes," said Eric, "one short sharp shock, as Gilbert and Sullivan have it, by somebody who knows how to inflict it in a telling spot."

"Jujitsu," Toni said. "Yes. And I am such a fast learner. Isn't that what I told Captain Torrent just now?"

"You did," Skeets said, "He is a dear, isn't he?

CHAPTER 5

WHEN TONI went back to Lais the next morning (it was Thursday), her uppermost emotion was that of curiosity. The House of Lais was—must be—shaken to its very foundations by the blow dealt it by an unkind fate. Its very appearance should be different.

Of course no such thing was true. Everything was the same. The house of Lais was like a veteran lady of pleasure after a night's orgy, presenting an unchanged face to the curious world, with only perhaps the blue circles under the eyes to betray her. In the salon itself, under Illona's vigilant eye, the girls behaved as usual. No little groups gathered to discuss yesterday's events.

The only material change was that the few remaining bottles of Kismet no longer graced the shelves, having been graciously given to the policemen stationed in the salon, who had been seduced by their ornate appearance. The last customer to order this overpowering perfume was an oriental looking woman, clearly a proprietress of an Istanbul bordello, who bought the perfume in order to cater to the Arab trade. Toni shuddered at the thought of decent Irish families drenched in its purple fumes.

On Toni's floor the excitement cropped up mainly in the form of newspapers surreptitiously smuggled up and furtively discussed; their front pages bore in regrettably large type the words: FRENCH STAR SLAIN IN BEAUTY SALON. Also the clients all came on time. Without exception they came not to get exercises but a full and explicit report of the day before.

"To think," one of them commented with heartfelt regret, "that if I hadn't put off my treatment until today, I could have seen it all myself instead of having to depend on what you have to tell me."

Her tone implied profound disappointment in Toni's reportorial powers.

The third floor, when Toni visited it, was in a state of mild disorganization. Jeanne, who was busy taking calls at the desk, gave Toni a wan smile.

"What a morning," she said, having put down the receiver. "Do you know, these women are calling by dozens asking for the Winogradow treatment. All of them want to come to this floor."

"How charming," said Toni, and added, quoting the tabloids, "The murder floor."

"That's it, I suppose. One woman called and insisted on getting the room in which the murder was committed, otherwise she didn't want the facial. She sounded so—I don't know—nasty and hysterical. Ugh."

Apparently she was the only specimen of that kind, the others confining themselves to less morbid requests. Illona was at first only too delighted with this unexpected deluge, having in her innocence expected the opposite, until one of the clients turned out to be a tabloid press photographer. She quickly and efficiently photographed the room and the floor from all angles while everybody stood gaping and departed without bothering to take the treatment. After this distressing occurrence, Illona issued an order that all new clients bound for the third floor should be scrutinized with particular attention by the appointments desk and even, if possible, subjected to a little questioning. And under no circumstances should anybody be allowed to look into the room where Lili Michaud had died.

"Except, I suppose, Alicia Howe," Toni remarked. "After all, it's her room. I shouldn't imagine she'll want it, though, after what has happened."

Jeanne's blue eyes darkened strangely.

"She will want it, Toni. It'll make her happy to sit in that room and think of what has happened there."

"Look here," said Toni, "aren't you getting one of these obsessions about Alicia Howe? Next thing you'll say she did it."

"Supposing I do say it? Toni, when they had that fight, she threatened to kill her!"

"I heard her."

"Well?"

"Well, you can't take that sort of thing very seriously. I've heard you say that you'd like to wring Alicia's neck, but I don't think you would, even if you had a chance."

"Wouldn't I?" Jeanne's smile was crooked. "I wouldn't bet on it."

"In any case, you oughtn't to show your dislike of Howe so openly. Particularly not to the police. Why? Because if you have any damaging evidence against her they'll discount half, because of your attitude."

"But I did tell them the truth."

"And that was...?"

"I told them I saw Howe going up from the second floor. I was waiting for the Kyria. And I saw Howe sneak out of the doctor's room and go upstairs, when she was supposed to be resting. I knew that heart attack was phony," she added contemptuously.

"When was that?" Toni wanted to know. So that was the reason for Torrent's questions about Alicia Howe's character.

"About five or ten minutes after I came down. I was behind the showcase and she didn't see me. Do you really think the policeman didn't believe me, because he could see that I disliked that woman?" Jeanne's smooth forehead creased. "Surely they will know that I said the truth...

"I knew even then she was up to no good. And the minute I saw that Lili Michaud was dead, I knew who had done it. Excuse me," she added somewhat anticlimactically and turned to answer the telephone. "Yes, Miss Gorham. No, Hortense isn't back yet. No, she didn't know when they'd be through with her. Of course, I will, Miss Gorham. People have been asking for Hortense the whole morning," she said turning to Toni. "I suppose because she was taking care of Michaud yesterday."

"Well, where is she now?"

Hortense, it seems, had been summoned to headquarters early this morning. She had gone in a very nasty and uncooperative mood. For one thing, she wasn't sure that the time spent by her in aiding justice would not be deducted from her pay, the management of Lais being pretty close with money.

"I don't think they'll deduct this time, though," Jeanne mused, "because isn't this like jury duty?"

"More like an act of God," Toni returned. She was wondering what it was that Torrent was trying to get out of Hortense and whether it had anything to do with what she had told him.

Hortense sat in the hard-backed chair at Torrent's office and wept
expertly into a small handkerchief. She was weeping, she averred, because Captain Torrent was doubting her word. Torrent, unimpressed, let
her go on for a while. That was his usual technique. There was, he knew,
a limit to how long a woman can go on shedding bitter, passionate, effective tears. After a while the tear ducts dry up, sobs turn to sniffles and you
go on with the questioning.

There were two questions he wanted to clear up. One was why
Hortense left the floor for such a long time, namely from 1:00 to 1:30, and
the other was what she was doing with herself until she came back. "During those thirty minutes," he pointed out, "somebody killed your client.
Now the sooner you tell me these things the better. If you don't I'll just
naturally have to assume that you were doing something you don't want
the police to know about."

Hortense blanched and drew a perfectly dry-eyed face away from
her handkerchief.

"Listen, I don't know what you're trying to say…"

"Don't bother guessing. Just let's go over your movements again."

By dint of careful questioning he got her out of Michaud's room at
12:55, off the floor at 1:00. Then they got down to the second floor, where
Hortense saw Dr. Berchtold coming out of his office. More questioning
committed Hortense to the beautiful spectacle of herself and the doctor
walking up the stairs together to the fourth floor. Here Hortense stalled
for a bit until Torrent reminded her delicately of what was presumably
happening on the third floor in the meanwhile. Then she told Torrent that
she and the doctor had been engaged in conversation until 1:25 when he
went in to see Princess Lubescu, to reassure her that she was not allergic
to the new hair dye. As for Hortense, she finally picked up the hair atomizer and went back to the third floor.

Questioned about the nature of her conversation with the doctor,
Hortense said it was something personal. Torrent, noting the mulish
expression on her face, did not press her. He turned to something
else.

"How is it," he asked, "that you were taking care of two important
customers like Michaud and Sterling at the same time"

"I wasn't." Hortense denied it vehemently. "I was through with Sterling at twelve-thirty, before I took Michaud on."

"Yet she sent you out on an errand."

"Well, it's customary to come in and ask your client if there's anything
you can do for her before she goes home."

"Otherwise you were free to attend Michaud?"

"Of course I was. I was all through with Sterling. Except, of course, to get that atomizer for her hair."

"Now once again, there was nothing you needed to do for her except get her that atomizer?"

"Of course not. Why, she was all dressed and everything. She even went home before I came down."

"Yet it took you thirty minutes to get that atomizer. Isn't there something funny about your keeping a customer waiting for thirty minutes for you to put the last touch on her before she goes home, while you talk to Dr. Berchtold about personal matters?"

Hortense, trapped, glared at him malevolently. You could see her busy little brain running through excuses and swiftly discarding them one by one. Into her confusion, Torrent shot a well-placed arrow. "How much did Mrs. Sterling pay you to get that atomizer for her?"

"It's none of your business how much she—" Hortense stopped again. She shrugged her shoulders and in an entirely different voice said, "All right. She wanted to have a talk with Michaud and she asked me to keep away until she had a chance to do so."

The two questions were answered. At the end of the interview, Torrent replaced them with two others. One, what did Hortense have to ask Dr. Berchtold? The other, why was she at first so eager to protect Mrs. Sterling, only to turn about and give damaging evidence against her with the utmost readiness, once she admitted being paid to stay away from the floor? The first question he decided to clear up immediately by telephoning Lais and asking Dr. Berchtold to come down to headquarters. The second he filed away for future reference.

"Hortense?" Berchtold said. "Oh yes. I picked her up on the second floor, and we went up together to the fourth. We talked together there in one of the booths before I went in to see Princess Lubescu. That was, I believe, at one-twenty-five, because that is when the Princess's treatment started and she wanted to speak to me before it did. I came down ten minutes later. As a matter of fact, I remember passing Toni—the exercise director, you know—on the stairs. Directly upon coming down I met the Kyria, who had just come down by the back elevator, and we talked until I was called upstairs to see Mlle. Michaud."

Torrent wanted to know what the conversation with Hortense was about. Berchtold hesitated and turned his charming smile full force on the unimpressed policeman.

"You know, Captain, doctors are something like father confessors. I'd much rather not tell you unless it's absolutely necessary. Is it sufficient to say that the matter was personal?"

"You mean Hortense was consulting you as a doctor?"

"That's right, Captain. Many people in the organization do so."

Torrent looked at Dr. Berchtold and wondered why he disliked this genial, pleasant-mannered individual. Dr. Berchtold's icy blue eyes shone with the spirit of cooperation. He was a handsome figure in his dark suit, with a rich pearl pin glowing pleasantly in his immaculate mauve tie, and a mauve corner of his immaculate handkerchief peeping out of his pocket. Torrent asked him about the state in which he had left Alicia Howe in his office and was pleased to see a slight shadow pass over the doctor's face. He spoke vaguely about nerves, a heart condition. Torrent interrupted him.

"What I am trying to find out, doctor, is whether Miss Howe was sufficiently recovered to get out of your room by herself."

Dr. Berchtold hesitated and Torrent, who watched him narrowly, guessed that he was weighing the advisability of answering in the negative. He could almost tell to the second when Dr. Berchtold discarded that as a bad idea. He remembered, Torrent said to himself, that Toni had left her almost recovered and that other people probably heard her screaming at him.

Dr. Berchtold answered slowly, "Yes, I think she was, Captain. She was certainly well enough to go home, although not to indulge in any strenuous activities."

Like killing Lili Michaud, you mean, Torrent said to himself. He ushered the doctor out politely, conscious of not so much a certainty that the doctor was not entirely open with him as that he personally would very much enjoy catching him in a lie.

Left alone, he buzzed Moran in. "I want you to send somebody over to Lais to check on the fourth floor. I want to see if anybody saw Dr. Berchtold and this girl Hortense talking together and if so for how long. And I want to look again at that list you got from the girl stationed near the exit."

"Okay," said Moran. "We located that dame and brought her in. The Howe woman. She's waiting."

"Oh?" Torrent thought a minute. "Let her wait a while, and get me that list."

The list was carefully arranged from the testimony of the girl whose name was Brigitte (in private life Bridget Murphy) and who ordinarily worked in the salon. The names of people who came in and came out were written down separately in the sequence in which they arrived.

It looked something like this:

People who went up the stairs from 12:30 to 1:40 (time when elevator was stuck):
Suzette (operator on the third floor) at 12:30, came back from lunch.
Imogen (manicurist on the fourth) 12:45, ditto.
Mrs. Glendenning for her 1:00 o'clock appointment.
Hilda (masseuse on the second floor) at 1:05.
Dr. Winogradow at 1:10-1:15
Marthe, the elevator operator, 1:35.

People who came down the stairs at the time elevator was stalled:
Mesdames Smith, Carroll, and Nash (clients from the fourth floor) at 12:30.
Mesdames Parmalee and Flynn (clients from second floor) 12:45.
Evelyn (masseuse, 4th floor) 1:00—going out for lunch.
Alicia Howe at 1:10-1:15
Mrs. Sterling at 1:20.
Dimitri from the fourth floor at 1:35.

"The only people about whose times she was definitely sure," said Moran, pointing with a stubby finger, "are the employees, on account of she was posted there for the purpose of noting down at what time they went out to lunch, so that the organization shouldn't get cheated of a minute of its time, God forbid. Others we worked out with reference to these known times. Like she took the time of Hilda the masseuse and then Howe came out about ten minutes later, which fixes her at about one-fifteen. I checked up the clients' times with the appointments desk besides."

"Good," Torrent said. He drew lines through some of the names. "We are not interested in people who left before one, because we know that Michaud was alive then. We are particularly interested in people who were going either up or down the stairs from one to one-thirty. And of course we've got to check on any interfloor activity at that time. Better get some men on that, Moran, and let me know about it." He stopped suddenly. "What do I see? A man with the same name as that Godawful stuff on Michaud's face seems to have been hanging around during the crucial time."

"That's the company chemist. The girl," Moran volunteered, "thought it was kinda funny. He usually goes straight to the sixth floor, where he's got a lab."

"We shall have to have a talk with him," said Torrent. He set a check near the chemist's name. "And with this lady, too." He checked Mrs. Sterling's name and his pencil hovered over the name above hers. "And with this one. Send her in, Moran."

Alicia Howe walked into the office, sat down at the desk, lit a cigarette and, without replying to Torrent's greeting, said, "Well?"

Torrent, who had risen to his feet, sat down, too, and began his examination without further ado. "Miss Howe, did you know Miss Lili Michaud personally?"

The columnist stared at him as if he had just crawled out of a crack in the wall and she simply must speak to the landlord about it.

"Hell, no."

"Then the first time you met her was yesterday?"

"Yes."

"I understand you had a disagreement with the deceased."

Alicia Howe's haggard face twitched. "You know damn well I did."

"Could you tell us something about it?"

"No." Miss Howe's nostrils fluttered a little. "You've probably heard the story a dozen times and I have no intention of wasting my time repeating it again for you."

"I see." Torrent looked at her more closely. Unquestionably she was going to be difficult. "People usually prefer to give their side of the story. You might want to later, yourself, don't you know."

"How considerate!" Alicia Howe laughed unpleasantly. "Quite the gentleman policeman, aren't you? Quite the Sir Roderick Alleyn of Scotland Yard!"

Torrent disregarded this flattering comment. "What I am chiefly interested in is your activities after your quarrel with Miss Michaud and during the time of the murder. Dr. Berchtold took you down, didn't he?"

"Yes, to his office on the second floor. I wasn't feeling well."

"Did he stay with you all the time you were in his office?"

"No," said Alicia after a hesitation. "He went out soon after."

"And you?"

Miss Howe didn't answer at once. She plucked a cigarette out of her cigarette case with careful though not entirely steady fingers and waited for Torrent to light it before she answered.

"I stayed in the office for a while until I felt better, then I went home."

"I'd like a little more detail, Miss Howe. What time did you leave the office?"

"I haven't the slightest idea."

"Well how long do you think you stayed there after he left?"

"I don't know, I tell you."

"Was it nearer an hour or ten minutes?"

"The latter."

"Do you think it was more or less than ten minutes?"

"What the hell does it matter?"

"I am afraid that it does matter, Miss Howe."

"Well, I can't tell you more exactly."

"Can't or won't, Miss Howe?"

Miss Howe crushed her cigarette out savagely. "I can't remember whether it was ten, fifteen, or twenty minutes."

"Very well. Did anybody see you as you went out?"

"I don't know. I am not particularly concerned whether any of those little—"

"I see. Then you went—where?"

"Out," said Alicia Howe flatly.

"Using the stairs?"

"Yes."

"Did you stop anywhere on your way down?"

"No."

"Not to pick up your coat or something?"

"I had my coat with me."

"I see. Then you went—where?"

"I took a taxi and went for a ride."

"Did you go through the salon exit or did you use the employees' exit?"

"The latter."

There was an almost imperceptible sag of relief in her shoulders, as Torrent asked her a few more questions about her ride home. And then he sharply doubled back.

"Miss Howe, you say you went straight downstairs without stopping."

"That's right. What are you trying to do, play ring-around-the-rosy?"

"Yet one of the girls saw you go upstairs after you left the doctor's office."

Alicia Howe straightened up in her chair slowly, like a snake about to strike. "That's a lie. What girl? I didn't see any girl around."

"There was one around, nevertheless."

"I don't care if there were a thousand of them around. What are you trying to do, damn you? How dare you doubt my word? How dare you sit here goggling at me and insinuate— Whom do you think you're talking to? One of your prostitute floozies? I'll have you off the force so fast you won't know what hit you. I—"

"Shut up," said Torrent. His voice had suddenly grown cold and savage. "Cut out the hysterics, or I'll paste you one."

The woman choked and blinked, staring at him with unbelieving amazement. Her mouth fell open foolishly. Moran stared too. Never before had he heard his chief use this tone of voice to a woman, not even to those of the species to which Alicia Howe had alluded so warmly. "Limey" Torrent was known on the force for his polite ways with the ladies.

"I—I—" began Alicia Howe, spluttering.

"Now listen here. This is a murder investigation and you are under suspicion just like anybody else. Don't kid yourself. You're in a pretty bad spot unless you can answer my questions without stalling and lying. And if you were as bright as you think you are, you'd know that it isn't smart to give me ideas about your homicidal temper. Not unless you have a pretty good alibi."

The columnist stared at him in fascinated terror.

"Wh—what do you mean?"

"Isn't it true that you used the following words during your quarrel with Mlle. Michaud: 'Get out of my room or I'll kill you?' "

"I—"

"An investigation among the Lais employees shows that you lose your temper fairly easily and that you don't care what you are doing when you get sore. That is, you hit out at people and throw heavy objects at them. Do you see what I am driving at, Miss Howe?"

Apparently Miss Howe did. She collapsed like a deflated balloon, and burst into tears.

"All right," said Captain Torrent, after waiting a minute. "Pull yourself together and let's get this over with. Did you go to the third floor at one-ten?"

"I tell you I didn't! I heard Rudolph going upstairs—"

"Rudolph is Dr. Berchtold?"

"Yes—and I followed him a little way."

"Why?"

"I wanted to speak to him. He was going upstairs with Hortense."

"But you didn't speak to him?"

"No! I didn't really want to. I just wanted to see that he wasn't go-ing—" She stopped as if trying to collect herself. Torrent didn't give her a chance.

"Going where?"

"Going to the third floor."

"To Michaud, you mean. Is that where you thought he was going?"

"Yes—no…What are you…"

"Why didn't you want him to go there, Miss Howe? Is it because you were jealous?"

"I wasn't—I tell you I wasn't." The columnist's pale cheeks were covered with splotchy red. "I just didn't want him to—you have no right to say this to me," she ended weakly.

Moran grinned quietly. This weak defiance was very different from the cool arrogance in the beginning of the interview. Torrent went on in the same efficiently brutal manner.

"Well, and did he go to the third floor?"

"No, he didn't. He and Hortense went on up to the fourth."

"Did *you* go to the third floor?"

"No, I didn't. When I saw that he had gone on, I was I was satisfied and I went on down. As I told you."

"Why did you use the employees' entrance instead of going out through the salon?"

"Because I looked a mess. I mean, my hair, and my face wasn't done."

"Miss Howe, isn't it the truth that you had your quarrel with Lili Michaud because you were jealous of her as well as because she had inconve-nienced you?"

"This is ridiculous," Alicia Howe protested, her hands shaking. "Rudi didn't even know her. I mean, I was simply furious because the little tramp had taken my room."

"I see." Torrent rose to his feet, followed by Moran. "Just another thing. You keep on talking about 'your room.' Does it mean that it actually is yours? That nobody can use it even while you are away?"

Alicia was beginning to recover from her beaten state. She straight-ened up slowly. "It *is* my room. The furniture in it is mine. I even keep some of my papers there."

"Isn't it rather an unusual arrangement in a beauty salon?"

"I insist on comfort and privacy for myself and I go where I can get it."

"Quite," said Torrent. "Well, that is all so far, Miss Howe. We'll let you know if we need you again. Good day."

The door closed behind Alicia Howe's ignominiously fleeing form. Moran shook his head in admiration. "You certainly put that one over."

"A pipe," Torrent answered carelessly. "The only way to deal with female bullies is to outbully them. Besides, I had to work fast. Next time she won't walk into this office without a lawyer." Torrent tapped his pencil on his notes. "She's a nasty woman, Moran. And she's scared silly. Maybe she has reason to be. We'll see."

CHAPTER 6

LATER THAT SAME DAY Captain Andrew Torrent and Detective Moran waited patiently in the hall until the butler reappeared to lead them to the rosy boudoir of Mrs. Sterling. They found her reclining on a chaise longue in a pose reminiscent of Mme. Recamier, and a handmaid was combing out her ash-blond tresses. The two men advanced toward her doggedly across the dove-gray carpet, unwilling sailors lured by a somewhat ripe Lorelei.

"Do sit down," said Mrs. Sterling in dulcet tones. "And do forgive this informality but I simply must be getting ready for a luncheon. Mitzi, you bad thing, did you hurt the nice mans?"

"Not really," said Torrent, grimly detaching an enraged Pekinese from his ankle. Its mistress beamed at him benevolently and again begged him to sit down.

"I hate to see a man towering over me. It does dreadful things to my ego," she confided. The two detectives looked around helplessly. The truth was that there were no chairs worthy of the name in the room. At last Moran let himself down cautiously on an enormous satin pouffe, while Torrent found himself ludicrously craning his neck over the back of an old-fashioned loveseat upholstered in salmon pink.

"As you may know, madam, we are making an investigation about the death of Lili Michaud. Since you were on the scene you might help us, don't you know?"

"Are you Scotch?" Mrs. Sterling inquired.

"Ma'am?"

"Your way of speaking and then you look a little like Lord Argyle, with that little mustache."

"But Lord Argyle isn't Scotch," Torrent said helplessly.

Mrs. Sterling cocked her head coyly. "Not even on his mother's side?

(How did I get into this? thought Torrent in exasperation.) I knew you were British in some way, with that little mustache."

"As a matter of fact, I was born in North Ireland. If you don't mind I'd like to ask you a few questions."

"Of course, Inspector—what's your name again? Stebbins did tell me..."

"Captain Andrew Torrent, and this is Detective Moran." Moran tried to get up from his pouffe but gave it up. "Mrs. Sterling, according to my information, your room was two doors away from that occupied by the deceased?"

"That's right, Inspector."

"Captain," Torrent corrected her. "You were aware of her presence on that floor?"

"Aware? Such fanfares, my dear Inspector! You'd think a circus had arrived. So vulgar! You're pulling my hair, you little slut," she added to the maid in the same tone of voice. "And of course as if that weren't enough, she has to get into an altercation with the Howe woman just as—"

"We'll come to that presently. I should like first, as a matter of routine, to check your own time of arrival, etc. Now your appointment was for when?"

With exquisite skill Captain Torrent extracted from Mrs. Sterling the facts he wanted, steering her away from unnecessary digressions the way a veteran sheep dog does a particularly giddy sheep. The times seemed to check with those provided by the appointment desk, vaguely, because Mrs. Sterling loathed the idea of time, and preferred to forget it. She did, however, give a spirited description of the scene between Alicia Howe and Lili Michaud.

"And then?" inquired Torrent, after waiting vainly for her to go on with her narrative.

"And then?" Mrs. Sterling raised a pair of limpid blue eyes to his. "Then I got dressed and went home."

"According to you, then, the last time you saw Lili Michaud was when you came out to look at her during her quarrel?"

"Yes, of course. Now really, Inspector—"

"But we have information to the effect that you saw her later. That, as a matter of fact, is what we'd like to hear from you about, don't you know."

Mrs. Sterling walked to her dressing table, sat down at it with her back to the detectives, and picked up a little crystal sprayer, which she presently directed on herself.

"It really is in your interest to tell us," said Torrent, mildly. "In the first place you don't want to give us an impression that you are hiding something. In the second place, we'll merely have to resume our conversation down at headquarters, under much less pleasant circumstances. Now then, you told Hortense that you would like to speak privately to the deceased and asked her to stay away so as to provide you with the chance to do so?"

Mrs. Sterling swung around to face Torrent who ducked with a wary eye on the sprayer, from which hissed a delicate spray of perfume. "It just goes to show," said Mrs. Sterling, "that one can't buy loyalty. When I think of the Christmas gift I gave that girl last summer..."

Torrent shook his head a little as if to clear it and hung on doggedly to the implied admission.

"Then you do admit that you made arrangements to see Miss Michaud. Why?"

"Really, Inspector, you don't expect me to bare my whole personal life before you."

Torrent shifted ground. "Have you seen this before?" Torrent laid the clipping from Alicia Howe's column on the mirrored top of the dressing table. Mrs. Sterling glanced at it and flicked it disdainfully to the carpet, whence Moran rescued it.

Mrs. Sterling said, "There! I knew I had grounds for libel. Everybody knows it's Chester. Even you knew it and you don't know Chester."

"Then you recognized this as dealing with your husband?"

Mrs. Sterling looked resigned. "Very well, so I did. Marie, you can bring Mitzi back."

"Is that what you called Mr. Sterling in Washington about?"

"Yes. He told me it was all nonsense but I told him that I was going to speak to that woman anyhow."

"And what did Mr. Sterling say to that?"

"He said, 'Oh, my God,' and hung up. Poor Chester is so inhibited. I thought a talk with that woman would be more satisfactory. Have you seen *The Women,* Inspector? Not that I'd ever divorce Chester, of course. Do you, know, I've never divorced anyone and yet this is my third marriage. Both my previous husbands died."

"And that," said Torrent grimly, "brings us back to Miss Michaud. You went into her room at what time?"

"I told you how I am about time. Really, you can't expect—"

"Was it soon after Hortense left you?"

"Oh, just a little while after—I had to change my lipstick—about five or ten minutes."

"And then?"

"I looked out and nobody was around, so I thought that was a good time to do it. I *was* a little nervous," said Mrs. Sterling with an amused reminiscent smile, "so that I almost went into the wrong room and disturbed whoever was there. Then I went into Alicia Howe's room."

"What," asked Torrent in a restrained manner, "happened there? Please tell me in detail."

"Well, there was this little tart, with her Winogradow mask on, with just her hair showing, and I must say from what I saw, Dimitri did a good job on it. I was even thinking of having mine done like that, only now of course it's—where was I? Oh yes. I said, 'Hello there,' and she didn't answer me. Of course she was sleeping—that Winogradow treatment is the most relaxing—anyhow, I decided I was going to wake her up and show her Alicia's column."

"And did you wake her up?"

Mrs. Sterling looked a little sheepish. "No, I didn't, Inspector."

"What did you do?"

"I turned around and walked right back to my room."

"I see," said Torrent relaxing. He saw Moran relaxing too. It wouldn't have surprised him in the least if Mrs. Sterling had said brightly, "Why, Inspector, then of course I just killed her. Really." There was no telling about Mrs. Sterling.

"What made you change your mind?"

"At that point, it suddenly occurred to me that I couldn't very well talk to the woman, because I don't know a word of French, so of course we couldn't have our little talk. So I went away."

"I see," said Torrent. He mopped his forehead with a handkerchief, and was silent, calculating. "Mrs. Sterling, thinking back to when you were in that room, would you say Michaud was dead or alive when you saw her?"

"Why, I really couldn't tell you, Inspector— What do you mean, dead?" Mrs. Sterling did a double-take that would have done credit to Edward Everett Horton. "You mean..."

"Well, she died sometime between one and one-thirty. Either you had come in after she was already dead, or you were the last person to see her alive—except the murderer, of course. That's why it's so important, Mrs. Sterling. Think now. Did she make any motion or a sound when you spoke to her?"

"Why, I don't— She was wearing the mask, of course."

"Yes, I know. But did you notice if she was breathing?"

"I—really, Inspector, I don't think I can—Oh dear, go away! Do go away."

Mrs. Sterling had turned faintly green, Torrent noticed with some satisfaction. He motioned to Moran who struggled up from the pouffe into which, being something more than sylphlike in weight, he had been steadily sinking, and they made their adieus. As they went out, they heard Mrs. Sterling bidding her maid in agitated tones to cancel the luncheon engagement and to make one with her psychiatrist, instead.

"My God," said Torrent, as they emerged into Park Avenue. "What a screwy dame. Do you suppose she's too dumb to be true? Now we might as well stop at the salon and have another talk with the old lady. From one sweet-smelling boudoir to another—what are you grinning about, you big ape?"

"Talking about sweet-smelling," said Moran with glee, "that describes you to a T, Captain. That dame got some of that perfume on you. You better take it off before one of them Fifth Avenue characters falls on your neck and kisses you."

At the salon Torrent was told that the Kyria was home, indisposed, and he repaired there forthwith. Lais Karaides occupied three floors of a building very near the salon and here too Torrent marked the impact of her lavish, luxury-loving, slightly monomaniac personality. Like the salon, it was built around her, perhaps even built up to her. There was the same classic sweep of staircases and Greek statuary.

It was a cold abode, slightly out of the world, full of endless rooms with a strange, unlived-in look, packed to the ceiling with art treasures. Some of them were beautifully arranged with that soulless perfection that only the services of a professional decorator can achieve. Others were Daliesque jumbles, with here a wan Picasso glimmering dimly over a gem-encrusted ebony statue of a Moor and there a fifteenth-century suit of armor cheek by jowl with an atrocious example of 1920 constructivism.

An old woman in black, whose bleak face held traces of vanished beauty, opened the door to Torrent and Moran and guided them silently to the library. A slight, youngish man with very white hands and a skullcap of polished black hair looked up from a silver vase in which he was, with minute care, arranging a cluster of fabulous tulips. The old woman spoke to him in Greek and he turned to Captain Torrent smiling.

"I understand you are from the police. You wish to speak to my mother?"

Torrent looked at M. Maurice with redoubled interest.

"Yes," he returned. "I did not find her at the salon."

"Of course not. Yesterday's business shocked her rather and today's developments—I suppose—ah"—he consulted the card Torrent had put on the table—"Captain Torrent, is it absolutely imperative to interview my mother? She is—shattered."

"I am afraid so," said Torrent, and added, "Sorry."

"My dear man, I quite understand," M. Maurice exclaimed, and Torrent's eyebrows lifted an imperceptible fraction of an inch at the lilt of his voice. "We all have to do things we don't like. Just wait a moment." He lifted the receiver, dialed swiftly and, after a pause, broke into melodious French chatter. He replaced the receiver and smiled at Torrent brightly. "There! She will be down very soon and I shall entertain you in the meanwhile. Now how shall I do that? Oh I know. I shall show you the vases. Do come along. You too," he added to Moran, graciously.

"You can add to my entertainment," said Torrent, following his host, "by giving me a little information about yesterday."

"Anything you like, Captain. Of course, I don't know very much. Luckily I wasn't around when Mlle. Michaud was discovered. I should have hated to see her. Brutal things like that—shatter me."

"This one didn't look very brutal though," said Torrent. "A rather businesslike affair, don't you know. A sharp powerful blow across the throat that fractured her larynx and that did not even show superficially. It's a pretty well-known jujitsu trick."

"They say, however," murmured M. Maurice, "that it shows in people's faces when they are murdered, a rather unpleasant expression that is absent when they die a natural death."

"In this case, of course, the expression was nonexistent, the face being covered with that strange concoction you call Winogradow's pack."

"Of course, I forgot," Maurice shivered a little and laughed apologetically. "My dear Captain, you make it sound worse than ever. A dead woman, without an expression on her face—one might say, without a face. I am glad I missed that bit of Daliesque fantasy."

"You did meet Miss Michaud yesterday, though, didn't you?"

"Yes, I did." Maurice stopped before a showcase in which nestled a lovely Greek amphora. "There, look at that. Red figured *lekythoi* of the fourth century. Very lively, aren't they? Take this one, for example. On this side a satyr is chasing a nymph, and here, as you see," he gave a high-pitched giggle, "he's got her!"

"He certainly has," said Torrent dryly. "What was your impression of Miss Michaud?"

"A natural sequence of thought," Maurice commented. "Oh, I thought she was rather like most of our customers—a pampered little tramp. On the whole I am not surprised at her demise. Her kind is always wallowing in an emotional mess and finally getting her throat cut by some man who couldn't take it any more. Only I am sorry that it had to happen in our place."

There was no malice in M. Maurice's rather extraordinary statement. It was quite matter-of-fact, even a bit absentminded. It was as if he had come to take the natural awfulness of women for granted as well as the fact that his profession brought him in contact with it.

"You sound as if you knew her very well," Torrent commented. Maurice shrugged his shoulders.

"Saw her yesterday for the first time. This vase is my favorite," he said suddenly, gently, and lifted it out of its nest with tender hands. The figures on it were those of young men, boys with long clean limbs, riding archaic horses around the delicate rim of the vase. "The lines-—are nice."

"They are, rather," said Torrent. "Those guys apparently knew how to ride. They're all riding bareback. Something else I wanted to ask you: it was about that elevator. I understand it was about twelve-thirty when you stalled it."

M. Maurice replaced the vase in the showcase and broke into a plaintive rebuttal. He did not stall the elevator. He knew perfectly well where Captain Torrent had gotten the story, but Mlle. Illona's ridiculous charges notwithstanding, the trouble was with the elevator, not with him.

"It stops by itself," he complained. "Once it stopped when I was in it and not running it, mind you, and I had to spend half an hour in the extremely boring company of Mrs. Glendenning, who unfortunately fills the elevator to *overflowing.* I've been begging mother to have it overhauled, but she keeps it because of a nostalgia for the unspeakable elevators she used to have in her Paris salon. To return to your question. Yes, I do believe it *was* twelve-thirty, because Mrs. Fairchild had just come in for her appointment. Since she and Illona were in the midst of a fascinating talk and no sign of emerging from it, I grew impatient and took the elevator myself. I often do it. All I need to do afterward is press the button that sends it down again."

"We have the statement of the girls on the second floor that you were released at one-forty. What did you do then?"

"I was taken up to the sixth. Then I dumped all the things in my office and went home. Silly of me, but I was annoyed by my misfortune and I felt I couldn't do any more work. Is there anything else I can tell you, Captain?"

"No, sir. This is just routine, don't you know."

"Then," said Maurice, with a charming smile, "I will show you more vases."

"That will have to be later," said the Kyria's icy voice. "I believe these gentlemen have business with me."

Torrent's first reaction was that of amused surprise because the Kyria was wearing the same floating draperies she wore in the salon. Torrent had judged them then as the inevitable trappings of the role she had assumed. He realized now that it was apparently a role she played constantly. He noted too that she looked even worse than yesterday, so much so that her face seemed to be crumbling away under the protective shell of skillful makeup.

Behind her loomed a tall, untidy man of about sixty, with a straggly beard and tie, whose curiously discolored hands immediately caught Torrent's quick eye.

"Yes, mother," M. Maurice muttered. He removed his hand from Torrent's arm and busied himself with closing the showcase. His crestfallen countenance reminded Torrent irresistibly of a kittenish old maid whose pleasurable excitement at entertaining men is cut short by an uncharitable rebuke. The Kyria seated herself slowly, regally, without introducing Torrent to her companion. She answered questions listlessly.

"No, I didn't know Lili Michaud personally. Naturally as one of the most glamorous women of France she is—was—a welcome client. Using her for the purpose of advertising our new creations like the Winogradow pack and the Hermes coiffure was entirely Mr. Skeets' idea. It would have been good publicity, if this horrible thing hadn't happened."

"It's gotten you on the front pages," Torrent remarked dryly. The Kyria looked at him blankly. She was a dreadfully humorless person, Torrent thought, completely absorbed in her business and indifferent to any other aspects of life. Apparently to her the death of Lili Michaud was merely a publicity stunt that misfired disastrously.

"Do you suppose that we want publicity like that, Captain Torrent? Do you know that until you gave the press facts on how she died, some of the reporters had the temerity to suggest that something might have been wrong with the Winogradow pack?"

Torrent supposed that she was referring to a tabloid paper which had photographed their own model with a mud pack on her face and had added the following caption: "This is how Lili Michaud died."

"Our bureau of analysis," he said mildly, "found nothing wrong with your stuff."

The Kyria pursued her grievance with the fervor of a lioness defending her young. Her eyes flashed with an almost sacramental flame.

"Why should they? Any claim of malicious persons that the Winogradow pack may be harmful is a pack of lies. Why, we always try our new creations on our employees before they are used on our clients."

Torrent's mild gaze flickered, but his amiably inquiring expression did not change.

"Don't your employees object to being used as guinea pigs, madam?"

The Kyria drew herself up to her majestic height. "Loyalty," she said icily, "is the slogan of this company."

Maurice said, smiling, "The captain is shocked. Bless you, Captain, don't you know how women love to experiment with their faces? Here those little snips are getting these expensive treatments for which others pay money. They love it. And the stuff is pitifully innocuous. Why, take this Winogradow pack—it's made up mostly of herbs and—what is the name of that clay, Serge?"

"Kaolin," said the bearded man in a short gruff bark. His voice had a strange hollow quality. "Generates warmth and produces a most interesting scent."

"Am I," asked Torrent, "by any chance addressing the—er—creator of the Winogradow pack?"

The tall chemist nodded, with a disagreeable scowl distorting his bearded face, and shambled away to the window as if to escape Torrent's candid interested gaze.

"I'd like to speak to you later, sir," said Torrent to his stooped back. "All I'd like from you, madam, is the account of your movements. Routine, don't you know."

The Kyria's immense cerulean eyes turned to him slowly. "Really," she said, "I am afraid I can't help you. I haven't kept track of time."

Torrent said, "Perhaps if we begin at the beginning." He thought the Kyria was not nervous but cautious, as if she were feeling her way along an unknown path. She confirmed that she wanted Jeanne to wait for her on the second floor, but she did not come down until later.

"I don't know exactly when. The elevator boy, perhaps—" she said in a curiously tentative manner. Torrent asked whether she always used the back elevator to go down.

"Of course not," said the Kyria frowning. "But I was told that the other elevator was stalled." She stopped and Torrent, out of the corner of his eye, saw M. Maurice make an involuntary gesture of dismay.

"You see," said Torrent smoothly, "we are getting somewhere. This means at least that you came down before one-forty, because the front elevator was stalled until that time. Now then, perhaps, if you'll remember what you did when you came to the second floor?"

The Kyria hesitated and floundered a little and M. Maurice stepped neatly into the breach. "Didn't you tell me that you spoke to Berchtold?" he asked blandly. "That should help Captain Torrent because Berchtold is so time-conscious—a German trait, you know. He always knows what time it is."

His chatter covered the Kyria's momentary indecision. She slowly inclined her white regal head, without deigning to throw a glance at her helpful son. "I spoke to Dr. Berchtold directly upon getting out of the elevator. We discussed Miss Howe's indisposition. We were still talking about it when the call came from the third floor. I don't believe there is anything else I can tell you, Captain Torrent."

He was being dismissed. The Kyria closed her eyes wearily. With her white eyelids covering her intense eyes she looked more than ever like a statue. It was an affected gesture but Torrent thought with a little shock of surprise, "By George, she does look genuinely tired."

Dr. Winogradow was still standing by the window, his hands locked behind his stooping back. Torrent thought that anybody questioning him would have to give up any idea of learning anything from his facial expression. His face was so camouflaged by the straggly beard and the thick glasses, behind which his eyes had a swimmy and totally unreal appearance, that one might as well be talking to a mask. Torrent's mention of the fact that he was seen going up the stairs at about one-fifteen drew from him merely a short assenting grunt.

"Where were you going, Dr. Winogradow?" asked Torrent, adding perfunctorily the talismanic words, "Just a routine checkup."

Dr. Winogradow was bound for the fourth floor. A new hair dye was being tried out on one of the girls and she was awaiting his examination before drying her newly colored hair.

"It came out beautifully, Lais," he said, turning to the Kyria. "Blond with a faint greenish tint. A spectral look, as if drowned." There was positively a ghoulish gleam behind the thick lenses, and the Kyria intervened uneasily.

"Don't be extravagant, Serge. The dye is to be used only on that long lank hair that is such a trial to women. It'll give them a fragile look. We shall call it blond Nereis."

"And use a faint salty scent. Very delicate and pure. Like jasmine saturated with sea water," said Winogradow softly and his hands made a tender movement as if holding something precious. His camouflaged face tilted toward Torrent. "I am most interested in perfumes. At present I am trying to evolve the perfect perfume."

Torrent said that that was very interesting and did Dr. Winogradow know what time he came upstairs. Surprisingly Dr. Winogradow did know. It was exactly one-eighteen. That was when the dye was supposed to be washed off and he had timed his lunch so as to be there at the right moment.

"Just one more thing," said Torrent getting up to his feet. "Did you know the deceased?"

Dr. Winogradow gave a short sharp sardonic bark of laughter. "No. I don't know her. I don't know anybody."

He again presented his stooped back to Torrent.

Torrent escaped from the house, followed by Moran, who was breathing hard. Neither ventured a comment until they were in the car.

Then Moran said simply, "My Gawd!" He brooded for a while and added, "They're all bughouse, ain't they, Cap? That Winogradow—he gave me the creeps. And the old lady...Crazy? My Gawd."

"Crazy like a fox," Torrent told him. "Nobody who pays an income tax of a million bucks is completely crazy. But they sure are a bunch of neurotics. Maybe except this Maurice."

Moran emitted a falsetto hoot and mincingly crooked a little finger.

"I know," said Torrent. "But still he's a smart little guy." He remembered a look of amused sympathy that Maurice had thrown him. "However, this is going to be a mean case."

He summed up quickly what he had learned during the interview. If the Kyria did not lie about her conversation with Berchtold, she had come down after 1:30, that is, after the crucial period when the third floor was left unattended. Torrent knew that already from Berchtold's testimony, but something about the way the information was given did not satisfy Torrent. As for Winogradow—wasn't it a little odd that a vague gent like that should know exactly the time he arrived upstairs? That would also have to be checked.

And of course there was the incredible Mrs. Sterling, who was on the spot at the right time.

"Moran," he said aloud, "Did you pick your fancy?"

Moran's answer was prompt and emphatic. "The Howe woman. She's the one. She did it."

During the next forty-eight hours Torrent found himself grudgingly inclining toward Moran's point of view. Grudgingly, not because of any special affection for Alicia Howe, but because this solution left many un-explained blind spots and Torrent liked his cases to be clear and above-board. But it did look as if that was the only possible explanation and with the press and the D.A. howling for action, there was no time to moon over the weird aspects of what came to be called the "beauty murder."

The trouble was that although all of the suspects had plenty of oppor-tunity, nobody had a real motive. Henri Barrat was presumably the only one who knew the volatile Lili sufficiently to harbor homicidal designs on her, but also he was the only one who had a good alibi. Even had he wanted to kill his wife, it was impossible for him to find her in the salon without outside assistance.

Mrs. Sterling, Torrent had to admit, looked good at the first flush if only because she was on the scene of the crime. But Torrent could see what a good defense attorney would do to any case that could be built up around her. That this lady, on the strength of a vague little squib in a gossip column (which Torrent suspected she did not really believe), should calmly do away with a woman whom she had never met, and that after obligingly telling Hortense about her intention to visit her "rival," seemed fantastic. Mrs. Sterling had apparently been trying to arrange an emotional talkfest. The murderer who had oblit-erated the pretty Frenchwoman with such cold, scientific ferocity had obviously very little to say to her.

Alicia Howe—that was a different matter. She had already come into physical conflict with Lili Michaud and was ignominiously worsted. And her squib had indicated a certain amount of ill will toward the latter be*fore* she ever met her at Lais. Moran, whom Torrent had sent to do more supplementary questioning at Lais, kept on bringing home morsels of gos-sip throwing light on such endearing characteristics of Alicia Howe as her ungovernable temper, her occasional sadistic outbursts, and her posses-sive jealous infatuation for the bland doctor.

"This girl Alice," Moran reported, "told me that when the doctor was examining Michaud he sure did take a long time and the way they were laughing and carrying on in there it sounded like more than examination." Moran looked at his fingernails. "Not that I blame him," he said unexpect-edly, "That dame was hot! Anyhow Alice says she was telling that to another girl, Hortense, and Howe had come up behind them and she is sure that she had overheard them talking."

Torrent nodded and mentally brushed in another stroke in the slowly growing picture of Alicia Howe as the murderess. It would do in a pinch, but unlike a well-known brand of cigarettes, it did not satisfy.

"The trouble is that we don't know enough about the setup," he told Moran. "We need a guide to it. Somebody to explain all the screwy little things that don't make sense and that bother me."

Moran nodded glumly. "Trouble is there were too many people walking about for no good reason during that half hour," he said. "If we could narrow that down…"

"One thing is clear," said Torrent. "Before I make any sort of case for the D.A., I've got to find out more about those people." He smiled a little wryly. "Maybe I had better go to the ballet again."

"Whadja say?" inquired Moran.

"Nothing," said Torrent. He didn't go to the ballet that night, but at six o'clock his car was parked on Fifth Avenue near the entrance to Lais. He was waiting for Toni to come out.

He picked out the slim figure in the blue coat trimmed with gray Persian lamb from among a small crowd that burst out of the employees' entrance. Young Skeets was with her and they were talking together so earnestly that they almost walked by Torrent without recognizing him. When they did see him their reaction was a strange one. They looked at him with awe, then at each other. Then Toni laughed and said, "All right, I give up. It must be fate."

"Greet Captain Torrent nicely," said Skeets. "See, your bad manners have saddened him. The truth is we were just talking about you. Toni's got a clue and she refuses to surrender it to the police in spite of all my pious exhortations."

"So?" said Torrent noncommittally, falling into step with them. Toni laughed again.

"That's right, go ahead and sow dark suspicion in Captain Torrent's breast. It's just that I am perfectly sure that the police know all about it, and I don't want to make a damn fool of myself pointing something out to them that they already know."

"Really?" Captain Torrent's smile was unexpectedly warm. "You mean to say you don't think that the police are bungling fools and that all the crimes are solved by helpful amateur sleuths? Miss Ney, you amaze me. Nevertheless, I'd like to hear about this."

Skeets told him that they were on their way to dinner and would Captain Torrent join them? Captain Torrent consented with alacrity and in a few moments they were seated in a retired corner of Larrabee's and Toni was telling her story.

"You may have gathered that Mrs. Sterling is rather fond of talking. She came in to take her exercises today and as a result, I am afraid," said Toni with a faint twinkle, "I know as much about her visit to Lili Michaud's room as you do. Something she said bothered me a little. You remember, she said she was so excited that she almost blundered into the wrong room and startled the occupant. Well, that seemed funny to me because the two rooms between her and Howe's room were empty at the time. So I thought maybe she walked in the wrong direction, although that seemed impossible because Alicia Howe's room is sort of a landmark. Everybody knows where it is and it's just opposite the elevator, so you can't miss it. But Mrs. Sterling said no, she went in the right direction and the room she almost went into was the one before Howe's. So I asked her how she knew that somebody was in it. And she said, well, she had a little trouble opening it and when she looked up, the lamp was lit. Do you know about those lamps, Captain Torrent?" He shook his head. "Well, whenever anybody is in a facial room and the door is shut, the light goes on outside the door. You must have seen it, it's one of those fluorescent bars shaped like an L. When nobody's in it we leave the door open a crack and that prevents the light from flashing on. So the question is, who could have been in that room? I asked all the girls and they said no, they weren't. And by the time Hortense came back it was already gone. As a matter of fact Pauline, who had stuck her head out into the hall before Hortense came back, doesn't remember seeing any light next to Alicia Howe's. Well, that's all," Toni ended abruptly.

"It's quite a lot, I should say," said Torrent.

"You mean to say," Skeets demanded, grinning wickedly, "that this has escaped the attention of the police? That the amateur sleuth is triumphantly vindicated?"

"I am afraid so, Mr. Skeets," Torrent admitted.

"Don't be bratty, Eric," said Toni severely. "How could anyone spot it unless he knew about the lamps?"

"Thank you for those kind words. I will admit in confidence that we are a little handicapped by our ignorance of all your peculiar little customs. As a matter of fact, that's what I wanted to see you about. I wanted you to give me—well, shall I say the atmosphere of the place, don't you know."

"I am so relieved," said Toni demurely. "I thought it was perhaps about my elementary knowledge of jujitsu."

Torrent gave a shout of laughter. "That hasn't been bothering you, has it? It shouldn't. With your rockbound alibi you could know black magic and not be implicated. But to come back to what you told me. It's very important, you know. I think we may consider, until proved otherwise, that the person who was in that room was the murderer."

"Wow!" said Skeets, like a little boy whose favorite ballplayer makes a home run. "You sure got something that time, baby."

"You are very quick, Miss Ney."

"Dear me." Something like mockery shone under Toni's demurely lowered long lashes. "If I weren't wedged here so comfortably I'd get up and make a low curtsy. Captain Torrent, does this mean that Lili Michaud was already dead when Mrs. Sterling came in to see her?"

"Not necessarily." It was Skeets who answered. "The murderer might have been waiting for her to leave before paying his visit. But anyhow it must have happened very soon before or after Mrs. Sterling came to see Michaud. Incidentally, why do you take it for granted that Mrs. Sterling couldn't have done it herself? It seems silly but possible."

"Mrs. Sterling," said Toni, "told me of some amateur theatricals they had last summer at her country home in Connecticut. You know what they played? *The Women* by Clare Boothe. Mrs. Sterling particularly liked the scene where the wife confronts the mistress."

"Is that the role she played?"

"No. She carried a spear, figuratively speaking. Unfortunately she starts giggling the minute she gets on the stage. But she wanted the role of the wife very badly, and I think she couldn't resist the opportunity the other day."

Torrent said morosely, "No wonder I'm beating my brains out here. Everybody in this case is nuts. And that reminds me. Miss Ney, Winogradow is definitely cracked, isn't he?"

"Well, he's queer about perfumes. He's got an obsession about creating a perfect scent. He goes off to tropical countries every summer and comes back laden with peculiar herbs. He's already made Lais famous. All the rest of the stuff he just tosses off, and he is mildly interested in dyes. But his perfumes are just divine. Is he a possibility?"

"Yes, anybody who was hanging around the third floor is a possibility. But so far there is not a shadow of a motive. Winogradow claims that he does not know Lili Michaud."

Toni and Eric looked at each other and Toni made the little saluting gesture with which a dancer introduces a partner to the stage. "*A vous*," she said. "Captain Torrent, Eric has got something to say about that."

Skeets complied with alacrity. Torrent listened without comment to his story of Winogradow's refusal to let Lili Michaud into the laboratory, merely shrugging his shoulders when Toni protested that it was quite possible for Dr. Winogradow not to have noticed Michaud.

"Women are quite unreal to him," she pointed out. "They are dim shapes without meaning. I don't think he even sees those girls on whom he tries his dyes and things. He just looks through them."

"Perhaps. Now there's something else I want to ask you. Would Hortense be likely to ask medical advice from Dr. Berchtold?"

"Hortense?" A tiny frown creased Toni's brow. "I thought she was in the best of health, as far as I know."

"Perhaps under that healthy exterior she is concealing a nameless disease," said Skeets. "So many people I know are nothing but whited sepulchers."

"I don't know. Perhaps. Of course the authorities frown on the girls coming to Berchtold for professional advice. He is sort of consecrated to the clients, if you know what I mean. Who said that she was consulting him?"

Torrent sighed wearily. Another little inaccuracy, another lie, not important in itself but adding to the twisted, evasive character of the whole business.

"Till I caught you telling—those little white lies," Eric hummed softly, with reckless disregard for the tune. "But maybe it's true. The dear doctor is known for his willingness to please the ladies."

"Hortense is not his type although, now I come to think of it, they *have* been having a lot of conferences," Toni said. "She's a sort of thin but wiry type. He likes them young and tender, when they are working girls without any other attractions but their sweet selves, that is."

"You don't like Dr. Berchtold, do you?" Torrent asked idly.

"Well, no. He's attractive, I suppose, in a repulsive sort of way. But I find that the only way I can make myself stand him is by remembering his predecessor. That was a scientific gentleman who used to hie him to the slaughterhouse every morning and pick himself a little bouquet of various glands which he'd boil in a soup." Skeets ostentatiously moved away his dessert and directed a reproachful look at Toni. "Aha, you shrink, my weak-stomached friend. Not so the Kyria and her clients. They drank that nauseating brew by gallons, hoping to be rejuvenated thereby."

"That," said Torrent, slowly, "is the damnedest story I've ever heard."

"It's true, though. He flourished at Lais, until the medical association got after him. Then dear Alicia brought Dr. Berchtold, who tries to make the ladies feel young by the more usual methods. You can't blame me for finding Dr. Rudi a bit sinister because I can't help thinking, what reputable doctor would work in this place?" Toni sighed. "I understand that he and Hortense have made each other a nice durable alibi."

"You sound regretful."

"I am not, really. My favorite suspect would be Alicia Howe, because she is such a—however, if you'll be able to ring the dear doctor in as accessory, it's okay by me."

"This callous modern generation," said Eric. "I think, darling, you've given Captain Torrent enough information about the beauty business to make his hair curl. Besides, we have to run along."

Captain Torrent dexterously scooped up the checks from under Eric's clutching fingers and got up. "You've been very helpful again," he said gravely. "I had a hunch you'd be. I might call on you again for—atmosphere, don't you know. You are both very bright young people."

The bright young people declared themselves completely at his service any time.

"And we'll remember," said Toni, with another of her swift elfin smiles, "we're not amateur sleuths, we're rather consulting experts. Correct?"

"Quite," said Torrent grinning.

CHAPTER 7

THAT WAS FRIDAY NIGHT. All during Saturday Toni waited for news of startling developments. These did not arrive, however, and the story was shifted from the front pages of the tabloids. On Sunday, Eric Skeets called on Toni in her apartment tolerably early, to the great indignation of Tom Jones. He categorically refused to indulge in any more conjectures about the murder and added, unnecessarily, that he could think of many more interesting things to do. They spent the afternoon lolling on the couch in front of the fire, telling each other the story of their lives, and sipping at cocktails prepared by Eric, while the gray November sky blanketed the window. Only in the evening did Toni break the tabu by wondering irrelevantly whether the Homicide Bureau worked on Sundays.

This artless question would have drawn a bitter grin from Torrent, who was spending the day of rest (as he had the previous day) getting the goods on Alicia Howe. Toni's contribution had advanced matters considerably. The murderer had definitely been in the room next to that occupied by Lili Michaud at approximately 1:10. At 1:05 Alicia Howe was seen going up to the third floor, and there was only her word to show that she hadn't gone in. Howe stuck grimly to that story. She came to Torrent's office in the company of a lawyer, whose purpose apparently was to watch Miss Howe's blood pressure. Miss Howe did not seem to need him very much. She sat there calm, if somewhat livid. Her light blue eyes had an impenetrable glaze and her blond curls hung lankly over her sallow forehead under her severe Quaker hat. Only her thin fingers worked unceasingly in her lap as Torrent grilled her implacably about the gossip item in Wednesday's *Globe*. Miss Howe was particularly averse to vouchsafing information on that point. It was just a piece of gossip which she had remembered and put in her column. No, she was not activated by any feeling of malice, it was just part of her job. No, she couldn't tell Torrent her source of information. She didn't really remember herself.

"Of course," said Torrent, "that makes it impossible to check," and as the columnist shrugged her shoulders with a thin contemptuous smile, he went on silkily, "It could just as well be made up, couldn't it?"

"What would be the point of that?"

"I don't know," smiled Torrent. "The only purpose it could serve that I can think of is to throw suspicion on Mrs. Sterling, in case something happened to Lili Michaud. What do you think of that, Miss Howe?"

At this point the lawyer remarked coolly that she did not need to answer that question. Alicia Howe did not. But she was visibly shaken, and that was why Torrent's next question caught her unawares. "You seem to have been very interested in Lili Michaud's past. Would it surprise you to find that Dr. Berchtold was a part of it?" Almost as dirty a trick as asking a man whether he had stopped beating his wife, but it worked. Alicia Howe ground her teeth and an exclamation that sounded vaguely like, "I knew it!" was forced from her throat. That was the only time he was able to draw blood. But Torrent said to himself that with her unpleasant character and her bad nerves she would make an excellent witness—for the prosecution.

In the meanwhile he went ahead collecting evidence to show that Alicia Howe was emotionally perturbed on the occasion of Lili Michaud's visit to the salon, and the reason why. It wasn't any too easy to get this evidence from the Lais employees, who, while undeterred by any personal affection for the columnist, still feared her influence in the salon. Dr. Berchtold was also a bit of a thorn in the side, having apparently decided that he would be a gentleman even if it hurt, but Torrent was pretty sure that he could be easily handled by the prosecution on the stand. After some gentle prodding from the D. A.'s office, he set Monday as the day on which he would take Alicia Howe into custody either as material witness or on a charge of murder. This promised to be a sensational case and he did not want anything to go wrong for lack of preparation.

Until then it would be very useful to have Alicia Howe stew in her own juice for a while. "Soften her up," said Captain Torrent, using a military term well known in the Blitzkrieg type of warfare.

It would have been hard to say just how the salon had found out about Alicia Howe's plight. Nevertheless, it did so. By some mysterious grapevine the word had been spread around that the Howe woman was on the spot. Already on Saturday the girls were pointing out to each other the obscure paragraphs in the papers dealing with new questioning. The *News* had mentioned the fact that among those questioned about the Lili Michaud murder was Alicia Howe, the barbed-tongued columnist of the *Globe,* while the *Mirror* played up the story of the scrap between Howe and Michaud. Of course it was the columnists in the other papers who really went to town. Alicia Howe was apparently less than popular in her profession. The attack upon her was carried without any name mentioned, but was nevertheless quite explicit and ranged from the most delicate of innuendoes to a blunt query about, "What well-known contributor to the gossip columns of Gotham press has a murder charge hanging over his or her head?" One of the facial operators contributed to everybody's happiness by starting a scrapbook where she religiously pasted everything that was printed about the murder. And nothing but the fear of being immediately fired kept the girls from talking to the reporters who were still hanging hopefully around the salon.

Into this atmosphere of frenzied conjecture Alicia Howe came briefly on Saturday, apparently unaware of the interest she was creating. Marthe, from the fourth floor, had been summoned to the sixth floor to see the Kyria, who had finally recovered enough to come to the salon. While waiting outside she was startled by the appearance of Alicia Howe who had brushed by her and gone into the Kyria's office unannounced. To judge from the sounds that issued from behind the closed doors, it was rather a stormy interview. At the end of it Alicia left quite abruptly, slamming the door, and the Kyria found herself unable to see Marthe and tottered home, looking very ill indeed.

The consensus of opinion was that Miss Howe had held the salon responsible for the adverse publicity she was receiving and had withdrawn her patronage. However, she was back again on Monday for her appointment. Toni, who was putting her cautiously through her paces in the gym, thought that she gave no indication that anything was wrong.

Her manner was not pleasant but it had never been. And if her sallow, arrogant face had a livid cast to it, that could be explained by the fact that her powder had been laid on thickly over heavy foundation cream to conceal her acne, which apparently had been brought back by the nervous disturbances of the past week.

"I haven't gained an inch around here." Alicia Howe fretfully patted her regrettably meager chest. "Those exercises of yours are phony, aren't they? For all the money I pay." She subsided into ominous silence. With many other women of her class she shared the comfortable delusion that the mere act of paying money was the equivalent of exercise and transferred all the responsibility to others. Toni let it ride.

The Howe woman's insolent stare was making her uneasy. There seemed to be a special malevolence in it today.

"Something I meant to ask you," said Alicia Howe. "Does the Kyria approve of your doing work for the police on the side?"

Toni stared at her. "I beg your pardon?"

"You know what I mean. I saw you having dinner with that policeman at Larrabee's on Friday. I should imagine that he finds you quite invaluable as a spy. Now don't bother to deny it. I saw you there."

"Really?" said Toni. "Would you like to go on with your exercise, Miss Howe?"

Two unattractive red splotches appeared on the columnist's sharp cheekbones. "The hell with my exercise!" She paused for a moment, evidently trying to fight down a mounting rage. "Come on, now," she said. "Quit stalling. What lies have you been telling about me?"

"Miss Howe," said Toni, "I am afraid I don't know you well enough to tell lies about you. And it's very hard for me to understand your interest in my personal affairs."

"Your personal affairs," the Howe woman mimicked savagely. "What the hell do you suppose I care about them? When I see an employee of Lais having dinner with a policeman, it's pretty obvious that it's something the Kyria ought to know about, and I'm going to see to it that she does something about it, you sneaking little stool pigeon."

Toni sighed. "Do whatever you please, Miss Howe. I can't control your actions any more than you can control mine, or those of the police. Only don't you think you are being pretty imprudent right now?"

"What do you mean?"

"Well, what is to prevent me from reporting your rather strange concern, if I am really a police spy, that is?"

"You wouldn't—" Alicia Howe began and stopped. Her complexion reverted again to the greenish pale, and there was real fear in her eyes. She got up from the mat, put her wrapper on and left the gymnasium abruptly.

After a while Toni followed her. It was part of the Lais etiquette that at no time should a client be left alone. She caught up with her at the opposite end of the corridor, at the small hallway which led to Dr. Berchtold's office. Alicia was standing there motionless, as if waiting for her, but the rigidity of her body and the strange, tense attitude of the head and neck, bent to peer at something, drew Toni's eyes in the same direction.

In the bright rectangle of the door at the end of the dim hallway two figures were framed: Dr. Berchtold, in his white coat, and Jeanne, momentarily welded together in a passionate kiss. Upon completing it, Dr. Berchtold went into his office, pushing her out with a final caressing little slap on the rear, an intensely personal gesture, which, if accepted with equanimity by the recipient, invariably establishes a sense of intimacy that cannot be mistaken.

Jeanne came down the little corridor as if her feet were walking on air. Her face was radiant and wore a bedazzled blind look. She did not notice Alicia Howe until she had practically walked into her and recoiled with a little gasp, as if she had stepped on a snake.

"I—I beg your pardon."

"Watch where you are going, you little slut," said Alicia and slapped her face hard. Jeanne took it without defending herself. She was so completely caught unawares that she just stood there while Alicia freed her other hand from the folds of her cape and swung again. This time she was prevented. Toni caught her hand in midair.

"Let go of me," said Alicia. There was a note of incipient hysteria in her voice, and a little red spark of madness glowed behind the china-blue surface of her eyes. In a moment, Toni knew, they would be the midst of a monumental scene.

"Come, come, Miss Howe," she said, "you must learn to control that homicidal temper of yours. We don't want another scene like last week."

Apparently any mention of Alicia's temper worked like magic. There was a flicker of fear in her livid face. When she spoke again it was in the accents of an icy, civilized, controlled rage.

"Let go of me."

Toni did so, promptly. Alicia Howe chafed her bony wrists. She looked pleased. She said, "I am going to see to it that both of you are fired—today."

Jeanne's eyes grew enormous in her white face, the pupils blacking out the azure irises. She said slowly, and her accent had grown perceptibly, "You are a horrible, wicked woman. You think you can harm everybody and nobody touch you. But you will be punished."

Alicia Howe laughed and turned away. They watched her going away and heard her shrill chilly voice speaking briefly to Hortense, who had come down on one of her periodic trips and was obviously puzzled at the sight of a client walking unattended through the halls of Lais. She threw a baffled glance in their direction as she took Alicia Howe into the solarium. Jeanne sank down on the bench and began to weep, bitterly.

"It isn't just losing my job," she explained to Toni, who tried to console her. "It's just that it was so horrible and disgusting. It made me feel dirty all over. And I was so happy only a minute ago."

"Yes, I saw you," said Toni dryly. "So did Howe. She didn't like it a bit."

"She is a horrible, horrible woman. She is a murderess. Why doesn't somebody do something about it?"

Toni shrugged her shoulders. "Probably somebody will. Look, darling, snap out of it, will you? In the first place, we are not necessarily fired just because Howe said we are. That's just the way Alicia Howe feels about it. She might not be able to make it stick."

"She always has before, hasn't she? And, oh Toni, it'll be very bad for me if I lose this job. I owe a lot of money—I've had to send a lot to mother—and it's difficult to get another one. Particularly when one is a refugee. But I could stand that. It's that she should so cheapen my feeling for—for…"

And Jeanne wept again. Toni threw her hands up in exasperation.

"Honestly, I could spank you. Don't you see, you little dope, that she couldn't have made you feel that way if there weren't already something cheap about the situation? How you can be so blind about this Teutonic Casanova?"

Jeanne lifted reproachful tear-drenched eyes. "There, you see, you are so prejudiced just because he is German. You are all wrong. He is good and kind. Just because you don't like Dr. Berchtold—"

"That's right, I don't like Dr. Berchtold. But—"

"I am desolate, Toni," Dr. Berchtold remarked, materializing noiselessly beside them. He was grinning like a big Cheshire cat. The grin disappeared after a look at Jeanne. "Anything wrong?"

"Well, rather." Toni told him with disagreeable frankness. "Miss Howe slapped Jeanne's face and said that she would see to it that she was fired."

She was rather pleased to see the irresistible doctor's face lengthen. "When did it happen?"

"Right here and now," Toni told him, with a delicate emphasis on *here*. A swift look backward to his own office told her that he understood. He swung toward Jeanne with an expression of lively dismay on his handsome face.

"Was Miss Howe very upset? Did you tell her that it was—well, did you have the wits to pass it off as a joke? No, you wouldn't, of course," he answered himself with a sort of contemptuous impatience. Jeanne's face turned to him, slowly, incredulously.

"Rudi, I—" her hands went to her tear-streaked face with a childlike gesture of grief and despair.

Berchtold shrugged his shoulders. "It's no good doing that now. Where did Miss Howe go?"

It was Toni who answered him. "She's having a treatment in the solarium."

Berchtold checked himself. As a doctor he had access everywhere; but he anticipated a scene that might be overheard.

"Well, let me know the minute she is through." He shot an exasperated look at Jeanne. "And for God's sake, pull yourself together. My God—women!"

Toni watched his virile, white-clad figure retreating to his office.

"And that," she said, "is that." She turned a rueful eye on her companion, who was now beginning to sit up, in a state of cold and dry-eyed despair.

Jeanne remarked in a cool dispassionate manner, "I want to die."

"There, there," Toni said, stroking the soft honey-colored curls. "How about washing your eyes and powdering your nose and trying to look human? It can be done, you know. Just remember—it's probably callous of me to say this—but in a surprisingly short time all this will seem faintly amusing."

"If you mean I'll know what a fool I've been," Jeanne said dully, "I know it right now. I'm sorry that you—"

"Think nothing of it. As a matter of fact, I have a hunch that nothing will come out of dear sweet Alicia's threat to fire us. Telling the Kyria about it will make her look an awful fool, and she has other reasons for not wanting to appear to be a jealous fury."

Toni's hunch proved to be right, although not precisely for the reason she advanced. Alicia Howe did not lodge any complaints with the Kyria for the simple reason that an hour later she died in her room.

It happened at about 3:30. Jeanne had showed a tendency to cling distractedly to Toni's skirts and was dislodged only by a call from the third floor, where she was supposed to be in the first place. They wanted her to come back, first stopping at the Ambrosial Bar to get some refreshment for the clients. "Tomato juice for Glendenning, apple juice for Smythe and orange juice for Howe. And tell her to step on it." Jeanne went down listlessly and Toni was left alone, to her secret relief. There distinctly is a limit to what one can say to a tearful blonde whose life has just been blighted and it is a strain to keep on fighting the unworthy impulse to say, "I told you so."

At 3:30, however, she felt worried and decided to go up and see for herself how Jeanne was bearing up under the strain. As she went out of her office she saw Berchtold charging down the corridor, his face so ghastly that she cried out involuntarily, "What's the matter?" His answer as he passed her was indistinguishable. Something about the third floor. "Jeanne!" shot through Toni's mind. She followed him, breathless with fear, and darted into the waiting elevator just in time. She was treading on his heels when he strode swiftly into Alicia Howe's room.

For a moment she had a crazy idea that somebody was running time backward like a film that was being rewound on the reel. She was again, incredibly, living through last week's scene: the figure slumped in the chair with the monogrammed cape thrown on it and a crown of blond locks tumbling over a face whose features were obliterated by a layer of gray clay. Complete, even to Hortense babbling and wringing her hands.

"What happened?" snapped Berchtold, and added brutally, "Don't stand there like a fool, get that stuff off her face."

It was Alicia Howe's face that appeared as the Winogradow pack was wiped off by the towel in Hortense's trembling hands. She was dreadfully pale, so pale that the faint patches of acne started purple against her skin. But her thin vindictive mouth had relaxed and lost its cruel petulant expression, and her face had a curiously peaceful look.

"Help me, Toni," said Berchtold, as Hortense exploded in hysterics. Toni, moving deftly and quietly, helped him to disentangle Alicia Howe's inert body from the enveloping cape. She remembered how the columnist disliked being touched and thought again that her body looked that way. It was the body of a spinster, meager, thin, unripe.

Behind her, Hortense was delivering her weepy recital of what had happened, punctuated by Berchtold's curt commands as he busied himself with the columnist. Miss Howe hadn't been feeling well, complaining of headache and being irritable and jumpy. She had quieted down after the

Winogradow pack was applied and hot towels were placed on her back and neck to relax her. Hortense had left the room but stood outside the door in case Howe wanted her. She thought she had heard a funny sound and came in to find Howe in the midst of a heart attack, writhing in her chair and clutching at her heart. Before Hortense could do anything, she had stiffened and then slumped in a faint.

Berchtold was rummaging in a bag. Toni saw him picking up a hypodermic needle, but his movements were perfunctory, almost uncertain, as if he knew that it was no use. Toni surreptitiously put her hand on the columnist's inert wrist. Not the thinnest thread of pulse beat responded to her searching fingers.

"Yes," Toni said halfheartedly, fishing for an olive in a martini that Eric had prepared. It was evening and the fire glowed comfortingly in the diminutive fireplace. "She was dead, all right. Heart. Dr. Berchtold examined her and proclaimed her dead from natural causes. It was—"

Toni saw again Berchtold straightening up wearily. A strange expression had flickered over his face like distant heat lightning over a bland sky. It went, and his face had resolved into the lineaments of decent grief almost before Toni had a chance to diagnose it as an expression of relief.

"It was what?" asked Skeets. "Don't look so vague, Toni. Come back from Shangri-la."

"Oh, just peculiar. I—I don't know."

"Was there any monkey business? Come on, tell papa."

Was there? Toni wondered to herself. Surely it was quite natural for Dr. Berchtold, all unnerved as he was, to upset the half-full glass of orange juice that was standing there. It was perhaps a little less natural for him to want to pick it up and start carrying it with him. Of course, people do such strange things when they are caught unawares. Look at the perfectly idiotic things people rescue when fire breaks out in their homes.

She explained to Eric about the glass of orange juice.

"Did he actually take it away?"

"No, sir. He was going down the elevator with it and I took it out of his hand saying sweetly, 'Never mind about that glass, Doctor. I'll take care of it.' He looked at me with a sort of cold hard stare, then at the glass as if he didn't know that it was there. Then he surrendered it. Do you feel that is sinister?"

"I don't know. Where is the glass, incidentally?"

Toni shrugged, "Well, if you must know, I didn't know what to do with it so it's still in my room. I felt kind of silly."

"I would have let him take it out and see what he did with it."

"Now wait a minute, wait a minute. Do you really think that something might have been wrong?"

"I don't know. I wasn't there." Eric's tone seemed to imply that people who had been there weren't keeping their eyes open.

"Well, but look. Alicia does have a bad heart. I've seen her have heart attacks by the dozen. There certainly were no outside marks on her. This business about the glass seems to indicate poison. But while I was looking her over, I didn't perceive any smell of bitter almonds or orange blossoms, or whatever it is. Eric, she just didn't look poisoned."

"How do you think poisoned people look?"

"In a minute I'll know how poisoned cats look. Stay out of my drink, angel pussy." As Tom Jones recoiled in dignified disdain from the glass, she added, "See, I told you, you wouldn't like it."

Skeets remarked scornfully, "Your cat is a moron."

"Nonsense. Tom Jones is a smart cat. Any cat that wakes you up every day at eight o'clock so you never get to work late, and lets you sleep late on Sunday, is very bright, you must admit."

"I admit that his duties are arduous for a cat," said Eric. He leered elaborately. "I stand ready to take them over any time you want."

Toni looked at him thoughtfully. "What you need is a mustache that you can twirl when you say these things. Seriously, Eric, I hate to hear you talk about poisons and stuff in connection with dear defunct Alicia. This time I am afraid I qualify as a suspect."

"How?"

"Well, she was going to get me fired. Who will believe me when I claim that I've been trying to get myself fired from Lais for simply ages?"

"Have you? Isn't it simpler to quit?"

"It's very difficult to quit a good paying job for no reason except that it's too rich for your blood. Every once in a while I say belligerently that I want a raise or I'll quit, and they give me a raise every time."

"That must be provoking," Eric grinned at her. "Well, now that I am here you are not to think of leaving any more. Anyhow, wait until I do. We shall go out into the unknown hand in hand. Did I ever tell you that you have beautiful hands as well?"

"As well as what?"

"As well as beautiful—eyes."

This lyrical beginning was interrupted by the doorbell. Toni went to answer it and to her surprise found Torrent, who was conscientiously rubbing his snow-sodden galoshes against the doormat. He gave her his cheerful grin. His pleasant face was ruddier than ever and snowflakes were melting on his broad shoulders.

"I was in the neighborhood and thought I'd drop in," said Torrent. "Er—is it all right?"

Toni assured him that it was all right and took him into the living-room where Eric was already preparing a drink for him. Torrent took it with grateful alacrity and looked around him.

"Very pleasant," he remarked. "I say, that's a fancy cat you've got. Here, pussy."

"Don't waste your time," said Skeets. "He's a snob. Won't go to anybody."

Tom Jones looked at Skeets coldly and then suddenly leaped up on the armchair where Captain Torrent was sitting and leaned against his shoulder in an ostentatiously affectionate manner. Toni laughed and Eric looked sheepish.

He said airily, "Probably has a police record that he doesn't want revealed. What do you think of what happened at Lais, Captain Torrent?"

"Matter of fact," said Torrent, "I've just been viewing your latest corpse." He peered at his drink thoughtfully. "Most inconsiderate of Miss Howe. Our favorite suspect dying like that, don't you know. Well, I suppose it will save the state a trial."

"You were pretty sure about her then," said Toni.

"Why, yes," said Torrent quickly, and, Toni thought, a little defensively. "By the way, I don't think I told you how helpful you two have been about this case. You are the sort of witnesses people in my profession pray for. You have helped me to see the setup as nobody else could. And you are so nice and modest about things. I mean you don't go in for amateur sleuthing even if there was a murder in your salon."

Skeetes remarked lightly, "Oh, we know our place. So you think the case is closed?"

"Oh, we'll go pegging along for a while, clearing up the details. Getting an actual confession would have been more satisfactory. And, of course, if it were suicide that would be a tacit admission. This way, just popping off with a bad heart…" Torrent shrugged his shoulders. "Of course, we'll claim that the nervous strain of her guilty secret was too much— that sort of thing."

"Everybody in the salon regards it in the light of divine retribution. And she knew that the police were after her, all right," said Toni. "She even accused me of spying on her for you." She told Torrent briefly about their little clash.

Torrent nodded. "Yes, she knew all right." He hesitated. "I suppose I might as well tell you kids. We were going to arrest her today. Only she called in the morning and told us that she was coming down to talk to us herself, later in the afternoon." Torrent coughed. "She—er—claimed that she knew who the murderer was and she was going to tell us. Got quite upset about it and said she wasn't going to take a rap for anyone. I think she had the wind up and was sort of striking out wildly."

"Whom do you suppose she was going to accuse?"

"We have an idea it would be Mrs. Sterling. I think she had rather expected us to go after her anyhow."

"But—" Toni was beginning, when the telephone rang. She flitted into her room to answer it, shutting the door behind her. She did not immediately recognize Dr. Berchtold's voice. It had an unwonted, clipped, harsh quality that was amplified by the telephone.

Dr. Berchtold was worried. It seemed that just before leaving Lais he had noticed that a bottle of nitroglycerin was missing from his cabinet. (It took Toni a few seconds to realize that he was talking not about a well-known explosive but about a heart stimulant.) He remembered seeing Jeanne going out of his office right after their—er—talk. He had thought at the time that she was merely trying to see him and talk to him so he had sidestepped her, not wishing a repetition of the previous distressing scene. Now he wasn't so sure.

"You mean you think—" Toni began, conscious of a disagreeable chill at the pit of her stomach.

"Precisely. Now, Toni, you are a sensible girl. I want you to talk to that little fool and see if you can get her to restore the bottle quietly. I have reasons not to want any fuss, so I won't say anything to anybody. You understand?"

"Big of you," said Toni frigidly, "seeing that a suicide on your account would be bound to raise your stock among your clients."

"Suicide!" said Dr. Berchtold, "Yes, my God! Get hold of that girl and—and talk to her. I don't even know how to reach her." His voice dropped to a cajoling note. "You were right, Toni. I should have listened to you and not have had anything to do with her."

Toni said curtly, "I'll speak to Jeanne," and hung up. She would have been boiling mad if she weren't so scared. She called Jeanne's number and was answered by the girl who lived with her. The girl told her that Jeanne had come home terribly upset, went to bed early, and was now sleeping. She seemed somewhat puzzled by Toni's concern and her insistence that she should watch over her friend, but promised to do so.

Toni hung up and sat for a minute on her bed gnawing her nails and thinking furiously. Berchtold had said, "Suicide." But there was something else. Toni suddenly remembered that it was Jeanne who had brought Howe's orange juice.

Torrent was putting on his coat when she went back to the living room and discussing the merits of the newest ballet with Skeets. They both agreed that they preferred good corny stuff like *Giselle,* where there was less emotion and acrobatics and more honest ballet. Finally he departed, after patting Tom Jones on the head.

"You fat, fluffy wretch," said Skeets, shaking his fist at Tom Jones, who looked smug. "What are you trying to do, ruin me? Toni, I swear I've met cats before and they've liked me. This is a dastardly scheme to discredit me in your eyes. He dropped to the couch. "Don't you think that methinks Torrent protested too much? About his being sure of Alicia's guilt? Whistling in the dark, sort of? Incidentally, we never did tell him about the orange juice episode. I remembered just as he was going but I had the impression that you didn't want him to hang around."

"Did you? Oh, I didn't mind ," said Toni vaguely. Eric grinned ruefully.

"There I go again, trying to maneuver you into admitting that you like being alone with me. We can tell him about it tomorrow anyhow."

"No," said Toni, and then as Skeets looked at her with surprise, she said, "After what he said about amateur sleuthing? Not on your life. We're the pride of Torrent's heart because we stick to being advisory experts. I'd feel like a damn fool if I were to lose his regard because of a harmless glass of orange juice."

Skeets agreed but wanted to know what if it wasn't harmless. "Of course," he added slowly, "we could have it analyzed ourselves. Any drugstore…"

Yes, Toni thought, it was true. Any drugstore would be able to tell if there was, say, nitroglycerin, in the drink. But she would have liked it better if she were the only one who knew about its existence. Skeets meanwhile was getting more and more excited by that idea. He walked around the room, ruffling his dark hair.

"We ought to do it soon," he was saying. "Clues don't improve with age. Do you suppose we could pick it up tonight? Could we get into the building? It's only ten-thirty."

Toni thought they probably could. She had gone into the building before when she had forgotten something and one of the charwomen had let her in without any trouble.

"If there is any trouble about it," she said, "we can say that we wanted to work tonight on that exercise booklet you sent me the copy for this morning, and that I had forgotten it on account of today's excitement."

"How virtuous of us! Come on, Toni. What are we waiting for?"

CHAPTER 8

IT WAS LATE when Eric and Toni approached the building. It had snowed and stopped, and the sky was mauve with another impending snowstorm. Against the pale winter sky the heavy, violet-blue cubes of buildings stood out sharply, perforated with tiny, pale yellow rectangles of windows to show belated office activity. The snow under their feet crunched dryly and glittered like the diamonds in the Marcus miniature show windows.

Skeets said softly, "It's a lovely street, isn't it? Fifth Avenue, I mean. Like a pretty woman, not quite conventional but extremely chic."

"With very expensive taste in jewels," Toni added.

"Yeah. I used to think of Fifth Avenue in the trenches. Silly, isn't it? I kept on wondering what kind of flowers they were planting in Rockefeller Plaza, and what sort of display Saks Fifth was putting on—"

"Trenches!" Toni turned startled eyes to her companion. She fluttered her eyelashes to get rid of a stray snowflake that had settled on them.

"In Spain," Skeets said briefly. He smiled reminiscently. "There was another New Yorker there and we were both homesick. Well, here we are. Think we can get in?"

Toni's reflective green eyes turned from Skeets' face to the closed door of the salon. From the relief above it, the marble Aphrodite rising from the seashell smiled emptily and invitingly into space.

"I think so." Her fingers found the button and a hollow ringing reverberated through the building. After a long time a faint light went on in the salon and the highly unromantic figure of a cleaning woman materialized behind the glass pane of the door. She opened the door, recognition dawning in her face as she saw Toni. Toni explained that she wanted to get into her room to get something she had forgotten. The woman nodded and moved away from the door to let Toni come in. Skeets tried to follow and was stopped by a mop that barred his way somewhat like a halberd.

"Now wait a minute, young man. I don't know you."

"He's with me, Mrs. Halloran."

"You don't want me to wait outside and catch pneumonia, do you, Mrs. Halloran, a kind lady like you?" said Skeets, turning on the Skeets charm.

"Are you goin' to wait downstairs?" said that lady warily.

"Frankly," said Skeets and smiled at her, "no." Gently but irresistibly, he propelled her to the elevator, at the same time pressing a dollar bill into her hand.

"Well," said the cleaning woman, an indulgent smile beginning to tug at the corner of her mouth, "well." She tucked the dollar bill into her pocket and led the way into the elevator. The elevator went up with a fretful yawning sound and stopped on the second floor.

"I'm gonna leave you here," she said. "We're still up on the fifth floor and it'll take us a long time to clean up. People who works on that floor is certainly wasting plenty of paper and we're the ones gotta clean up after them."

"That's you, dear, Toni said. "Mr. Skeets works on that floor, Mrs. Halloran."

"Oh, does he now. Now dearie, I didn't mean it in the wrong way. Listen, sometimes the other floors are so filthy, in spite of all them creams and soaps, that it's more like a pigsty than a beauty salon. Well, I guess you don't need me here any more."

"Just one thing," said Eric. "Can we get to the third floor by using the stairs or is it closed?"

"Nope, all the doors are open. You don't have to call me until you're ready to leave. Just ring for the elevator when you're through with what you're doing." After pronouncing these last words with what almost amounted to a leer, Mrs. Halloran was wafted upstairs cackling faintly.

"An evil-minded old person," Skeets remarked virtuously. Toni regarded his guileless face coldly.

"Are you trying to—to compromise me?"

"Don't hurry me," Skeets replied airily. "Everything in its own time. First we'll get that glass. Then I'll see."

"I have a good mind," said Toni, "to let out a good healthy yell and then see what you will tell your girlfriend upstairs when she comes down."

"She won't come down." Skeets followed Toni along the shadowy corridor. "She'll know that you didn't mean it. Is this your little cubbyhole? This is very exciting, like being behind the stage or dipping into the Eleusinian mysteries."

Toni, though she didn't say it, liked it too. There is something exciting and pleasurably blood-chilling in creeping with a friendly accomplice through a deserted building, particularly when it's night and all the familiar nooks and corners assume a mysterious, aloof expression and refuse to recognize you.

"Here's the clue," she said taking it out of a drawer. She also took out the copy and the photographs for the booklet and stuffed them into her purse. "As you see there's very little stuff left in it."

Eric took it, looked at it in the light, sniffed it, and shrugged his shoulders in a gesture reminiscent of the eldest Ritz brother in his Dr. Jekyll-turning-into-Mr. Hyde scene. Out of the mild confusion on Toni's desk he drew a small box with the gaudy emblems of Lais and a red elastic. He put the glass with its yellowish residue into the former, packing it firmly with tissue paper to keep it upright, and snapped the latter around it.

"Shall we ring for Mrs. Halloran and allay her evil suspicions of us?" Toni inquired.

"Presently, dear. That jovial hag seems to worry you overmuch."

"Well, what else is there to do?"

"Plenty." Eric smiled wickedly. "Darling, do you realize that we are alone at last—alone? There's always been somebody around. But now I've got you away from your cat." He twirled an imaginary mustache, carefully put the box on the table, and kissed her. Almost immediately he drew back and looked at her suspiciously.

"Why are you laughing?"

"Well, it's so absurd. After spending the whole day here, to maneuver me here again at night to kiss me."

"You have a point there," Skeets conceded, rubbing lipstick off. "The atmosphere is distinctly unromantic. I did it all for Mrs. Halloran, bless her bawdy Irish soul."

They were out in the hall again, their voices reechoing in its dim emptiness. Eric lingered with a strange almost sheepish expression.

"Well?"

"Well," he said slowly, "I feel a little peculiar about this. I am going to make a very unusual suggestion and I don't know how you'll take it."

Toni's eyebrows went up, and after one glance at her face, Skeets burst into laughter.

"I can see that I am making myself very clear," he said dryly. "In a word, I would like to take a look at the doctor's room." He added more seriously, "I don't know what it is. Must be my bloodhound blood beginning to tell, but I am awfully set on it somehow."

Toni stared at him. "You're mad," she said flatly. "Why, we wouldn't even know what to look for."

"I know, but I've got a feeling."

"I've got a feeling that we'll look awfully silly rifling through the doctor's possessions. All right, let's go."

"What a girl," Eric muttered happily, following her into the doctor's office. "What a pal."

"I hate to think of what Torrent would say. He'd be terribly disappointed in us," Toni said, leading the way.

"What he doesn't know won't hurt him. Besides, why should he have all the fun? Now let's see, what have we here?"

The feeling of illicit elation forsook the two criminals very soon. The doctor's office was unpromisingly neat and impersonal. It presented a polished surface beneath which it was impossible to penetrate. The desk was one of those modern affairs consisting of an exquisitely polished strip of wood with one end resting on a bracket in the wall and the other on a unit of three drawers. An intensive search through these drawers brought nothing except a tray of three by five cards covered with notations in Berchtold's neat handwriting. Toni recognized them immediately.

"These are personal cards, so called," she explained. "The regular records are in that file cabinet but he keeps the cards with personal observations on their idiosyncrasies in his bureau drawer. The remarks are so personal that he never shows them to us. What he does is put a little asterisk on the record and that is a sign that the woman in question is a special case for one reason or another and to consult—Why are you looking at this?" she interrupted herself.

"I am interested to see what the doctor has to say about the principals in the case. Let's see." He shuffled through the cards rapidly. "It's alphabetically arranged. Glendenning—Mrs. Howard. What's it say here? '*Vorsicht! Nympho! Nur im Beisein von Zeugen.*' Now who would have thought it? Tsk, tsk, tsk . . . What does it mean?"

"You're being nosy," Toni remarked severely. "It means that Mrs. Howard is impulsive and he is never to see her alone and it's none of your business, Eric Skeets. Mrs. Howard is not a principal in the case."

"True. Howe ought to be next, but—there is no Howe. Odd, isn't it, that he shouldn't have any special remarks about Howe?"

"Not at all. Those are just things he ought to remember about the clients, and there isn't much chance of his forgetting any of Howe's many endearing characteristics." Toni paused and shook her head. "I keep on talking about her in a nasty way, as if she weren't dead."

"Yes—*de mortuis,* and so on. I am going to look up Sterling. Starret, Sterns—hold hard! He seems to use downright code on some of these. At least I can't make out head or tail of these abbreviations. I suppose these are the real unmentionables. Here is Mrs. Sterling: '*Kindisch—leicht zu überreden; Allergie zum—*' I can't read that word. Not terribly important."

"No. Of course, the complete record can be found in the regular files. I know that Berchtold keeps the active file here. It's usually open in daytime. I wonder—"

"Let's try."

To their pleased astonishment the file cabinet was open. They regarded rows of large cards in cellophane envelopes filled with notations in typewriter and handwriting.

"It's no use going through all these in search of God knows what. I'm just going to find Alicia Howe's folder and call it a day," said Skeets, thumbing through the files. He stopped. "Hey, there is no Alicia Howe folder."

"That's impossible."

"Look for yourself. Howard—Howatt—Howell—Isserman—no Howe."

Toni looked. "Peculiar," was her comment.

"Yes, isn't it? I know she's dead, but isn't it a bit precipitate to throw her file out before her ashes are cold? Insufficient respect for the dead and all that. Where is that damn folder?"

"Maybe it's mislaid."

Skeets looked dismally at the rows of folders before him. "Take a long time to look through these, wouldn't it? Mrs. Halloran will have a fine tale to tell her cronies." He stood a while in thought, like Lewis Carroll's beamish boy, then brightened up. "Look, I have an idea. Why don't I show myself upstairs on the fifth floor? There's a book I forgot that I wanted to pick up. You can look through the files meanwhile and see if the Howe record got misplaced somehow. This way we'll save your reputation and lose no time."

"I think," said Toni, "you're just trying to get out of work."

Skeets chucked her under the chin and disappeared.

Toni turned back to the files and her fingers ruffled swiftly through the folders. The files were arranged with German accuracy. It took her a very short time to convince herself that Alicia Howe's folder was indeed gone. She slid the drawer shut and sat down behind the desk to wait for Skeets' return. She felt that he was attaching overmuch importance to the folder's disappearance. After all, why should anybody want it? With a twinge of tender conscience, she admitted to herself that perhaps it was with an ulterior purpose that she encouraged Skeets to follow that line of reasoning.

"I am not obliged to tell him everything," she reflected defensively. Her eyes lighted on the package with the glass and she sighed. "Besides there is no reason why I should worry him about Jeanne. She—well, she's my responsibility."

Her eyes again wandered to the package.

"But," said Toni grimly to herself, "I've got to *know.*"

Then she had an idea. As long as she was going to snoop around she might as well be the spy complete. The key to her locker below fitted others, she knew. It might fit Jeanne's. It was worth while to take a look and see if—if what? Toni shook her head impatiently at herself. "Just take a look and see," she said. "Sufficient unto the day is the evil thereof."

She went out into the hall, opened the door to the stairs, and stepped out on the landing. As the door closed, she found herself in complete, blind, Stygian blackness. Toni gave a little gasp. She had an irrational sense of panic, as if she were suddenly struck blind. She had let the door-knob go. She now groped for it in vain. There probably was a switch nearby, but she hadn't the slightest idea where it was. This was absurd. Toni stayed where she was, waiting for her eyes to get used to the darkness.

It was then that she heard someone coming downstairs toward her. The light steps reechoed faintly and hollowly through the stairway, in a swift staccato patter, broken by two firmer steps whenever they came to a landing. Eric—it was probably he—was apparently not disturbed by the darkness, Toni thought. Then the steps approached, and the darkness sprang back, as the light was switched on, a few landings above hers. The steps reached the third floor. Toni was just about to call out when there was another click of the switch. Simultaneously the door on the floor above her slammed, darkness again enveloped her and all was silence around her.

Eric had gone to the third floor instead of coming down to the second. Toni's curiosity was strongly aroused. Also she was rather indignant. When you go on a prowl with a friend it is definitely not playing the game to wander off on an investigation all your own. She started toward where she supposed the stairs were, having seen them there the last time, was met by them halfway and sprawled noisily, barking a shin and an elbow.

"Blast," said Toni. "My good stockings." She went on possessed by a definitely unfriendly feeling toward Eric with his mysterious forays. She was by this time fairly well oriented and her eyes accustomed to the dark. Keeping a firm grasp on the handrail, she made her way to the third floor without any further mishap.

The third floor was as black as the stairway. But across the length of the loggia the luminous L was softly glowing. Toni stared at it, curiosity gnawing at her vitals. What in the world was Eric Skeets doing in Alicia Howe's room? She walked over to it, feeling like a cat pouncing on a mousehole. The closed door of Alicia Howe's room faintly reflected the bluish light of the lamp above. She opened it and instantly heard a faint click of the switch. The light in the room went out so fast that it seemed to linger in her bewildered eyes.

"This," said Toni with decision, "is very silly." She stretched her hand to the switch.

The next moment her outstretched hand was caught and held around the wrist. Toni stood quite still, panic tightening around her heart as if it too were gripped by those iron gloved fingers. She said in a small frightened voice, "Eric?" There was no answer. There was something terrifying about the complete motionlessness and silence of the presence near her, as if the evil blackness around her had materialized into that menacing hand that reached out and gripped her. Then suddenly Toni sensed a change, a movement toward her as the grip tightened, then shifted. The two hands were on her throat. Later, Toni was to remember with justifiable pride how swift her reaction was. There was only one thrashing futile movement on her part. Then her hands went to the hands around her throat, not the wrists and not the cruel pressing thumbs, but the little fingers. She found them and yanked viciously. There was a gasp and her throat was freed.

She twisted away with the desperate agility of a trapped wildcat. She stumbled against the wall, fell, and scrambled to her feet, every nerve screaming for flight. A little gasp escaped her. Flight! Where? Her straining eyes made out a blacker splotch against the darkness barring the way back to the door, in time to arrest her first instinctive movement which would have brought her into those implacable hands. She drifted backward, putting distance between her and her assailant.

There was a little advantage on her side. She was now facing the loggia, that was lighted by a large window above the couch. The shades were down but even so a little light trickled in, so that the shape of her assailant was a tiny bit blacker than the background behind it. Toni could sense its movements. She could maneuver until the attacker either got tired of the whole business and put the lights on, or cornered her at the far end of the hall.

Back, back—putting one foot down after the other—with infinite caution. Into Toni's head there swam an absurd fragment from *The Pirates of Penzance.*

With catlike tread
Our cautious way we feel...

But what good is catlike tread, when your heart is hammering so loudly that surely anyone could track you by its sound, and your breath escapes in shrill gasps through your cold lips? Quiet, heart. And thank God for soft, soft carpets. Toni stopped, keeping her eyes on the black blur that drifted toward her. She slipped out of her shoes and moved back on soft feet, and was soon rewarded by hearing the person who was following her stumble over her shoes. A few feet further back the wall broke off and she realized that she had turned the corner of the L-shaped corridor. Her hand brushed the edge of an open door. Only a little while longer and she would reach the end of the blind alley.

Suddenly, out of sheer cold desperation, Toni knew what to do. She dug into her pocket for her gloves, crumpled them into a ball, and threw them at a wall a few feet ahead of her. She heard the steps pause, as the gloves struck faintly, and then there was a rush in the direction of the sound. In that moment Toni had slipped into the room and closed the door behind her. She waited for the footsteps to pass. When they reached the end of the hall, she would slip out again and run.

The footsteps continued, faintly audible, but deliberate and terribly menacing. Then they stopped. A silence, with the blood drumming in her ears, and then—the sound of a ghostly chuckle. At that moment Toni realized what she had done. Now she was really trapped. A luminous L above the door of the room where she was crouching—the lamp that went on whenever anybody closed the door—proclaimed very conveniently where she was.

For a moment she knew that she was going to faint. She knew she ought to do something, anything. Put on the light, look for some weapon, scream, but the hand she lifted to the switch was as heavy and slow as if weighted by lead. It was exactly like a nightmare, the same feeling of hopeless futility. Her legs and arms had gone as nerveless as sausages. And when she tried to scream the only sound that issued from her bruised throat was a sort of a rasping hiss. She could only stare at the door in front of her, as its surface slowly, inexorably slid away from her and the person on the other side of the door stepped in.

It was probably the fact that she was so close to the door that saved her. Her attacker, who apparently expected her to be huddling as far away as possible, was taken unawares by her desperate rush. She ducked under an outstretched arm, her face brushed the rough tweed material of a coat, something clinked and jingled. Then she was out of the room running, running and screaming. She hurtled against the door and miraculously found the doorknob. As she flung it open, a hand caught the skirts of her flying coat. And then the darkness burst into a thousand flying sparks, unbearably, achingly bright, that settled as she plummeted into the blackest blackness of all.

CHAPTER 9

SHE WAS LYING in a dark narrow room outside of which people were at work. She heard their voices lifted in low casual talk. But the horror of it was that they were pushing the walls in on her. Already the heavy stone was crushing her head. She wanted to scream, to let them know that she was there, but her vocal cords had withered away. At last, with a superhuman effort, a shriek tore out of her throat.

"She's coming to," a voice said, and Toni heard her own voice moaning feebly. Her eyes fluttered open for a moment and closed as a bright light seared across her eyeball. As from a vast distance she heard a familiar voice saying wildly, "Darling, are you all right? Darling, speak to me. Darling—" It sounded exactly like a broken record. Toni opened her eyes, for good this time. Eric's white agonized face hung over hers. As she looked, an almost ludicrous expression of relief overspread it.

"She'll do now, I think," said another voice, also familiar. Toni jerked her head in its direction, wincing as she did so. She winced again under the disconcertingly unsympathetic stare of Torrent's cold blue eyes. She thought of closing her eyes again and saying, "Where am I?" Instead she smiled feebly.

"Captain Torrent, I presume. What are you doing here?"

Torrent's face was expressionless, yet Toni somehow sensed anger and suspicion behind the bland surface. "I was wondering the same about you," he said pleasantly. "What happened, exactly?"

"That's what I want to know myself." Toni tried to sit up and gave it up. Her head hurt so terribly that tears came to her eyes. A white-sleeved hand gave her something to drink and over the rim of her glass she looked at a fresh-faced intern. Young Dr. Kildare. He grinned at her cheerfully.

"You got a bad rap on the head," he told her. "Luckily it was just a glancing blow."

"Don't tell me," said Toni with a weak grin, "that it was the blunt instrument—"

"Supposing," Torrent suggested softly, *"you* tell us something about it. What were you doing there in the first place?"

Toni found herself telling him the version that she and Skeets had prepared before they descended on Lais. She was aware of Eric's puzzled frown and kept her eyes away from him. It was difficult to talk. Her head was a huge balloon tied to her shoulders by a single thread and any movement threatened to dislodge it.

Torrent said, "Any idea who?"

"No. I guess I really don't even know whether it was a man or a woman. Except if it was a woman, it was an awfully strong one. He or she wore gloves and sort of a loose tweed coat. My face brushed against it when I got out of that room."

"But you said you grappled with whoever it was. Couldn't you tell?"

"Not really. First there was that one gloved hand gripping mine. Then two hands at my throat and I pulled them away. Then that coat— There was something else but I can't remember." Toni closed her eyes. "Nobody saw the—that person get out?"

"No. Skeets heard you yell on the stairs as he was coming down from the fifth floor. He sprinted down and there you were sprawled on the stairs, out like a light. He thinks he heard a door slammed downstairs but he didn't investigate, being too much concerned with your situation." Torrent's voice was dry. "There's something else I want to ask you... O.K., Doc, I won't then, if you think she can't take it any more. What is she supposed to do now?"

Young Dr. Kildare suggested going home to bed. "As long as you've been able to walk away from it," he told her cheerily. "Stay in bed tomorrow. You'll have one hell of a headache."

Toni found after a few attempts that if she sat up and moved very gingerly her head would not fall off. Torrent insisted on taking her home, and by the glint of his eye this was something more than mere gallantry. Accordingly she went home in a police car, wedged between Skeets and Torrent. The siren howled, and Torrent sat next to her in forbidding silence. The trip was a fast but weary one. When they came to her house, the two men carried her up the stairs in spite of her protests.

"You get into bed," said Skeets, who still looked white and shaken. "I am going to run down to the drugstore to have this prescription filled—the sedative the doctor gave her, you know," he explained to Torrent. Torrent nodded his permission and he hurried off. Torrent looked after him with a cold and disapproving expression and Toni had a feeling that a nasty chill seemed to be creeping into their beautiful relationship.

Torrent started to the door and turned to look at her. "I am stationing a policeman outside of your apartment," he told her. "So if you are worried about another attack…"

"Thank you, Captain Torrent," said Toni wanly. "I don't think—"

"I don't either. People who don't go where they are not supposed to don't usually get into trouble. But just in case…"

Toni sighed. There was an unmistakable emphasis in his words. "Good night, Captain Torrent."

"Good night," said Torrent curtly. "I'll be back tomorrow."

That had a definitely foreboding sound. The door shut behind him and Toni staggered into the bedroom. Tom Jones followed her disapprovingly. "Pickled again," his manner seemed to imply.

The doorbell rang and she let in a contrite Skeets.

"I thought you might have gone to bed and here I was getting you out of it again. But I didn't know what else I could do. I had to bring you your medicine. Why aren't you in bed?"

"My bed isn't even made," said Toni morosely. "And I think I am going to throw up."

She did. Ten minutes later she was in bed, made for her by Skeets in an elaborately impersonal manner. The pillow felt soft and cool under her aching head. Skeets, still in his coat, was administering the sedative. After she drank it, he bent to imprint a chaste kiss on her brow.

"Sleep well, my dear. And don't worry, there's a big policeman outside, just in case. I'd stay here too if I didn't want your reputation to remain as pure as driven snow in the eyes of the police department."

That brought a dim memory to her mind. "How is my reputation with Mrs. Halloran?" she said drowsily. "You certainly had a long talk with her, didn't you?"

A funny tremor passed over his face.

"Yes, much too long. Good night, dear."

After he left, Toni lay in a drowsy daze, her headache jolting to a stop. From the foot of the bed came a tiny purring snore. Tom Jones was in possession again. Her eyes dropped shut. The images of the day twirled in her mind in an ever accelerating kaleidoscope. She had almost dropped asleep when a galvanic shock brought her upright in the bed, every vestige of sleep gone and her heart pounding.

She had forgotten the glass of orange juice in Dr. Berchtold's office!

That was bad. In the first place, it would certainly tell Dr. Berchtold that somebody had gone through his room. And then after all the fuss to be as far from knowing the contents of the glass as ever—that was too provoking.

"Hell," said Toni, clutching her aching head, "hell, hell."

What to do? Eric—she snatched the receiver off the hook and dialed his number. But the idea died an early death while his telephone was ringing. Skeets couldn't go down to the second floor early and walk into the doctor's office without all of the girls noticing it and wondering and later commenting about it. She replaced the receiver slowly, thinking that apparently she would have to go to Lais herself. That was the only solution. Her spirit moaned at the thought, but there was nothing to be done about it. The thing to do was to fall asleep as soon as possible and kill that headache. Toni grimly took another pill and lay back. Sleep seemed impossible. Her eyelids kept on popping open like a sleeping doll's, and every movement started anew the anvil chorus in her skull. So that it was with a feeling of vague surprise that she finally fell asleep, plunging into a sea of dreams, doubts and vague but galvanic alarms.

Tom Jones' soft paw patting her soothingly on her cheek awoke her at eight the next morning.

"Thank you for nothing," she said sourly, and crawled out of bed. She felt awful. Her headache had retreated, but she was sure that very little would bring it back in full force. Her eyes felt like boiled onions and her eyelids as if they were propped up by matchsticks. She staggered into the bathroom, shuddering at the doleful face that met her scrutiny in the mirror.

"Circles under my eyes down to here. A fine thing. Oh why, why couldn't I stay away from sleuthing, like mother told me to?"

She struggled painfully into her clothes and dragged on her coat. In the hallway she bumped into a tall burly man who was sitting on a chair and staring at a ceiling. He got to his feet and nodded to her.

"Good morning," said Toni, at a loss. "Do I know—? Oh good heavens." She remembered Torrent's last remark. "You poor man," she exclaimed, in honest sympathy. "You mean to say you sat in that uncomfortable chair the whole night? Why didn't you come in? I could have made you perfectly comfortable on the sofa."

A blush, faint but unmistakable, mantled the startled countenance of Toni's guardian. He said bashfully, "Aw, Cap wouldna liked that, girlie. It was okay."

"No, it wasn't. He needn't have put you to all that trouble... Well," said Toni brightly after a little pause, "The night is over and nobody got me, so I guess you can go home and sleep now."

The detective didn't seem to greet that idea with the enthusiasm that it deserved. Instead he eyed Toni askance, "You ain't going out, are you?"

"Why yes, I'm going to my job. I'm much better now."

"Well, I don't know. The Cap said you should stay in."

Toni explained patiently, "That was because he thought I'd still be ill. But I'm all right now."

The burly detective shook his head. "I don't know. He said that if you wanted to go to work, I should stop you. Besides, he's coming in to see you at ten."

"Look," said Toni in exasperation, "I am not under arrest, am I? This is a free country, isn't it? I can go out if I—" She stopped, suddenly realizing the futility of arguing. She might as well try to explain the situation to a humorless but dutiful great Dane parked on her threshold. Captain Torrent seemed to have neglected to tell his watchdog that the idea was not to keep her in but to keep somebody else out.

The watchdog looked at her and grinned. "Whyn't you go in and wait for the Cap, Miss?" he said not unkindly. "Get back to bed, will you? You look as white as a ghost."

There was nothing to do but go back. Too much insistence on going to Lais might be suspicious. There was just another thing she could do and she did it. She called up Jeanne and was lucky enough to catch her just as she was leaving. She didn't tell her anything about the night before, merely that she was unable to come to work, that yesterday she had occasion to go into Dr. Berchtold's office and had left a package there.

"Something personal," said Toni. "I'd like you to get it out before anybody comes in."

"All right," Jeanne said. Her voice sounded a little hoarse, as if she had been crying. "I'm sorry you're ill, Toni. I shall come in and see you during lunch hour. And I'll bring the package."

"That'll be fine," said Toni. "I want to talk to you, anyhow." After she had hung up, it occurred to her that perhaps it wasn't such a terribly good idea, with the police hanging around. There was also the possibility that Jeanne might look into the package. Toni didn't think she would, somehow, but if she did, the way she would act about it would tell Toni a great deal. At any rate she was not going to worry about it. She poured some milk for Tom Jones and went back to bed. She had a feeling that it might be a good thing to look helpless when Torrent came around.

He arrived at ten, his ring at the door awaking Toni from the first really refreshing sleep she had. Tom Jones made a protesting little noise when she got up. He had made up his mind that this must be Sunday, after all, and resented these unwonted interruptions. Torrent came in, ruddy and odiously cheerful, shaking the snowflakes off his coat.

"Do you mind if I go back to bed?" Toni asked pathetically. In her heelless slippers, her childish quilted robe, she knew,or at least hoped, that she looked fragile and innocent.

"By all means," Torrent said heartily. "Make yourself comfortable. I have a lot of questions to ask you." (That's bad, Toni thought, pattering off to bed.) "Feeling any better this morning? You do look a bit done in. Have you had any breakfast?"

"Well," said Toni, "no. I've nothing in the house, you see. I have thought of asking my landlady to get me some. But I was afraid she would get wrong ideas about your watchdog outside."

"O'Malley?" said Torrent, laughing too heartily. "Nonsense! What wrong idea?"

"For example, that I am under arrest. Incidentally," she asked delicately, "am I?"

"Good Lord, no. Whatever made you think so?"

"Well, O'Malley wouldn't let me out this morning. Your instructions."

"My dear young lady," said Torrent, "you amaze me. You must have misunderstood O'Malley. I merely suggested to him that if you didn't feel well and still wanted to go out in spite of doctor's orders, that he should remonstrate with you. Why, he has no authority to keep you here." There was a little pause while Toni looked a little foolish. Then Torrent said gently, "Incidentally, Miss Ney, why are you so anxious to get to Lais? I had an idea you didn't like the place. Yet there you go prowling about it at night, getting yourself almost killed, and the next morning you're practically rushing to get there although you're still obviously unwell. Why all this loyalty and attachment to the salon?"

"Aha," Toni thought and mentally rolled up her sleeves. She said sweetly, "I wasn't thinking of going to Lais this morning particularly, Captain Torrent. I merely wanted to go out and get some breakfast."

"That wasn't the impression O'Malley got."

"O'Malley," said Toni gently, "probably misunderstood me just as I misunderstood him."

They eyed each other warily, like two fencers trying out each other's blades in a tentative swordplay. Then Torrent rose and stepped out into the hall.

"I have sent O'Malley for some breakfast for you," he said on returning. "In the meanwhile you might tell me about yesterday."

Incongruously enough, Toni was conscious of a positive longing to tell him all about yesterday. She was pretty certain that Torrent would not be too pleased about the little matter of burgling the doctor's office. But that she could have braved. It was the other matter with its dark implications that kept her silent.

"I think I told you everything about last night."

"Let's go over it again. Why did you go there in the first place?"

"I told you, to pick up the copy and photographs for the booklet. If you'll give me my pocketbook—" She dug them out of the minute chaos while Torrent watched expressionlessly. "Here they are."

Torrent gave them back without any comment but with a definitely disbelieving look in his eye. However, he seemed to drop that subject for the time being and went on to recheck the story that she had already given him. Under his adroit questioning, while eating a hearty breakfast brought in by the grinning O'Malley, she found herself recalling details that had escaped her memory the first time she told the story. She remembered, for example, how light and quick were the steps she had heard going to the third floor.

"That's why I thought at first that it was a man—you know, women as a rule walk down the stairs rather heavily and with their heels clicking."

"Yes," said Torrent slowly, "but it might have been a woman wearing low heels. Could you swear it wasn't that?"

Toni found that she couldn't. "And I suppose that impression I had of a loose tweedish coat doesn't mean anything either. Women wear that sort of coat too. Now if I had the presence of mind to stop and see if there were pants under the coat..."

There was no answering smile on Torrent's cold face. He made no reply and Toni went on, "That reminds me of something else. When I brushed against the coat, there was a sort of funny sound—tinkling, you know."

"Like change?" asked Torrent. He put his hand in his coat pocket and jingled the change tentatively. Toni shook her head.

"N—no. It was different—something else—I know!" her face brightened. "It sounded like glass. That's what it felt like too. A bottle. I thought of that last night when Eric came in with that medicine bottle in his coat pocket. Let's try that. I've got an empty cream bottle in the kitchen."

The experiment was more or less satisfactory. "That was it, all right," Toni said. Then her face fell. "Not that it tells us anything. Captain Torrent, have you any idea? Is it anything to do with—with the murder?"

Torrent favored her with an enigmatic glance. "Which one?" he asked.

Toni caught her breath and looked at him. "Then you think there was something strange about Howe's death?"

For a moment Torrent seemed to forget that he no longer liked Toni. "I don't know. On the surface there seems to be nothing in it except the fact that she did call me to say that she was going to tell me who the murderer was. But that attack on you last night seems to show that the germ is still active, in a manner of speaking. As for Howe's death—well, she did have a heart condition, according to the folder Dr. Berchtold showed me at Lais this morning. But an autopsy will clear it all up, right enough."

Toni sat up bolt upright, discarding the fragile air. "Did you say Dr. Berchtold showed you Alicia Howe's medical record this morning?"

"Yes," said Torrent in mild astonishment. "What's so surprising about that?"

"Because—because—"

At that moment the telephone rang.

It was Jeanne. "Toni? I am terribly sorry but I cannot come, I think. I'll try to drop in after work."

"That's all right," said Toni, acutely conscious of Torrent's thoughtful gaze.

"And Toni—I couldn't find that package. I couldn't get down to the second floor until later and it wasn't there. Was it important?"

"No, not particularly. Then I'll expect you later. Goodbye."

She hung up, resisting the impulse to press frantic hands to her whirling head. Torrent did not ask her who had called her, as she half expected him to. Like a good hunting dog he had kept his point.

"What surprised you so much about my seeing Dr. Berchtold's records?"

Toni took a deep breath and told him. Not everything, because now there was more reason than ever to say nothing about Jeanne and the glass of orange juice. Luckily, the story of the missing folder was one she could tell without involving Jeanne.

Torrent listened to her stonily. It was obvious that he wasn't impressed and Toni could almost hear him saying to himself bitterly: "Amateur sleuths."

When she finished, he said in a dishearteningly suspicious manner, "I suppose you've told me all you know, eh?" He waited a moment before continuing. When he did his voice was hard and cold. "That's the trouble with getting to like people when you are on a case. You're bound to be disappointed. There's no place for personal feelings in my work. Now, you've been very useful to me, Miss Ney, and I prefer doing things the nice way, naturally. But there are other ways of finding out what we want to know. This is a murder investigation, and not tiddleywinks. Good day."

Toni let him reach the door before she called him. She wanted to know whether O'Malley was going to remain on guard and whether there was going to be another misunderstanding about her going out. Torrent answered curtly that O'Malley would no longer bother her and added, perhaps unnecessarily, that the next time she was detained there would be no misunderstanding about it. He slammed the door behind him, so loudly that Tom Jones got up to peer after him in a surprised way.

The morning that began so badly wore on drearily. At noon there arrived a huge horseshoe-shaped wreath of roses, regrettably gaudy, and bearing greetings "From the Boys," in Skeets' scrawly handwriting. It was closely followed by Skeets himself, bringing more gifts, to wit, a box of candy and a woolly panda, which he threw on Toni's bed. To Toni's jaundiced eye, he looked unnecessarily cheerful, as if he had nothing on his conscience.

"Eric, you idiot!" She indicated the rose-decked horror in the corner of the room. "How could you possibly?"

Skeets grinned. "Isn't it a lulu? I told the florist to whip up a little floral offering that would be suitable for a gangster's funeral. No reflections on you, darling. How do you feel?" He surveyed her with an anxious and proprietary eye. "My God, you gave me a fright yesterday, sprawled down the stairs, all limp and lifeless. I tell you I lost my head. It was La Halloran who finally called the cops. Are you sure you're all right now?"

Toni admitted to a headache.

"Well, you look lousy," he assured her candidly. "A mere wraith of the flowerlike girl who used to grace my revels."

"I've been questioned by the police," said Toni. "You wouldn't look flowerlike either under the circumstances."

"Wouldn't I?" said Skeets with a trace of smugness. "That's what you think. I was questioned by the police too."

"Really?"

"Yes, really. Our pal Torrent gave me a going over."

"What did he ask you about? What did you tell him? Did you say anything about . . . ?"

"Steady, there. The answer to all these questions is no. I looked as enigmatic as a sphinx and lied like a gentleman, very much against my conviction, I must admit. But last night I got the idea that you for some unknown reason wanted secrecy about our nefarious activities. And I didn't get a chance to see you until now so I just played dumb and didn't know from nothing. Isn't that loyal and devoted behavior? Now supposing you tell me what it's all about."

Toni hesitated. "It's just that I don't want to burden you with my troubles."

"Lady, at this point you can't help it. At this late date your troubles are mine, as one Siamese twin said to the other. What did Torrent have to say to you?"

Toni told him. When she mentioned the missing folder turning up again, Skeets jumped from the chair and began pacing the room excitedly. "That is very interesting. So our friend Rudi the Rat has taken to conjuring tricks. Did you tell Torrent about the orange juice?"

"No, I didn't."

"But for God's sake, don't you see how important that is? Torrent has got to know."

"I don't know how important it is. There's probably nothing in it."

"Torrent has got to decide that for himself. Holy smoke, Toni, you aren't going to protect that louse?"

Toni's back straightened into a ramrod. "I'm not protecting Berchtold!"

"Then who are you protecting?"

"Whom, you mean."

"Never mind my grammar. Come on, Toni. If you want me to keep my mouth shut, I am entitled to some explanation, don't you think?"

Toni sighed and told him the whole story. Skeets' face darkened slowly as he listened, until at the end he bent a wintry look on Toni.

"Nice work," he remarked coldly. "I would have sworn that you weren't holding out on me."

"You mustn't feel that way—"

"How do you expect me to feel? Here I'm basking in a fool's paradise of perfect understanding, fellow conspirators and all that bunk, while the truth of the matter is that the minute something really serious comes up you don't consider me worthy of confidence. I suppose," said Skeets bitterly, "you were going to have the stuff analyzed and the results would have been negative, so far as I was concerned, no matter what the truth was?"

"Perhaps," said Toni steadily. She had gone a little pale.

"Tshah!!" said Skeets explosively and strode away to the other end of the room.

Toni spoke after a moment's silence. "That's why I didn't want you to be involved in this. I just couldn't throw Jeanne to the wolves even if—I don't say she did—but even if... As a matter of fact, I think whoever rid the world of Alicia Howe is a benefactor," she ended defiantly.

"What about Lili Michaud? Is her murderer also to be considered a candidate for a medal?"

"Do you think there is a connection?"

"Perhaps. We can't tell, and certainly Torrent can't until he is in possession of all facts. And now Berchtold has got that glass and will probably get rid of it before the police have a chance to do anything about it. Toni, I think you're wrong to keep anything back at this point. You're getting yourself in trouble. Our friend Torrent is no amateur. He's going to get to the bottom of this. He'll find out all the things you are hiding from him, only meanwhile you will have gotten yourself into serious trouble. And Torrent is suspicious already. His attitude toward us is entirely different."

"I think," said Toni, nastily, "all you're worried about is that he won't let you play the amateur sleuth any more."

Skeets flushed and Toni had a suspicion that she had flicked him on a sensitive spot. He said coldly, "Your business, of course, but I think it's a very silly thing to allow yourself to get so emotionally involved that you can't think straight. A murder is a murder. If your friend Jeanne is a poisoner, are you really prepared to go to any length to shield her?"

"I don't believe she is."

"Then you're doing her an extreme disservice in not letting it be cleared up as soon as possible. Women," said Skeets, warming up, "are always unwilling to accept realities. You think she's innocent and you act as if she's guilty and you think that's logical."

Nothing can make a fellow creature as unlovable in your eyes as an uneasy suspicion that you have acted unjustly toward him. Toni moreover resentfully found herself agreeing with Skeets' remarks. In pure self defense she decided that he sounded intolerably righteous and should be taught a lesson. She flashed an oblique glance out of her green eyes, which should have put him on his guard.

"You have kept quiet about all this to Torrent, haven't you?"

"That's right. I told you why."

"Because you thought I wanted you to, isn't that right? One might almost say you were protecting me. Is that logical, in view of your convictions?"

Skeets flushed again. His eyes grew angry. "Well, I'll be damned! Women are all alike. Do something for any member of your unscrupulous tribe and you can be sure that it would be used as a reproach or as a hold on you."

It was Toni's turn to redden. "I didn't mean to use it as—as a weapon. I just wanted to show that one can't always be logical when—"

"Emotional factors enter? You're quite right. I probably ought to teach you a lesson and remedy my mistake."

Toni's eyes were challenging. "By telling Torrent about everything? Pray do. It'll at least absolve me of any obligation to you."

"That too is a typically female trick. Get your responsibilities off your shoulders and feel righteous about it."

"I think it's you who have been righteous."

"I have *not* been righteous!"

"No?"

They glared at each other. "I have a good mind to shake you," said Skeets slowly. "I think you're deliberately fomenting this." He made a step toward the bed. There was an outraged yowl followed by a yelp from Skeets. His leg shot up in the air and Tom Jones, who had been clawing at it, sailed through the air and landed in the far corner, where, dazed but indomitable, he rose to his haunches and shadowboxed.

Toni said accusingly, "You kicked him!"

"I didn't."

"Yes, you did. I saw you. Taking your temper out on an animal."

"I didn't! He clawed at my leg and I—"

"You enjoyed doing it! I saw you. Besides, you said once that you'd enjoy kicking him because he has such a nice f—furry b—behind." To her intense disgust her voice broke. Skeets shook his head in a dazed way as if to clear it and made another step toward her. His face was such a study of conflicting emotions that suddenly Toni wanted to laugh. "In a minute," she thought with horror, "I am going to be hysterical." The anvil chorus had started up in her head again.

"Toni, darling—"

"Go away," said Toni vehemently, waving him out of sight. "Just go away."

He stared at her again, until anger was uppermost on his expressive face. "All right," he said and left. Tom Jones came from behind the horseshoe wreath dusting his paws, as if to say, "We sure got rid of him fast."

"Damn," said Toni morosely.

CHAPTER 10

IT WAS NOTICED in the Homicide Bureau that Torrent returned from his prowl not in the best of humor. The value of this knowledge was purely academic. "Limey" Torrent was not the sort of guy who took his temper out on his subordinates, and these were already working at their utmost capacity on what was conceded to be the screwiest case on the calendar.

Torrent was mostly sore at himself. As he told Toni, he felt he had been a fool to establish a personal relationship and expect it to work. A murder case does not provide a proper atmosphere to engender confidence and frankness. Torrent had to admit that up to a certain point Toni and Skeets had acted well. They had been modest yet candid, helpful yet retiring, all the virtues on a Boy Scout pledge. And what was more, they were useful, particularly Toni, whose knack for vivid humorous description and knowledge of all the mad, unbelievable eccentricities of the beauty business had made the whole peculiar setup come alive for him. The trouble with "advisory experts" of this kind was that criminal investigation was bound to go to their heads and start them off on their own, when, by getting their own theories and testing them, they got into trouble, grew secretive and generally served to becloud what already was an obscure and complex case.

Torrent strove to forget his grievances by burying himself in the incoming reports on the case, which, with the favorite suspect dead, now showed every sign of creaking to a stop. The reports on Alicia Howe's demise annoyed Torrent in an obscure way. He was fairly sure that the autopsy reports would coincide with the doctor's certificate, since it was a fairly obvious thing. Yet strange things had happened before and after her death, and the murderous attack on Toni coming as it did in what the press still called the "murder room" seemed to indicate that the trouble was still active.

Before returning to headquarters Torrent had visited the firm of lawyers who handled Alicia's affairs and had gotten some rather interesting information from them. It was an old and responsible firm. Its branch in Boston, where Miss Howe was born, used to handle her father's affairs, and the daughter kept her not inconsiderable account in their careful and conservative hands. Torrent had a fruitful interview with Mr. Dunnan, who was the head of the firm, an old gentleman with a bald pink head and a pair of shrewd eyes in a wizened, snapping-turtle face. Mr. Dunnan, who knew Howe when she was a little girl, seemed to consider her sensational demise as just another childish prank and to feel that Torrent was rather a cad to capitalize on it.

"Miss Howe was always a rather willful young lady," he remarked. "Exactly what kind of information do you want?"

Torrent wanted to know first and foremost the extent of Alicia Howe's connection with Lais. The answer did not surprise him too much. Alicia Howe was a part owner of the salon. She owned enough shares to have a considerable voice in the management of Lais. She had acquired this interest three years ago. Mr. Dunnan was rather vague about the whole transaction. It was one, he explained rather stiffly, which Alicia had done on her own. To acquire the shares she drew on resources which were outside of the company's ken, a transaction that came as a surprise to Mr. Dunnan who had thought before that he knew all of Miss Howe's resources.

The perusal of the will yielded another interesting bit of information. A brief and uncompromising statement, it left all the property which she possessed to Dr. Rudolph Berchtold, except for a sizable legacy and a house in Boston which was left to one Abigail Morton. "Her old nurse," the lawyer explained.

Torrent looked swiftly but efficiently through the effects of late Alicia Howe and his sandy eyebrows lifted slightly at the picture that emerged through the jumble of bankbooks, canceled checks and statements. Alicia Howe lived extravagantly, apparently spending more than even her large salary and returns from investments warranted, yet somehow there was always more coming in. He noted with a small glow of satisfaction that one of the ever-recurring items of expense was a sizable monthly check to Dr. Rudolph Berchtold. When Torrent finally left for headquarters, one of his assistants who specialized in accounting was busily at work on the Howe accounts with a view to analyzing her expenses and income for the past year. Torrent held a rather crass viewpoint that a good knowledge of the financial background was indispensable to any investigation.

Not that it meant neglecting other factors; at the same time, reports were coming into his office from men who were methodically going over the mountains of Alicia Howe's correspondence and notes, most of it, as sadly reported over the telephone, of a strictly libelous nature. At least one nugget was unearthed and expedited to Torrent's desk, where Torrent read it immediately upon coming back to the office. Detective Moran reported that he had found a rather interesting typewritten note in Alicia Howe's desk. It said, somewhat enigmatically, "What well-known beauty salon has a murderer on its staff?" Miss Bundy, the late columnist's secretary who had been kept standing by to explain things, told him that this was among the notes Alicia Howe gave her to type the morning she had died. When she handed the typewritten notes back to her employer the latter had flared up and called her a fool for typing that particular bit. According to Miss Bundy she had said, "You goddamn fool, next thing I know you'll be typing my telephone messages and sending them to the paper to be printed." Apparently that note was merely a doodle, or something meant for Alicia Howe herself. Miss Bundy had felt very badly about it because Miss Howe always used to scribble her notes on whatever piece of paper was handy and this one was not different. The original note was thrown out, but Miss Bundy remembered that it was on a Lais memo pad.

Later in the afternoon the M.E.'s office came through with a call. The news the medical examiner had to give was brief but enigmatic. Alicia Howe did not die of heart failure but something much more complex. Howe's heart, which should have been flaccid and relaxed if she had died of heart failure, was instead contracted and hard (like a fist, the M.E. remarked with some satisfaction), which no heart is supposed to be under any circumstances.

"And what do you make of it?" Torrent inquired, after taking in this strange piece of information.

"Looks like the effect of some drug. We are considering various possibilities. Be able to tell you better after a few tests. Nothing in her stomach. This points to the drug being injected, but there are no punctures outside of the one made by the post-mortem injection of adrenalin by her doctor. We are going to perform blood analysis and let you know as soon as possible."

"Well, there it is," thought Torrent grimly, hanging up. For a moment he harbored an unreasonable grudge against Toni. If she hadn't got herself knocked on the head, there would have been no autopsy and the case would have been closed instead of promising to be a bigger headache than ever. Then he admitted reluctantly that probably he should be grateful. He called Moran.

"About Alicia Howe's room in that damned salon—you've got it locked up since last night, haven't you? Well, have every single bottle and jar analyzed. Better print them first. Hurry it up."

Moran said, "Okay. The rest of them, you mean? I'd checked up on that Winogradow pack stuff."

Torrent told him irritably that he remembered that and that there were other angles. Of course, it was impossible to get hold of the actual preparation that was put on Howe's face. It was wiped away and the towel automatically thrown out. But Hortense had told them that she had opened a brand-new jar which had arrived directly from the supply room a few minutes before.

Moran went away, leaving Torrent to study the reports on what all the principals did last night, at the time when Toni was playing hide-and-seek with, presumably, the murderer. As he suspected, the alibis were highly unsatisfactory and proved absolutely nothing either one way or another. Dr. Winogradow, it is true, was working late at the Lais laboratory but he had left before Toni and Skeets arrived. At this point, Torrent groped in his drawer and brought up the folder with Alicia Howe's medical record.

He was genuinely puzzled. There really was no reason for Berchtold to take the folder home with him. There was nothing he needed to cover up. Any other doctor would have felt justified in signing a certificate as he did. The peculiar state of Alicia's heart which was now puzzling the M.E. could only be revealed by autopsy and there were no marks of violence or symptoms of poisoning. To him it looked like simple heart failure. That it happened to be a little more complex wasn't his fault. Nevertheless, the fact remained that he had taken the folder home. Torrent went over the few pages closely and failed to find any reason for that action. He shrugged his shoulders and rang for Moran.

"Have this sent out for analysis," he said. "No, not just prints. Look for changes, erasures."

"Anything special, chief?"

"No—I—don't know. Point is, the guy might have tampered with the record and if so I want to know what he did."

"Okay. You're supposed to go down to the house of the old lady, the madam."

Moran clung stubbornly to the simple translation of the exotic "kyria" and obviously cared not where the chips might fall.

Captain Torrent wondered at the whimsical fate that seemed to lead him from one boudoir to the other. It was not, he reflected, a locale designed to make questioning easy.

The Kyria's bedroom seemed the only lived-in room in the house. The toilette table was covered with a mess of bottles, lotions, cream jars, perfumes, tissues, rags, lipsticks and tubes, all of them showing signs of wear.

A tray with food, most of it untouched, Torrent noted, stood on a dainty little table near the enormous bed surmounted by a pink velvet canopy. The Kyria herself was in bed. Torrent's mind went back to the history books of his childhood with their pictures of dying monarchs. The Kyria, with a fur-trimmed velvet jacket covering her shoulders like ermine, seemed to exude the same odor of splendor and decay. She turned to him a ghastly face that seemed to be held together by the thin film of foundation cream and powder and answered questions about Alicia Howe with strange indifference. She admitted Alicia Howe's part ownership of Lais, admitted it without showing any surprise at Torrent's knowledge.

"Could you tell me more about that?" Torrent asked her. "About your acquaintance with Miss Howe, I mean. How long have you known her?"

"Six years," said the Kyria. "She came to Lais with a pretty bad case of acne. She was quite unhappy about it, poor girl. She seemed to think that that was the only thing that spoiled her looks," she added with weary malice. "Well, we cured the acne with my own Zephyr lotion. Poor Alicia was so grateful."

Poor Alicia, it seemed, was grateful to the extent of eventually pulling Lais out of a hole. Apparently wolves were howling up and down Fifth Avenue in 1937. Lais needed money badly to go on dispensing beauty. Dear Alicia talked one of her friends into buying part of Lais and as a reward insisted on some shares of stock for herself, which the Kyria gave her with great reluctance.

"I've always owned the business alone. Not even my son, who will eventually own the business, has any of it now. However, we bow before necessity," and she inclined her pale, cameo-like head.

Shortly thereafter the business boomed, and then Kyria was able to redeem the stock. However, when she tried to buy back the stock from Alicia's friend, she found that it was now in Miss Howe's possession and that Alicia didn't mean to give it up.

"I think," said Torrent, "I'd like the name of the person from whom she got those shares of stock."

"Sterling," said Kyria. "Chester Sterling. His wife is still a client of ours."

"I remember," said Torrent, his voice betraying nothing of his excitement. "But I didn't know that Miss Howe knew him so well."

A pale ripple of a smile ran over the Kyria's face. "Alicia Howe knew everybody."

"So it appears. Now, madam, what was your reaction to getting Miss Howe as a partner?"

The Kyria shrugged. "I didn't like it because, as I have told you, I am accustomed to being sole owner. However, Alicia did save the place for me. She was able to do a lot for me, as far as publicity went. And of course, as long as I had the controlling interest..."

"How much of an influence did she have on the actual policy of Lais?"

"It amounted to this—while she had no actual power, I listened to her advice. For example, about six months ago there were difficulties at the salon. I was thinking of selling. Alicia stopped me. And soon the difficulties ceased. Poor Alicia. She used to say that the salon was the only place where she felt comfortable."

"I see. I understand she came to see you the day before her death."

The interview had gone on smoothly until then, the Kyria answering all his questions in a curiously peaceful voice, as if nothing could hurt her any more. At his last question the atmosphere changed subtly. The Kyria's pale head stirred on the pillow. The rings on her fingers flashed as her hands tightened nervously on the quilt.

"Yes, she did."

"What was your conversation about?"

"Personal matters. Nothing important. I can't remember."

"Did the conversation touch on Mlle. Michaud's death?"

"It may have."

"Did Miss Howe express any opinion on it? Such as, for example, her ideas about the identity of the murderer."

The Kyria shook her head. It was an unexpectedly senile movement. "No, she didn't. It was just personal matters. I'm—tired, Captain Torrent. I am afraid I will have to ask you to leave."

"In just a moment." Torrent smiled his pleasant implacable smile. The Kyria's eyes avoided his and shifted restlessly around the room. Then an expression of relief relaxed her face so that for a second it looked like that of a very old woman.

"Dr. Manning," she stretched her hands to an elderly professional looking man who came briskly into the room. "I will see you presently. I am being—cross-examined." Dr. Manning put his hand on her wrist with a doctor's automatic gesture and his eyes went involuntarily to Torrent in a startled glance.

"Well whatever it is, it had better stop," he said. "We can't have too much excitement."

"I am not excited." The Kyria flashed an exasperated look at the doctor and dragged her hand out of his clasp. "I am just tired."

"Of course," Torrent rose. "Just one more question. I don't know if you are aware that Miss Howe seemed to think that Lili Michaud's murderer was someone on the staff of Lais." The Kyria looked back at him composed but deathly pale. He continued, "She wrote as much in a note, we believe, on Saturday, when she visited you." Torrent put down before the Kyria the typewritten note he got from Miss Bundy. "Do you happen to know to whom she was referring? We feel it possible that she has discussed the matter with you."

The Kyria lifted the note stiffly to the level of her eyes and read it. Then she dropped it as if it were a loathsome insect suddenly coming to life at her touch, and said with difficulty, "I have no idea."

Torrent said gently, "You must remember, madam, that this is still a murder case. And the murderer has not yet been apprehended."

"What about Alicia?" The words came tumbling out almost involuntarily. The Kyria leaned forward with disconcerting swiftness. "I thought she was—I thought you were getting *her*—I hoped with her dead, that was all over with!" She was almost petulant about it.

"Last night," said Torrent, "Toni Ney, who had come into the salon after hours to pick up something she had forgotten, was assaulted by somebody whom she surprised in Alicia Howe's room."

The Kyria asked soundlessly, "Who?" And Torrent shrugged his shoulders. "I hoped you might help by giving us the name of the person you and Alicia Howe discussed at your last interview."

The Kyria stared at him for a moment. With her mouth awry and her white hair disarranged, she suddenly looked like one of those distorted tragedy masks. Then she blew her top. She screamed at Torrent with a voice from which all velvet had been stripped. He was an incompetent fool. It was his business to track down murderers and to protect her and her customers from annoyance. She was going to speak to his superiors. She even remembered about being a taxpayer.

The last glimpse of her through the door, before the doctor had closed it after him with a very grave face, showed her still screaming hysterically.

This, Torrent reflected glumly, was definitely not his day for drawing truth out of witnesses.

Eric Skeets sullenly dialed Toni's number. As he waited for her to answer, he rationalized.

"After all," he said defensively, "she wasn't feeling any too well. That was quite a crack she got. Probably got all unnerved. Besides—oh, I know she's a little brute and I ought to just let her alone and see how she likes it, but what the hell!"

Nobody answered the phone. Skeets frowned, hung up and tried the same number again, with the same result. He remained where he was, glaring at the telephone in a baffled manner. Where the hell could Toni be? She certainly was in no state to be going out this evening.

"She'll do, now," said Dr. Berchtold, shutting the door gently behind him. He was immaculate as ever, even in his shirtsleeves. Looking at him Toni was more conscious than ever of her own disheveled state. Her head was again pounding with the headache that she had temporarily forgotten. Her hair felt dry and scaly and her face, she reflected, must be downright haggard without a vestige of makeup.

"Hot and cold stimulants," said Berchtold, judiciously, "were a fine idea." He might have been talking about first aid for a hangover instead of for an attempted suicide. "How did you know about it?"

"I don't know," said Toni honestly. "I've got a peculiar mind. All kinds of things both useful and useless stick in it." She sighed and slumped deeper into the chair. "Moreover, I had a morbid interest in books on medicine when I was a youngster, and it stayed with me the rest of my life. Whenever I come across the *World Almanac,* I turn to Poisonings, Antidotes to… Dr. Berchtold, are you sure she's all right now?"

"She will feel very unhappy for a little while, but she's out of danger. It's bad stuff, but luckily she didn't take much or give it a chance to work." Dr. Berchtold's thin chiseled lips drew back in a cold smile.

Toni thought of Jeanne's voice on the telephone that two hours ago had awakened her from uneasy slumbers and sent her flying into the cold snowy night. It had been such a small, apologetic, frightened voice. "Toni?" it said haltingly. "I—I have been very foolish. I have taken poison and now I don't want to—What shall I do?" And then the silly child had added in a quavering voice, "I am sorry if I woke you up." The voice died away leaving Toni shouting madly into the vacuum. It was lucky that Toni's call to Berchtold found him home. Having been disgustingly healthy all her life, Toni knew no kindly family doctor who would do his best and keep his mouth shut. She clutched at Rudi the Rat as a drowning man would clutch at even a rotten straw. And to do him justice the man did his share. He came over in a hurry (dropping a fairly important dinner party, as he petulantly remarked), and his ministrations were efficient. Jeanne had been too sick to care much about the fact that she was being taken care of by her idol, clay feet and all. She was far more concerned with the nasty effects that twenty tablets of nitroglycerin can have on one's constitution and regretting bitterly having taken same. (Toni touched the little bottle which she had put in her pocket.) And when she finally was put to bed considerably the worse for wear, looking as if all color had been washed out of her pale cheeks and hair, she had turned her head away from Berchtold and her lips had framed a faint, "Go away."

That's done it, Toni thought. Whenever she looks at him now, she'll think of that stomach pump.

Berchtold began putting on his coat. His manner was that of a good doctor, nothing more. Nothing to suggest that he might have had anything to do with what had taken place. It was, surprisingly, merely a doctor's eye that he turned on Toni.

"Incidentally, are you all right? You look sort of done in."

Toni reflected that she must look like the devil to provoke solicitude on the part of Berchtold. "I have a rotten headache," she said. But when she got up the floor tilted dangerously and she sat down again.

"You'd better go home," said Berchtold. "There's nothing else you can do. This young lady is going to take care of Jeanne, aren't you—er—Giselle?"

Giselle, a dark, somewhat sullen-looking girl with a mass of curly black hair, nodded in a dazed way. She had come in in the middle of things and simply couldn't get used to the idea that her roommate had tried to commit suicide. Toni decided to follow Dr. Berchtold's advice. The way she was feeling she wasn't much good to anybody. Giselle saw them to the door and received parting instructions in rapid German from Berchtold.

"I'll take you home," said Berchtold, and bundled her into his car that was standing by the curb. "It's on my way anyhow." He glanced at his wristwatch. "I still have time to drop in at that party. It didn't take so much time."

"How nice," said Toni. If she had felt better she would have walked out of the car. As it was she sat and seethed feebly. "I couldn't have forgiven myself if I had spoiled the evening for you."

"You are sarcastic," the doctor said calmly. "But I think it was very clever of you to call me. Keep it all in the family, eh? I dislike scandals."

Toni opened her mouth and shut it again. There was no use. Nothing could penetrate that thick armor of conceit and complacency. Apparently Berchtold was determined to be grateful to her for saving him from scandal. Him! Toni lapsed into sullen silence that lasted the rest of the ride.

Finally the car stopped before her own house. Toni leaped out of the car but not before Berchtold was there with a gallantly outstretched hand. He looked curiously at the old brownstone. "So that's where you live," he said. "Cozy, eh?" His eyes assumed a curiously reflective expression. "I am going to drop in on my—er—patient later and see how she is feeling. Shall I come up later and report ?"

"I'd be grateful if you called and told me how she is."

"You mean, by phone?" The doctor's voice was lugubrious. Toni finally got her hand away from him. Her patience suddenly broke.

"That's right, Dr. Berchtold, by phone. Remember? The famous invention of Don Ameche. Good night!"

The doctor said "Ha, ha" indulgently and watched Toni go up the stairs. Then the car slid away. Two dark figures rose from the stoop to meet her. Toni glanced at them carelessly and almost fell off the stairs.

"For goodness' sake," she said in utter surprise. "What are you two doing here?"

"Nothing at all," said Skeets, with perfect courtesy. His face was pale in the dark and he was shaking with rage. "Our mistake. We thought something might be wrong, but— Well, I hope you have had a nice time. Good night."

He pattered swiftly down the stairs, marring the dignity of his exit by ignominiously losing his balance and sliding down the last three snow-covered steps. He strode away, seeming to trample down with every step the long black shadow that fled before him. Toni watched him out of sight and then turned back to Torrent. Her eyes were shooting green sparks.

"Suppose you explain the meaning of this?" she asked.

"It's exactly as Skeets told you," Torrent said mildly. "He called you and there was no answer. He didn't think you were in a state to go out so the more he thought the more worried he got. He came here and tried to get in but your landlady proved very unsympathetic. Finally he called me about it, and put the wind up me too. After all, you *were* attacked last night, don't you know. So we came to take a look and just as we did you drove back with—Dr. Berchtold, wasn't it?"

"I shudder," said Toni grimly, "when I think of what sort of books my friend Eric has been reading."

"You didn't explain anything to him, you know," said Torrent.

Toni smiled a little disdainfully. "I don't have to explain anything to Eric," she said. Then she gave him a clear direct look. "But I'd like to explain certain things to you. How about coming up?"

They toiled silently up the stairs, Toni's mind churning wearily in a kaleidoscopic medley of reflections, conjectures and emotions. "Eric is acting like a damn fool—well, I can't help it. The main thing is Jeanne must be in the clear now. Silly to call Berchtold in to keep the police from knowing and then to tell all to a detective. That Torrent has a narsty grim look like a hanging judge but he'll act decent about it. Jeanne's poor little face—imagine killing herself for the sake of Rudi the Rat. That complacent look—I should have been nicer to him and won his confidence, found out what he has on his slimy mind outside of—yes, that orange juice glass—but I was so tired. Oh, *why* did Eric have to act like such a fool. It's worse than East Lynne. I wonder what Torrent is thinking."

Torrent, his eyes on his guide's lightly stepping feet, had emptied his mind of all emotions except anticipation. In her apartment, he divested himself of his coat and said "Well?" Toni fell into a chair, closed her eyes, and told him all, in the small monotonous voice of a little girl telling her misdeeds to a stern but just principal. At the end of the story she stirred in the chair, dug into her pocket, and pulled out a bottle of nitroglycerin, its contents somewhat depleted, which she handed to Torrent.

Torrent looked at it, his face expressionless, and pocketed it. "May I ask," he inquired, "what finally made you decide to confide in the New York police? Was it the fact that Jeanne's suicide made it less likely for her to be using the stuff for anything else?"

Toni opened her eyes and grinned elfishly. "There are no flies on you, are there, Captain Torrent? As a matter of fact, I called the homicide bureau before I got the call from poor little Jeanne. Only you were out. I had a nice nap and regained my perspective, you see. I kept on remembering The Shadow and how Crime Does Not Pay, so I figured I'd better tell you before you caught up with me."

"A very healthy attitude," said Torrent and for the first time smiled at her with something like the unaffected friendliness of their earlier acquaintance.

"Anyhow, now you'll have to get to work on Berchtold. What do you suppose he did with the glass of orange juice?"

"The glass?" said Torrent absently. He was thinking of something else. "Oh, yes, that glass. Well now, there was nothing wrong with it, anyhow."

"That's what I had hoped," Toni said. "But still…" She did a neat double take. "How do you know there's nothing wrong with it?"

Torrent came out of a brown study and smiled indulgently. "Because we had it analyzed last night directly after we picked it up. You had left it in Dr. Berchtold's office. And, my dear young lady, if somebody dies in a strange manner and a glass with remnants of orange juice she had been drinking shortly before her death is found carefully packed away, chemical analysis seems the thing to do."

"So you really knew all the time." Toni laughed on an embarrassed but relieved note. "This is beginning to make me feel very silly."

"I was pretty considerate with you," said Torrent. "I could simply have faced you with what we had and asked for explanation. But I figured that it was nicer to give you a chance to tell us yourself, don't you know."

"Yes, it's much cozier this way," Toni agreed. She felt subtly flattered. Without actually saying it, Torrent managed to communicate to her that he found her cooperation valuable enough for him to go out of his way to preserve the pleasant relationship which made it possible for him to call on her when necessary.

"What about Alicia Howe?" she asked.

Torrent was telling her something of the strange development that was baffling the research bureau when the phone rang.

It wasn't Skeets, as Toni halfway expected, but Moran, asking for Torrent. Torrent got on the phone hastily and listened to the news from the chemical analysis bureau. No special news. The boys had been busily testing Alicia Howe's blood for traces of strange and esoteric poisons but had not been able to find any. They would present a report embodying all their ideas tomorrow. Yes, they admitted to an idea or two. They were still working on all the bottles and jars from Alicia Howe's cabinet. But—and here Torrent stiffened to attention—testing for prints had brought out an interesting fact. All the bottles had fingerprints on them—Alicia Howe's, Hortense's and a third set as yet unidentified—except for one bottle which was unaccountably free of all prints. Torrent inquired about its name. There was a brief silence and then Moran painstakingly spelled out Zephyr de Printemps.

"Zeepheer de preentomps," he repeated, conscientiously pronouncing each consonant. "I don't know what the hell it's for. That's all it says and there's a picture of a fat boy with wings blowing fit to burst."

Torrent hung up and appealed to Toni for explanation. Toni identified the bottle as a special brand of acne lotion.

"The idea being that it purifies your blood like a spring breeze. The Kyria's own little gift to unsightly womanhood."

"I see. Do you happen to know whether the Howe woman used it lately?"

"She must have. She's been having trouble with acne again lately. Didn't you notice?"

"No," said Torrent. "Should I have? What is it anyhow"

"Just a lot of little pimples over the face, most often seen in adolescence. You probably wouldn't notice it on Howe because she wore a very thick foundation cream and powder to hide it. Didn't you see how sort of livid she looked these last days?"

"In that case," said Torrent, "how come there are no fingerprints on that bottle? It's damned queer. She couldn't have been handling it with gloves. Oh…" He paused. "Of course, it's possible that this was a new bottle not yet touched. No, Moran said it's three quarters full. But maybe she was using another bottle of that ointment. Whom do I ask about it?"

"Hortense, I should imagine, who usually takes care—or rather who used to take care—of Howe. And Jeanne or Alice. It's their business to keep the rooms on the third floor supplied."

"All right, I'll have to talk to them." Torrent scrawled in his notebook. "I want to talk to this Jeanne girl anyhow." He pulled Tom Jones' ears and got up. His shrewd blue eyes slipped over Toni's anxious face and he laughed. "I can see you have just remembered that suicide is a punishable offense. Well, don't worry about that. I have no intention of taking that poor youngster into custody. Just a few questions."

"I suppose you only punish successful suicides," said Toni, yawning irresistibly. She dragged her heavy eyelids apart and laughed at herself. "I'm sorry. This has been a hard day. Good night, Captain Torrent."

But as the door was shutting behind him she was on her feet in a flash calling to him. Torrent was startled to see a face from which all traces of weariness had fled. It was brilliantly alight with animation. Her green eyes sparkled.

"Gloves—bottles…Captain Torrent, remember, we decided that the person who attacked me must have had a bottle in his pocket. And he wore gloves too, and it was in the same room. And the next day we have a bottle without fingerprints. Don't you suppose…?"

"You're too damn sharp," said Torrent gruffly. "Can't keep a thing from you. Good night."

He departed in a hurry, leaving Toni staring after him bright-eyed.

CHAPTER 11

TONI GAZED without enthusiasm at the prostrate form of Mrs. Sterling, gasping pinkly at her feet. Naturally Mrs. Sterling had been late again. Reason: her chauffeur had overslept.

There was a sort of mad immutability about Mrs. Sterling, characteristic of the House of Lais in general. Empires might crash, universes reel, but Mrs. Sterling would turn up late but smiling in the timeless halls where "beauty and serenity" were peddled, the press and taxes notwithstanding. Toni, in spite of three years spent at this unreal establishment, could never take it seriously. Whenever she stayed away from it she half expected it to disappear in her absence like the fabulous castle in a Grimm fairy tale. But as always it was still waiting for her on the same place when she came back on Wednesday, after what she laughingly called a day of rest, and the gap of her absence was bridged by the gossip about the things that happened while she was away.

Mrs. Parmalee had got stuck in the chair again. The client of the day had been a dizzy young heiress who was to be married that same day, in a cathedral and with lots of lilies, who had come to Lais to get rid of a monumental hangover and to camouflage a gorgeous black eye. In spite of these handicaps the bride was in good spirits, hilariously referring to herself as an "all-American girl" because she had "made every team in the U.S.A." Mrs. Glendenning, the wife of a well-known oil magnate, finished her course of skin treatments and gave Alice a box of powder puffs in token of her appreciation. A reporter was caught sneaking up to the third floor and bodily ejected. A national picture magazine came out with a feature story about Lais, in which it was stated that murder had proved so profitable, providing the client as it did with just that needed fillip of sensationalism, that Arden and Rubinstein were seriously considering adding it to their list of attractions. Mlle. Illona was very upset by this statement and had begun writing a letter to that publication, reading, "Gentlemen—I have been in the employ of Lais for many years and I know that the Kyria is inalterably opposed to murder—"

And there was an interesting piece of gossip about Miss Illona—she had a boyfriend. Toni was gleefully begged to guess who, and, after having failed to guess, was told it was the little Frenchman who had been with Lili Michaud. He had come in to see her and was seen kissing her fingers in farewell while she blushed pleasurably. Margot, who understood French, had heard them make a date for the next day.

Toni was unable to see any softening effect of love on Mlle. Illona's beautiful egg face when she summoned Toni and called her down for having the audacity almost to get her neck broken within the sacred confines of Lais. Nobody else knew about that regrettable incident of Monday night, but Torrent told Illona about it in order to explain the sealing-up of Alicia Howe's room.

"If something had happened to you," said Mlle. Illona, her chiseled nostrils dilating faintly with horror, "think of the dreadful publicity, as if we hadn't been getting enough of it already. The Kyria was most upset about it. We feel you had been inconsiderate to the interests of Lais."

"But as you see," Toni retorted dryly, "I remembered them at the last minute, or you wouldn't be seeing me here."

Mlle. Illona dismissed her with an almost imperceptible ripple of a frown marring the placidity of her unfurrowed brow.

M. Maurice, who was present at that interview, was much nicer about it. Toni suspected that his desire to spite Illona played a large part in drawing from him the extravagant exclamations of sympathy, to which Illona listened with a prim lip and a chilly eye. The two of them were in the midst of another feud. M. Maurice had finally put through his favorite idea of his Greek vase exhibit. It was a timely one because of the new Winogradow perfume, aptly called Lethal, which came in exquisite tiny amphoras. M. Maurice wanted to have his beloved *lekythoi* shown downstairs in the salon. He thought it would be a good idea to tie it up somehow with the Greek resistance to the Nazi invader. Mlle. Illona stuck firmly to the policy of keeping Lais out of the war.

"My dear Maurice," she told him, "we don't want people to look at those things and think of a lot of Greeks *dying* all over the place. Besides, our snow-crystal jewelry exhibit is the important thing. I am sure the Kyria…"

The Kyria apparently had taken Mlle. Illona's side because the Greek vase exhibit was finally placed on the second floor in the loggia. M. Maurice himself designed it. It was to consist of a single slender stem of a Doric column broken just under the capital and encircled by a lucite spiral holding at different levels the Greek vases filled with fragrant oil. M. Maurice was very proud of the design, which he had tacked up on the bulletin board of the second floor.

All this gossip was duly relayed to Toni. But she had reason to believe that she herself was contributing material to the never-stopping mill of clacking tongues that functioned overtime at Lais. Skeets came down sometime during that morning to confer with Toni about the copy for the exercise booklet Lais was putting out. And his behavior was of such extreme and chilling courtesy that it was apparent to everybody on the floor that Something Must Have Happened. Toni looked at the dark head bent so diligently over the ridiculous booklet and longed to box his ears. This was a salutary impulse but one to which she couldn't yield. She was singularly unequipped to handle the situation. For one thing, she had a totally unfeminine horror of scenes. Lovers' quarrels with their rainbow tears and happy reconciliations held no charm for her. They were dreary things, lacking in human dignity. Faced with a sulking and frigid Skeets, she found herself shrinking inwardly. She could find nothing to say. His behavior froze the first words of explanation that had started to her lips. She gave Skeets cold look for look and they politely discussed layout and the merit of various photographs like well-mannered strangers. Before leaving, Skeets told her that he was meeting Torrent for lunch at Larrabee's and that the latter had asked her to join them. Toni had agreed to be there unless foiled by Mrs. Sterling, who was her last client before lunch.

At the rate at which Mrs. Sterling was going on she doubted if she could keep this appointment. That lady was in fine fettle and delivered herself of many fine conversational gems which Toni could have relished very much on another day.

"Such a day, my dear," she was burbling merrily. "I've been having such a time with my bank. They keep on sending me statements telling me that I am overdrawn and I immediately send them a check to cover the deficit. And the next time they send me a statement I'm overdrawn by that much again. Something must be wrong with them."

Toni looked at her client, opened her mouth and shut it again. Somehow she had a feeling that it was no use trying to explain. Silently she straightened out a feebly waggling leg. At least she could keep her in good physical condition.

"Something gone screwy in their system," Mrs. Sterling said brightly.

"Perhaps Mr. Sterling can straighten it out for you," Toni suggested.

"He's in Washington about converting steel," said Mrs. Sterling vaguely. "By the way, he got a call from—oh, what's his name—with the reddish mustache just like Lord Argyle—with a name like rain or a storm..."

"Captain Torrent?" said Toni with quickening interest.

"That's it. I think it's so funny. Here Chester has been cautioning me not to talk and he's the one finally had to tell all. Of course, she's dead and can't do any more mischief."

Toni, who had been recipient of many confidences about Chester and his occasional extracurricular blondes, thought she knew what it was about.

"You mean Lili Michaud?" she asked cautiously.

"Oh no, my dear. Chester finally convinced me that that was just Alicia Howe's malice. He knew Lili Michaud very slightly, not half as well as he knew many others I could name. No, I meant Alicia herself. Captain Tempest—isn't that the name? such a romantic name, my dear, just like Errol Flynn—wanted to know about the time Alicia chiseled us out of those Lais shares. You didn't know that I was a part owner of Lais for a little while, did you?"

Toni thought to herself, "I don't understand, but I've got to hang on."

Mrs. Sterling babbled on, intent on her grievances.

"I've always longed to get my hands on this place. I had such plans about redecorating it and then just as I got ready to do something about it and talk to the Kyria because, after all, we were part owners—presto! chango!"—the gorgeous solitaire gleamed as her hands flew in an explosive gesture—"who's got the shares? Alicia has. That made me really angry. And that's why I've never spoken to Alicia since."

"That must have been annoying," Toni breathed, afraid of shutting off the current.

"I should just think so. I didn't so much mind her forcing Chester to buy shares in Lais. It was her making him hand them over to her." Mrs. Sterling brooded for a minute and then said decidedly, "If it was up to me I would have said publish and be damned, like Washington—wasn't it?—but Chester is such a puritan about me. When one's hatred of publicity makes one do things one doesn't want to do, then it's time to do something about it. I never did care what people said about me—but then my psychiatrist says I am so beautifully uninhibited!"

Later, upon dazedly disentangling this mess of confidences, Toni thought she could see a little light. Probably Torrent knew all about it.

As she was about to go out she ran into a particularly disgruntled and discontented Hortense.

"It's getting so that you can't turn around without running into cops," she complained. "I'm combing them out of my hair. Every day they've got to know something else and I've got to tell it to them."

Toni devoutly hoped that they used the third degree on Hortense. "What is it now?" she asked.

"First they take away all the stuff from Howe's room," Hortense said. "Then they bring it back and ask Alice and me to tell them whether the bottles look any different from the way they did a few days ago. They're particularly interested in the Zephyr de Printemps. Now why should big grown men be interested in acne lotion?"

"And did it look different?" Toni asked eagerly.

Hortense shrugged her shoulders. "Not to me. Alice says there's more stuff in it than there used to be. That's just baloney, of course. She's just trying to be important. What's all this about, Toni? Do you know?" Her slanty eyes raked Toni suspiciously. "You're in the know, aren't you?"

Toni shrugged her shoulders and hurried on. Hortense fell into step. There was a little smile on her thin, too-narrow face.

"I hear you've had a quarrel with your boyfriend. Too bad. He's kinda cute." She added after a moment, her neck thrust out at an inquisitive angle so as to miss no detail of Toni's reaction, "He's already dated up Steffi Dunn. She'd come up to model for that ad for *Harper's Bazaar* and Mr. Skeets made a beeline for her. I heard him asking her if she would care to go to the ballet tonight. Steffi told me she thought he was kinda cute. I guess you've lost him for good and all. That girl is good."

"You're pretty good, too," said Toni, with equanimity. "The way you keep up with everything around here and all. I really think you're wasted on facials. With your special talent you should be doing Howe's gossip column for her. How come Howe never thought of using your services? Or did she?"

She spoke negligently, without thinking, her main concern being to get Hortense off the subject of Skeets. But the arrow shot at random apparently flew better than she knew. Hortense stopped dead and the look she darted at Toni was charged with apprehension and malevolence.

"What are you trying to say? What do you mean, Howe—why, I never..." After these disconnected remarks trailed off uncertainly, her ruffled feathers subsided and she managed an ingratiating smile. "Honestly, Toni, those cops have gotten me so mixed up, anything can get a rise out of me. You mustn't mind what I said about your losing your boyfriend. Steffi is beautiful but you've got brains and I got a feeling Skeets prefers the intellectual type."

"Thanks for the kind words," said Toni. She couldn't help laughing. Hortense's concern had been so obvious and she had used on Toni the sort of flattery that she had hitherto reserved for only higher-ups in the hierarchy of Lais.

"Sure you aren't sore? I was just kidding. Well, I'll be running along then. I've got Mrs. Pierson-Keith, Senior," said Hortense, much as if naming a rare disease with which she was for the time being afflicted.

As she trudged around the corner to Larrabee's, Toni asked herself what Hortense's information meant to her. She searched her bosom sternly for even a tiny pang and triumphantly failed to find one. Skeets might carouse with luscious redheads all he wanted. If he wanted glamour, sheer and unadulterated, unmarred by any signs of restless intellect, Steffi was his dish. Toni wished him good appetite.

Skeets and Torrent had already started on their lunch. They were so absorbed in their conversation that they didn't see her until she was upon them. Skeets rose to his feet and for a moment as his eyes met Toni's his face was the unguarded one of a sulky little boy who refuses to make up.

"I've been getting some atmosphere from Skeets here," said Torrent.

"About the time there was sabotage in the promotion department. It had seemed to disturb the Kyria very much."

"Oh yes," said Toni settling down. "I suppose that was the time when everybody talked darkly about loyalty and the Kyria threatened to retire and raise nudists. Has that any connection?"

"We don't know yet. We're interested in Alicia Howe's part in this. She seems to have been pretty ambitious about having a voice in Lais—just one of those loose ends we are trying to disentangle."

"Oh," said Toni. "That reminds me. I have not come to this conference with empty hands." She recounted the eerie conversation with Mrs. Sterling. At the end of it Torrent nodded, pleased.

"Yes, that rounds out things. Chester Sterling hinted at that much. He admitted that he had bought shares for Alicia Howe although he didn't say why."

"Then," said Eric Skeets slowly, "what really happened was that dear Alicia had something on the Sterlings—"

"Probably Mrs. Sterling," said Toni, "who is oh, so uninhibited."

"Anyhow, she used this as a means to force Chester Sterling to help Lais when it was going on the rocks and later to get the stock from him for little or no money."

"Isn't this what is called blackmail in polite society?"

"Why not? Apparently anything goes in your outfit. Thanks for your information, Miss Ney. It rounds out what we know nicely."

"Isn't it funny?" Toni remarked. "Like mending plates, or putting jigsaw puzzles together. You always have the big pieces and I have the little ones. But they fit together."

"Isn't it cozy?" Eric said nastily. His eyes slid over Toni as if she were a stranger. Then he had turned away from her and was talking to Torrent. He wanted to know about Alicia Howe. Was it a murder or not?

Torrent smiled at him amiably.

"Oh, it was murder, all right," he conceded, "but not a very promising one. I have a hunch that we'll do better to concentrate on the Michaud's murder. Howe's will be very difficult to pin on anybody because of the way it was done."

"Why?" asked Eric. "You don't mean to say that the murderer has used one of those obscure African poisons on dear Alicia?"

"I'm afraid," Torrent remarked, "that there are very few obscure poisons left nowadays. Modern science and all that…"

"Did it have anything to do with that bottle of Zephyr de Printemps?" Toni inquired. "Please don't look so mysterious. I've got to know."

Torrent thought that the kids were real bright. You had to be careful what you were saying or you found yourself telling them a hell of a lot more than you intended. There they were sitting across the table from him, eyeing him with alert interest like a brace of well-bred puppies.

"The name of the poison used was ouabain," he told them. "It's a glucoside that acts like a powerful heart stimulant. Its chief characteristic is that it contracts the heart violently and the heart stays hard and contracted after death. That's what the autopsy revealed in Howe's case."

Toni said, "I thought Alicia was too tough to die of mere heart failure. But how...?"

"Well, that's where your little set-to with the murderer helped us. Your memory of the bottle in the coat pocket of the person who knocked you out was very suggestive, in conjunction with the fact that there were no prints on the bottle of acne lotion we picked up for analysis the next day."

"I don't get it," said Skeets. "Was there poison in that bottle?"

"Wrong. There was nothing but acne lotion in that bottle."

"Of course," Toni cried. "Don't you see? The murderer took the poisoned bottle away after Alicia died. I walked in on him when he or she was putting the harmless bottle back. That's why there were no fingerprints on that bottle alone. He was handling it with gloves."

"Check," said Torrent. "We figured it that way. Of course, ouabain disappears from the bloodstream after a while, so in a way this is really guessing, but it's pretty high-class guessing. The only way poison could get into Alicia Howe's blood is through those little acne sores on her face and back. There were no other perforations. And the fact that somebody was meddling with the acne lotion—there is no other way to explain the lack of fingerprints on just that bottle, which we know Howe had been using to the very last—well, that was pretty conclusive. We know from Hortense that Alicia Howe put the lotion on as soon as she came back to her own room where she kept it. She died fifteen minutes later, which is about the time the poison takes to work. Of course we couldn't find any trace of the poison because it was washed off together with the Winogradow pack stuff when Alicia collapsed."

"What about her back? Wasn't any left on her back?" Toni asked and answered herself, "Of course not. Those hot towel applications took care of that."

"Damned ingenious," said Skeets. "Clever, these Chinese. Or rather these Japanese, because I take it Alicia was killed by the same person who knew enough jujitsu to do Michaud in so neatly."

"And Alicia knew who it was," said Toni, as Torrent nodded. "And now she is in her grave and oh, the difference to her…"

Torrent cleared his throat, "At this point, I'd like you to stop bothering your pretty heads about the second murder and turn to the first. I'd like to try a sort of screwy idea on you two kids. In this wacky case it runs a good chance of being right."

"Don't be apologetic," Toni reassured him. "After a day at Lais, neither one of us is liable to be shocked by a mad theory. The whole place has a through-the-looking-glass aura about it."

"Well," Torrent spoke again, slowly and with curious diffidence. "Hasn't it struck you that—well, I mean look at the convenient way Lili Michaud was murdered. First the elevator stalls. That gives the murderer an access to the floor. Then Jeanne is sent downstairs, leaving the floor unwatched. Then Hortense exits, leaving the victim alone. All the murderer has to do is come in and strike that blow. Doesn't it have a sort of deliberate look? As if it had been previously arranged?"

Toni nodded slowly, her green eyes bright, "I see what you mean. Of course it's a very common situation around here. Not that the elevator gets stuck every day. But people are constantly being ordered around, leaving clients in the lurch for the moment, with their faces covered with repulsive goo and their hair slowly shriveling away under the drier."

"Couldn't somebody easily create a situation like that? Incidentally, damned convenient for the murderer—"

"I know." Skeets scratched his dark thatch thoughtfully. "The time and the place and the loved one all together. Wasn't it Sterling who yearned to be alone with Michaud?"

Toni laughed. "Sterling wouldn't have bothered arranging things. She would simply have bashed Lili on the head and expected her husband to get her the *best* lawyers." Her voice lilted slightly in an uncannily accurate imitation of Mrs. Sterling. "What bothers me is that too many people seem to be acting on their own in setting the stage. Illona sent Jeanne down on the Kyria's orders. Sterling sent Hortense out for her own purposes. Maurice stalled the elevator out of sheer dopiness. Where's the common denominator?"

Skeets said thoughtfully, "It does seem to postulate a kind of superior intelligence manipulating puppets. Wait!" There was a queer note in his voice. Torrent thought with amusement that they were off in full cry now, noses close to the scent. He sat back and watched them placidly. "The murderer knows that at a certain time during Lili's treatment she will be left alone. That's right, isn't it? Sterling bribed Hortense long before the elevator stalled, didn't she, Torrent? Good. Then the murderer gets Jeanne out of the way during the same time and gets Maurice to stall the elevator. Don't interrupt me, let me just go on and see what we get. Then the stage being set, he or she comes to the third floor and finding the coast clear acts fast and gets away."

"Unobserved?" Toni inquired.

"We're coming to that. Now wasn't there somebody going toward the third floor at the same time? Creeping after the doctor and Hortense very quietly because she didn't want to be heard?"

"That, my learned friend, would be Alicia Howe."

"And where is Alicia Howe today?"

"Where," inquired Toni, "are the snows of yesteryear? I suppose you mean that the murderer might have run into her afterward and that's why— Now I'll ask you one, Socrates. Who the hell is this all-powerful individual who can get Jeanne off the floor and cause the elevator to stop…Oh." Toni stopped too.

"You're in the groove, honey," said Skeets, forgetting his mad in the investigator's fever. "Who in this organization would have the power to get Jeanne off the floor, and did? And who would have enough influence on Maurice to make him stall the elevator? In short, who is the superior intelligence that manipulates everybody at Lais like puppets? In the words of a well-known popular song—who?"

Toni shook her dark curls. "I can't see the Kyria messing up the salon with a murder."

"Nor can I," said Torrent, "without a rattling good motive, which we are looking for."

"Then you did have this in mind, didn't you?" Toni wanted to know.

Torrent admitted it. "Except that I wouldn't put it quite so bluntly at this stage. So far somebody seems to have set the stage for murder and it looks as if the Kyria might have been the one. Her movements certainly require explanation. For example, she sent Jeanne down because supposedly she wanted to speak to her, yet she never got around to it. Could it be that she merely wanted her off the floor? Then there's something peculiar about her alibi. Dr. Berchtold gave her one, saying that he spoke to her right after she came down in the elevator. But she didn't think of that herself when I asked her. It took her son to think of it and he practically stuffed it down her throat. Yes, he was mighty anxious to keep mother safely upstairs until one-forty. And about that elevator—Maurice was awfully concerned to have me understand that he didn't stall that elevator himself, that it stopped by itself. He kept on hammering it into me. It's a little thing, of course, but... Then what about that conversation the Kyria had with Alicia Howe on Saturday? My mere mention of it gave her the willies, don't you know."

"I was thinking," said Toni, "you would have to prove that the Kyria knew about Hortense being bribed to leave Michaud alone, before she started getting everybody else off the floor. And then—how could she tell Maurice to stall the elevator? He was downstairs the whole morning and she was upstairs on the sixth."

"Jeanne got her orders by phone," said Eric. "So would Maurice."

"So that would make Maurice an accessory, wouldn't it?"

"Perhaps, or perhaps he was just a dupe. He's pretty scared of mother, you know. Maybe he just did what he was told, his not to reason why, that sort of thing. And later he wouldn't be likely to talk."

"Maxine—that's one of the switchboard girls—always listens to conversations," Toni offered musingly.

"Much obliged," said Torrent, "I'll remember that when I talk to her. Well, thanks for listening to my theorizing. I shan't bother you any more today." He rose from the table, obediently followed by the two young people. "Incidentally, they're having a nice ballet program today. The *Sylphides*. I'm a sucker for that ballet. Are you kids going? If so I'll look for you there."

Having thus briefly transformed himself into Cupid and let fly an arrow, Torrent left them. By a bland twinkle in his eye Toni guessed that he knew about their little spat and was hugely amused thereby. Thus thrust out from the safe haven of impersonal discussion, they marched stiffly back to Lais. Skeets was at a disadvantage. Toni had a gift for being able to stay silent longer than anybody else. Besides, her mind kept on buzzing curiously over Torrent's strange revelations about the Lais murders. Skeets' thoughts also dealt with homicide, albeit not yet consummated. He was thinking how satisfying it would be to take Toni's slim neck between his hands and wring it. Under the circumstances he was bound to be the first to speak.

"Torrent has told me about last night," he said. "It seems I have made a fool of myself again. Please accept my apologies."

Toni answered the stilted apology in kind by assuring him stiffly that it was nothing.

"I would have told you yesterday," she ventured, "only—"

"Think nothing of it," Skeets in turn reassured her frigidly. "There is absolutely no reason why you should tell me things that you consider to be none of my business. After all, I have no special claims on your confidence, as Torrent has. And certainly to offer you advice would be fatuous. You're obviously perfectly capable of taking care of yourself."

Toni answered nothing. Suddenly she was so angry that she felt tears starting in her eyes. She was glad that her customary mask of impassivity hadn't slipped, that Skeets, tramping sullenly at her side, could see no sign of perturbation in her face. Of course, she had no way of knowing that it was that very maddening indifference expressive in every line of her still profile that was driving him to practically homicidal rage.

With these promising feelings raging in their constricted breasts they parted, Toni going to the locker and Skeets to the sixth floor to write purple copy about Lethal, the perfume that gets 'em every time!

CHAPTER 12

UPON RETURNING to the salon Toni found waiting for her a peremptory summons to go and see the Kyria at the house. Toni, who had just put on her leotard, glumly changed back into her street clothes and hied her to that house of gloomy splendor.

This was not the first time. Once before she had been summarily drafted to serve as a hostess when the Kyria threw the house open to the public for an exhibition of her surrealist collection. The house was furbished up for the guests then. This time Toni, following the silent guide to the Kyria's bedroom, was struck by the strangeness and coldness of it.

The Kyria was feeling stronger. She was sitting in a chaise longue near the fireplace. The firelight illumined her white hair and pallid face with a rosy glow, and a great quilted blanket dragged across her knees to the floor. Toni had barely the time to get over the shock that her employer's ravaged face had given her when she received another.

The Kyria screamed at her. She was beside herself with fury. The blue veins swelled and beat along her medallion-like temples, and her thin lips writhed over the accusations she was spitting out. Toni gathered that she was a traitor, a liar, a spy, and a viper in the breast of Lais, Inc., and should be trampled into dust where she belonged.

"What were you doing sneaking around my salon at night? Answer me, do you hear, *petite canaille*?" And as Toni shrank away from her, she went on with redoubled fury, "I want to know everything before I throw you out in the gutter where you belong!"

Toni had heard of the Kyria's occasional rages. In her Paris salon the girls used to go in mortal terror of her, and even in New York she retained a species of megalomania that caused her to see herself as a queen surrounded by helots. But this was the first time Toni had borne the brunt of royal displeasure and she did not care for the form it took. She told the Kyria baldly, "You must be mad."

"What! You deny having lunch with this policeman and telling him everything that goes on in the salon!"

"Hardly. I certainly tell Captain Torrent whatever he asks me. Policemen who are investigating murders are entitled to ask questions and to receive answers. And I personally have nothing to hide."

"You lie! Hortense told me—"

"Then you had better ask her the rest. I am not going to stay here."

"Wait!" The angry woman gasped at this *lèse-majesté*. "How dare you go before—I am not through with you yet."

"I am afraid, Kyria," said Toni stopping at the door, "you don't quite understand. The mere fact that somebody works for you doesn't give you the right to talk to her that way, and I am not even working for you. You have my resignation as of two minutes ago. Good day."

After this lofty pronouncement it was a little anticlimactic to lose one's way in the labyrinthine chambers. Toni was swearing mildly when M. Maurice caught up with her in the front lobby. His pale face under the skullcap of polished black hair was sweating faintly.

"Here you are," he said with relief. "Look here, you'd better come along with me. My mother wants you."

"Yes, I know," said Toni. "Like the ax wants the chicken. No, I'll be running along, if you don't mind."

M. Maurice caught hold of her muff and was standing there patting it nervously. He looked miserable. "I know you are angry," he said. "But, look, the Kyria is sorry. She thinks she has misjudged you after all. Please come back. It'll really be to your advantage."

"No, please—"

"But yes. My mother is a sick woman, Toni, a desperately sick woman. She's got to be humored. You'll go back with me if I have to *carry* you."

M. Maurice had a desperate look in his eye, as if he really meant to try, and Toni, who strongly doubted his ability to carry out his threat, felt that it would be pure cruelty to put him to the test. She didn't want to add to his already redoubtable array of inferiority complexes. Besides, she was curious, so she allowed herself to be drawn back to the Kyria's bedroom.

The Kyria, recumbent on her chaise longue, withdrew her lace handkerchief from a composed face and said, "Sit down, child." Toni sat down gingerly and the Kyria went on, "Perhaps I misjudged you. It is so hard to be sure. I realize now that you must have thought you were doing your duty and merely answering questions. Are you willing to swear to me that you weren't spying for that policeman when you went into the salon in the evening?"

"For goodness' sake," said Toni, exasperated. "This is downright silly. Like cheap fiction about international spies or something. If Torrent wanted to get anything out of the salon, he would have gone in and got it. Why should he have sent me?"

For some mysterious reason this rather rude retort mollified the Kyria. Her body relaxed and she suddenly launched into her lecture about loyalty to Lais. Toni, who had heard it many times, sat through it politely and rose to go when it was over.

"We will forget this whole incident," said the Kyria magnanimously.

"Of course," said Toni. "Incidentally, my resignation still stands. I am not going back to the salon."

The Kyria said with the air of one humoring a sulky child, "It is a good idea. You may have the afternoon off. You are probably still feeling the effects of your accident. I understand you don't know who attacked you?" And as Toni shook her head, she added, "Well, don't brood about it. Go for a walk, and change that lipstick, for heaven's sake. It's not your type. You are a good girl, Toni. You are sincere. I think I will raise your salary next month. You may go now."

Toni opened her mouth and closed it again. Apparently it was no use arguing. Besides, what did she expect from the Kyria, an apology? She left the room for the second time, not even wincing at the Kyria's parting shot, "See what you can do about that ungovernable temper of yours."

She spent the afternoon with Jeanne, who was still feeling groggy and a little foolish. After she came home, a young newspaperman she knew, who covered dance recitals and concerts, called her to say that he had tickets for the ballet and would she care to come along? Toni accepted with alacrity. Being fairly honest with herself she did not even attempt to say to herself that after all Torrent expected to meet her there. Instead, with a little smile of self-mockery, she went about picking an effective outfit: the strawberry-red ankle-length skirt of swirling velvet with a black jersey blouse and a jeweled belt.

She was looking for Torrent during the intermission when she saw Skeets with Steffi Dunn. Her heart executed a neat and unexpected *entrechat*. The redhead was depressingly stunning in diaphanous green, cut censorably low, and Skeets wore the pleased expression of a man who knows that the girl he is escorting is getting the eye from every man in the room. He was grinning delightedly, and Toni, watching him, thought that he had a terribly attractive smile. His white, even teeth flashed like a row of pearls in his dark face and his eyebrows swooped up in a droll slant. He saw Toni and, absurdly, blanched, looking for all the world like a little boy caught stealing jam. Then a look of happy anticipation came to his face. Toni knew he was hoping that her heart was being wrung.

She gave him a cool little smile and turned away with her escort. She didn't see Skeets the rest of the evening. Neither did she see Torrent, and she had a nice time, both at the ballet and later, giving Bill fine points of ballet for his review.

And incidentally she had firmly decided that she wasn't going back to Lais.

Of course, she went back the next morning. She knew she would, even while she was telling Bill that she was through and did he know of a good job and hearing his enthusiastic assurances that there might be a spot for her in his paper. The business at Lais was unfinished, and somehow she felt she had to be in at the end.

Her disposition was not improved by her constantly growing consciousness that Dr. Berchtold was furtively watching her every movement.

Toni had had little to do with him since Tuesday night when he brought her back from Jeanne's house. He had called her that night, as he had promised, to tell her how Jeanne was getting along and during the conversation had told her casually that he had been looking in vain for the poison bottle at Jeanne's. Did Toni happen to know where it was? Toni admitted that she had taken it with her and upon Berchtold's asking her sweetly why couldn't he drop in—it was 2:30 A.M.—to pick it up, she had replied succinctly, "Because I have already given it to the police," and hung up on his baffled silence.

The whole next day, until she left for her historic interview with the Kyria, she had felt his reflective eye upon her. Apparently by Thursday he had come to a decision, because from ten o'clock on his steady gaze was making her very self-conscious. It was a sort of involuntary strip tease. Every time she passed him she had a feeling she had a little less on.

The denouement came when he cornered her in the gym, where she had lingered after another chatty lesson with Mrs. Sterling, and asked her to have dinner with him.

Toni looked at him with startled green eyes and said, "This is so unex-pected."

"Not really," said Berchtold and showed his white teeth, "not to a smart girl like you, surely."

Toni looked at his large white teeth and decided to cut the discussion short. "Thank you, Dr. Berchtold, but I am afraid I am too busy."

"Always?" The doctor smiled again. His voice fell low and vibrated like a viol. "Why do you dislike me, Toni?"

Toni denied it politely, with a wistful eye on the door behind the doctor's wide shoulders. But the doctor would have none of it. "Yes, you do. Or you think you do. It's rather flattering, you know, when an attractive woman takes an unreasoning dislike to you." (Oh, Lord, Toni thought. Here's King Freud's head popping up again.) "But I want you to forget that non-sense now. I've always wanted—liked you, Toni. Can't you let yourself go, and like me a little?"

"Really," said Toni, "This is no place for—"

Berchtold disposed of her protest with a large and magnificent ges-ture. His voice had deepened until it had an organ-like quality and Toni had a feeling that he himself was being intoxicated by its sound. "Doesn't it mean anything to you that I want you so much, darling? That sullen little face—that lovely body that I can make come alive for me—only give me a chance…"

Toni looked at the handsome sensual face so close to hers and won-dered why all this display of passionate masculinity should leave her so cold. She remembered the sultry confidences of one Tamara, a Russian facial operator who had an affair with the doctor before Jeanne came along. Apparently the guy was good! Shouldn't she feel something? Could something be wrong with her? The trouble was that she was almost sure that she could see an ulterior purpose behind this pulsing appeal to what the Victorians used to call her baser senses. Dr. Berchtold wanted some-thing else from her besides the obvious thing. The thought of the irresist-ible doctor using his incontestably virile charms on her as crudely as Theda Bara used to vamp the boys in those naive days suddenly overcame Toni. She began laughing, her narrow hand against his chest to keep him away.

There was genuine amusement in her laughter and it infuriated Ber-chtold. The next minute he was all over her. His hand fumbled at her and his lips came down on hers, hot and odiously expert.

"Ugh," said Toni with heartfelt loathing. She used her meager knowl-edge of jujitsu for the second time that week. She put the heel of her hand under his nose and shoved. The doctor, not the first man to underestimate

Toni's strength, reeled against the opposite wall with a ludicrous look of astonishment on his face. Toni glared back at him, furiously rubbing at her lips.

At that moment Skeets walked in.

The next few minutes were packed with action of the most melodramatic kind. Skeets took one look, put two and two together with the inexorable accuracy of an adding machine, and swung a frantic and futile haymaker in the general direction of Dr. Berchtold's flushed countenance. A well-directed right to the jaw immediately laid Skeets out flat, dead to the world. Berchtold stood over him, nursing his knuckles, an ugly expression on his face. Toni felt certain that he was going to find an outlet for his harassed feelings in a kick at Skeets' inert body. It was in a purely reflex action that her sandal-shod foot flew out and connected with the doctor's well-padded shin. The doctor yelped in anguish, turned a harassed look upon Toni, and hurriedly limped out of the gym.

Toni dropped to her knees and bent over Eric. A pair of dispirited gray eyes sheepishly looking into hers told her that her hero was at least conscious. There was a moment's silence, then an unwilling grin spread across his face. Toni gave a feeble snicker. The next moment they were laughing maniacally, with helpless tears running down their faces.

"My fragile little flower," Skeets gasped out, convulsed. "What would you do without me? Where is that big brute? Did you drive him away?" He struggled to his elbow, still whooping. "It's no good," he told Toni, after the paroxysm had passed. "Here I've been practically praying for a setup like this, and look what happens."

"Never mind that," Toni said weakly. "How's your head? I heard it go bump when he—when you fell down."

"It hurts, all right." Skeets patted it with tender fingers. "Would you like to bind it with a strip torn from your petticoat?" he inquired gravely, his eyes wandering over Toni's skintight attire. Toni giggled again. All the constraint of the past two days had lifted and disappeared like a mist in bright sunlight.

"I'm afraid I can't oblige you that-a-way, suh."

"That makes me feel better. You aren't completely efficient and self-sufficient then. You know, that's what was driving me wild. You were so inhumanly self-sufficient, you didn't seem to feel any need of me. You wouldn't take my advice, you weren't even jealous and apparently you don't need me to defend you against brutes like Rudi the Rat." Toni noticed with alarm that he was again working himself up. "The only thing left for me to do is solve that murder. That'll show that you may have the brawn but I have the brains."

"But you don't have to prove anything," Toni protested. "It's absurd."

"Yes, I do." Skeets caught her hands. "Damn it, you're such a superior girl. I know there is no reason why you should need me or anybody. You're so bright, so quick, and so—so charming."

"If I had the looks of Steffi Dunn," said Toni gloomily, "I wouldn't have to be so damn charming."

Skeets stared at her; then a perfectly beatific smile illumined his features.

"Then you did mind," he said. "Sweet." He reached for her. That was why Odette, who had come in to tell Toni that her twelve o'clock had arrived, found her reclining dreamily on the mat in the encircling arms of Mr. Skeets from the advertising department.

"And it's no use telling me," Odette confided bodingly to her bosom friend Marthe on the fourth floor, "that she was teaching him her latest exercises."

CHAPTER 23

WHILE OUR HEROINE, as the eighteenth-century novels say, was mending her fortunes in the manner which is partly described in the foregoing chapter, Torrent was also wasting no time. If Toni had come back after her set-to with her employer she would have found him in the salon putting his theory to the test. Dr. Berchtold having left for the day, Illona had reluctantly ensconced Torrent in his office, where, hidden from curious eyes like a well-padded skeleton in the closet, he went on with his questioning.

He interviewed the two switchboard operators and got results from Maxine, the one who, according to Toni, was fond of listening in on conversations, a habit which Torrent at that point classified as one of the more amiable vices.

Maxine was another one of the Lais blondes, and had evidently gone to some pains to be one. She radiated the awful aura of refinement so characteristic of Lais, where the first step upon hiring a girl was to teach her to say "madame" instead of "moddom." But in spite of the super-sophisticated air attained by the generous application of Aphrodisiac Red lipstick, Cherubim powder and long, black, prickly looking artificial eyelashes, she had a healthy respect for the police. She strove hard to please. Of course, it was a week ago and hard to remember, but she was pretty sure that while she was on there was no conversation between M. Maurice and his mother.

"But I remember," she said, "the Kyria did try to get in touch with him once. She called from this very office, but he was stuck in the elevator." Maxine giggled. "Illona told us not to tell the Kyria about the elevator because she didn't want her to worry. But when the Kyria wanted to speak to Monsieur Maurice, I just had to tell her."

Torrent dismissed Maxine after thorough questioning. He had his information, all right, although not precisely what he was looking for. Obviously the Kyria couldn't give any instructions to M. Maurice about stalling the elevator if she hadn't been in touch with him before he stalled it. But this presented another complication. The Kyria had told him that she had come down to the second floor at the same time as Dr. Berchtold. That placed her on the second floor at 1:40, a comfortable margin of time after the murder, which took place at approximately 1:15.

But if her call from the doctor's office on the second floor was made while M. Maurice was still in the elevator, she must have lied about the time she came down. She was on the second floor much earlier than she claimed. And that explained why M. Maurice was so worried.

Now he had to find out whether the Kyria knew that Lili Michaud was alone upstairs. She knew that Jeanne was on the second floor because she had ordered her to be there. Did she also know that Hortense had likewise left her post? Another talk with Hortense was indicated. Torrent sighed resignedly and reached for the phone. Talking to Hortense was like pulling teeth. It was a strain having to be so tough all the time.

Mlle. Illona, when reached on the phone, told him frigidly that Hortense was busy giving a facial and could not be disturbed for the next half an hour. Torrent settled down in the chair. He thought irrelevantly that it was relaxing to sit by a desk uncluttered by mountains of reports. In the room next to him someone was arguing in a clear and imperious soprano.

"Of course, if you are going to allow the tape measure to hang, I'll never lose any measurements. Besides, I am perfectly sure that scale is wrong—why, I weighed myself in my clothes only four days ago."

Torrent listened, grinning. After a while he called up his office to see if there was anything for him. Moran told him that the report from the chemical analysis bureau on Alicia Howe's folder had finally come through. The boys were sorry about the delay but they had to do a lot of work on that particular job. They had gone over Alicia Howe's folder and found one eradication worthy of note. It was on the first page, where the doctor had put down his comments on Alicia's ailments. The words "heart condition" were written in ink that was much fresher than all the other entries and superimposed on the spot where chemicals had been used to eradicate previous words. At this point, with the help of various filters and screens, the chemical bureau had outdone itself and was able to report to Torrent that the previous words had been "false angina."

Torrent's face turned grave. The change was a significant one. It meant all the difference between a genuine heart condition and a nervous one. Berchtold had known that Alicia Howe's heart was functionally sound. He had no business signing the death certificate. Just another sinister little detail to be explained.

He had barely put down the receiver when Hortense entered. She looked anything but pleased to see him and Torrent didn't blame her in the least. This, he felt, would be one of their stormier sessions.

The hostilities began with Torrent asking Hortense in a civil manner whether she remembered telling anybody about leaving Lili Michaud alone. Hortense countered smartly that yes, she told Mrs. Sterling. Hadn't she and Torrent been through all this before? Nobody else? Nobody else. Was she sure? Of course she was sure. Torrent insisted mildly that they had information to the contrary. The answer came fast. Whoever gave him that information was a goddamn liar. Nevertheless, Torrent's practiced ear caught a faint tremor of hesitation. He immediately took another cue.

"You're a smart girl, Hortense. You ought to be able to see that it's silly to protect somebody else when you're in trouble yourself."

"I'm in no trouble," Hortense countered sullenly.

Torrent smiled. "That's what you think."

"I've got a perfectly good alibi and you know it. Why, the doctor will tell you that I was talking to him when Lili Michaud died."

"What about when Howe died?" Hortense looked at him in bewilderment and suddenly went so white that her freckles turned green. Torrent went on, "I'm going to put all my cards on the table and expect you to do the same, like the smart girl you are. Alicia Howe died as a result of poison that was put into her acne lotion."

"Into Zephyr de Printemps?" Hortense whispered idiotically through shaking lips.

"The same. Now then since you are the girl who put it on her—"

"But I didn't! She did herself."

"And later washed it off—"

"Dr. Rudi told me to—Dr...." Hortense whimpered. She lost all nerve, swiftly and shamefully. Her eyes went wild, and letting out a howl, she dashed for the door. Torrent caught her and unceremoniously clapped a hand on her mouth. With a brief flash of annoyance he thought that he should have questioned her at headquarters.

"Don't be a fool," he said brusquely. "Nobody is accusing you, yet. I just told you this to show you that this is no time for you to hide things. Now are you going to sit down and talk like a human being?"

He let her down into the chair. Hortense resumed her whimpering the minute he took his hand away from her mouth. "I didn't—I don't know anything about this, so help me God. You aren't going to frame me for this, are you? My God, what's going on here, anyhow?"

Torrent thought grimly that that was precisely what he wanted to know.

He repeated his former question and this time Hortense answered, fast. It was the doctor to whom she had confided that Michaud was alone. Yes, at the time when she was talking to him presumably about her health. Torrent wanted to know why Dr. Berchtold. The story came out grudgingly. She had a financial arrangement with the doctor. She was paid for recommending his services outside of the salon to the clients and also for telling him all the little items of gossip that she heard. He also wanted to be posted on anything out of the ordinary that took place in the salon. She also collected gossip for Alicia Howe. Being one of the oldest and most experienced facial operators she was given the pick of clients, thus providing Alicia Howe with good stories and Dr. Berchtold with profitable patients. She declined to describe the doctor's outside practice, saying merely that he was discreet and accommodating.

Torrent barely suppressed a whistle. He could see how the combination of a facial operator, a doctor and a gossip columnist would be a lethal one. He asked Hortense whether she knew how Dr. Berchtold used the information she gave him and she said that she didn't know because, virtuously, it wasn't any of her business. Torrent hurriedly returned to the Michaud business. It was a good idea to get as much as possible out of his victim before she recovered from her paroxysm of terror. But there was nothing to be learned here. Hortense claimed that the doctor was with her all the time until 1:25, when he went in to see Princess Lubescu, and that during that time he hadn't called anybody up. Finally Torrent let Hortense go with a stern injunction not to discuss this matter with anybody.

Hortense scuttled to the door. Her already skinny body seemed to have shrunk as if, having parted with her tawdry secrets, there was precious little left of her. She stopped at the door to spit out venomously, "I know who you got all this from. I'd like to tell her what I think of her, with her high and mighty manners." She disappeared without elucidating further. Torrent thought he knew to whom she was referring. He smiled a

little grimly. He only then realized that what she had told him hadn't surprised him unduly, probably because in the back of his mind there had
stuck a chance remark made by Toni the first time they had dinner together.

"Supposing I didn't know the time. I am not accustomed to clocking
my movements in my own salon. Besides, what does it matter if I came
down a little earlier? Of course, if you are going to go around encouraging
disloyalty among my employees—"

The Kyria confronted Captain Torrent with heaving bosom and flashing eyes. She had been moved back to her bed since her stormy interview
with Toni.

Torrent, who was sitting at a respectful distance, his face bland and
official, said mildly, "You mustn't disturb yourself, madam. This is routine,
you know. It was you, remember, and your son, who put such emphasis on
the time when you came down. My business is to check such statements.
What I'd like to know is this—wasn't this the very matter which Alicia
discussed with you before her death?"

"I—"

"She was blackmailing you, wasn't she, madam? With her knowledge, I mean, that you were downstairs at the time Lili Michaud was
killed. And to frighten you more, didn't she scribble down that note I showed
you yesterday in which she intimated that she knew who the murderer of
Lili Michaud was—"

"That note," breathed the Kyria, "I see. I see it all now. You think I—"

The nurse came out of the next room and put her fingers on the Kyria's
wrist with a significant frown at Torrent.

"Give me water," said her patient, her voice suddenly strong and vi-
brant. She drank it thirstily. "Now clear out." As the door closed behind
the bridling nurse, she turned to Torrent. "So your idea is that Alicia suspected me of killing Michaud. But that isn't true. We did have a quarrel,
but that was because she knew that you suspected her and she accused
me of protecting somebody else who would have made an equally good
suspect. You see, she knew the story of Serg. That woman," said the
Kyria grimly, "knew everything."

"Serge? You mean—?"

The Kyria meant the gaunt Dr. Winogradow, and the story that she
told Torrent about him went back many years, before Lais was even in
existence. She had known him in Paris many years ago when he was one
of the leading scientists, and, besides a distinguished career, boasted an

attractive wife, much younger than himself. He lost both one day when he killed the latter in a fit of jealous rage.

"Marianne deserved it," the Kyria remarked dispassionately. "She was a fluffy-headed blonde fool who gave Serge plenty of provocation. She really drove him mad."

An indulgent jury acquitted him on the grounds of temporary insanity ("you know how they regard *les crimes passionels* in France") and he was put into a lunatic asylum. When he was finally discharged, a broken and ruined old man, the Kyria took charge of him. "I liked him once," The Kyria's eyes grew soft and reminiscent. "*C'était un homme très distingué*—very distinguished in appearance." Under her care he recovered, but only working at chemistry kept him from slipping back. Silent and grim wreck of a man that he was, he suddenly developed an obsession for making perfumes, preferably out of the most unlikely media. The Kyria made good use of this unexpected development and paradoxically it was the work of the half-crazed chemist that made her venture a success. The House of Lais grew out of the salves, dyes, creams and perfumes Winogradow had evolved. Apparently the old misogynist found a certain grim humor in making products to heighten the attraction of the sex which had ruined his life.

Alicia had somehow unearthed this story and only the fact that she herself owned part of Lais prevented her from writing it up in her column. Winogradow gave her the creeps and she was only too happy to dub him the logical suspect in Lili's death. She knew that he had seen Michaud, though briefly, and claimed that the blonde French actress reminded him of his wife—"another cheap little blonde" she had said acidly—and caused a relapse. In her last interview with the Kyria she said she refused to be a scapegoat for a homicidal maniac. The Kyria was relieved by Alicia's death because she thought that she could keep the story a secret, but since she couldn't... The Kyria shrugged her shoulders. Ultimately, Torrent gathered, it was everyone for himself, since it seemed even she was not immune from suspicion

The Kyria leaned forward, clasping her bejeweled hands, and the stones sparkled in the firelight. "If I could prevail on you to leave Dr. Winogradow alone, Captain Torrent—you do not know what incalculable harm you maybe doing by upsetting him."

Torrent suspected callously that she was referring to the harm done to the Lais products rather than that done to Winogradow's psyche. He assured her that all would be looked into as quietly as possible. "But you can understand in view of what you told me that I will be forced to search

Dr. Winogradow's laboratory in the nearest future—tonight, even. It might be better to do this without his knowledge—won't upset him, don't you know." And as the Kyria nodded a reluctant consent, he continued, pleasantly, "And now about your own movements on the day of Miss Michaud's death, since your first version was—er—inaccurate."

The Kyria went over them obediently. She had gone down to the second floor to speak to Jeanne. But since upon leaving the back elevator she found herself close to the doctor's office, where Alicia Howe was presumably resting, she decided first to look in on the columnist. She hadn't found her there and was so upset by her absence that she just sat there telephoning around agitatedly until the noise outside told her that M. Maurice was being released from his durance vile. From then on her story followed the old version. She went out of the room and met Dr. Berchtold, who had apparently taken it for granted that she had just come down that minute.

"And you profited by that impression?" Torrent inquired coldly. The Kyria suddenly smiled at Torrent, a curiously fawning smile that affected him disagreeably.

"I am never clear about the time," she said. "And then Maurice— well, it seemed to trouble him so much that I should have been around just then that I simply let it go. It's quite understandable, isn't it?"

Torrent agreed and made his adieus, thinking that the Kyria in the role of helpless and bewildered old woman submitting to the domination of a masterful son was not very convincing. "All this crowd is a great bunch of buckpassers," he thought, making his way downstairs. Almost at the front door he ran into Dr. Manning. The gray elegant medico looked at him with disapproval and wanted to know how many more interviews there would be. They were not doing his patient any good.

A few minutes later Torrent continued on his way with a slightly furrowed brow. He had just been told that the Kyria's illness was incurable. Dr. Manning, with the cheerful pessimism characteristic of his profession, gave her a year at the outside. Apparently the Kyria, in her laudable desire to make more money than anybody else, had neglected herself, and when she came to see him last month it was too late. She was as yet unaware of her state, although the doctor felt it incumbent upon him to acquaint Maurice with it as long as a month ago.

Torrent, crunching through the frozen snow, thought gloomily that that tore it. His screwy theory was torn in several places, anyhow. The Kyria did *not* communicate with Maurice that morning and therefore could *not* have told him to stall the car, nor had she known about Hortense's absence from Lili Michaud's room. That being so, it was difficult to see her in the role of a stage-setter for the murderer.

The next thing to do was to tackle Dr. Serge Winogradow, who possessed at least two characteristics to qualify him as a murderer: being a chemist and a madman with a dislike for blondes. Torrent called headquarters and issued instructions. Some of his men were detailed to go to the salon and institute a search in the laboratory on the sixth floor, under the supervision of someone from the research bureau who would be apt to know more about the sort of thing they were looking for. He directed Moran to meet him before he went in to talk to Winogradow. If the man was really cracked, there might be trouble, and Torrent did not see the point of taking chances.

This precaution, however, proved unnecessary. Dr. Winogradow, who lived in a musty but distinguished hotel not far from Lais, let them in without any difficulty, and the fact that they admitted being there on police duty didn't seem to plunge him into any fits of passion. As a matter of fact, Torrent thought, in his disreputable old dressing gown and down-at-the-heel bedroom slippers, he looked like any crotchety old man, perhaps a little daft, but far from being sinister. Only his eyes behind the thick glasses had a disconcerting gelid appearance as if they would spill over any minute, an illusion due to the thickness of the lens. The room into which they were shown was monastically bare. The shelves were lined with thick professional-looking books, interspersed with strangely colored vials, and the walls wore a few peculiar Daliesque contraptions made up of retorts and bulbs.

Torrent plunged immediately to the heart of the matter by asking Winogradow whether he knew Lili Michaud. He added that although he remembered the chemist answering that question in the negative, he had reasons to think now that he was mistaken. Receiving a completely blank stare, he reminded him of the morning when Eric Skeets brought Lili up to his laboratory to be ignominiously turned away. A vague gleam of enlightenment penetrated through the doctor's thick glasses.

"Yes, I remember now. A sniggering little blonde with bedroom eyes," he said and added unexpectedly, "Now that I think of it, she looked rather like my wife."

Torrent experienced the same sensation as a man who, bracing himself to lift a pair of heavy dumbbells, finds that they are made of papier-maché. He looked foolish.

"Did that resemblance—er—upset you?" he asked upon recovering.

Winogradow looked startled. "Upset me? Why, not at all. You see, most women look exactly like my wife."

Moran made a strangling sound as if he'd swallowed a fishbone. Torrent threw him a baffled glance and the interview continued in the same unsatisfactory vein. It was interrupted by Winogradow's noticing Moran's furtive glance around the room.

"These," he said, "are various stages of my experiment in producing the Perfect Perfume. Of course, the actual work is done in the laboratory because dreadful smells must come before a pleasing scent is created. That is what fascinates me about perfumes. It seems like such an apt commentary on life. You know what the base for most perfumes is? Musk—derived out of the sexual glands of male deer—and male crocodile," he added conscientiously. "Or ambergris. That's nothing but the morbid secretion of a whale's stomach. We get an odor of lilac from hydroxycitronelol and mayblossoms from anecic aldehyde. I assure you, my friend, that you need a gas mask for those." Winogradow cackled with delight. "And to think that out of such stinks comes this!"

He dashed to a tiny vial, unstoppered it and thrust it under Moran's nose. Moran recoiled, then sniffed cautiously. A surprised and sentimental smile overspread his rugged face. An extraordinarily delicious, pure fragrance filtered through the room. It brought to mind white lilacs and water lilies swinging on crystalline pools.

"Say," said Moran, "that's a swell stink you've got there."

Winogradow cackled again and started unstoppering more bottles. He was firmly mounted on his hobby horse and was pouring out histories and compounds of various perfumes.

"Are you," asked Torrent, frantically trying to get through the barrage, "also by any chance interested in poisons?"

"Only the obscure ones," Winogradow answered in an offhand manner and was off again. He was gleefully telling the wincing Moran that the first lip rouge dye used by the ladies of the Renaissance was made permanent by uric acid in its natural form when Torrent intervened again.

"Do you happen to know anything about ouabain?"

"Why yes," said Winogradow, "that is a glucoside made from a special variety of strophantus. There's a tree for you. It can produce twenty-eight varieties. An infinite number of interesting drugs can be evolved from strophanti-semena—the seeds, you know. I have tried my hand at it myself."

Moran threw Torrent a glance which said plainly, "What are we waiting for?"

"You have been evolving poisons?" Torrent asked in a hushed voice. Winogradow gave a short bark which served him for laughter.

"I see you have the layman's unreasoning fear of poisons. What absurdity! Don't you see, in chemistry all is so mutable. Any of my perfumes has to pass through a stage when it is definitely toxic. And it all depends on amount and circumstances. There is such a small difference between a medical and toxic dose of any of your poisons. Even your highly potent vegetable poisons like curare or ouabain can be swallowed without even a stomach ache, unless you have a scratch in the area it touches. That's what is so fascinating, this change from the harmful to the innocuous, from the evil-smelling to—this." He fingered the little vial lovingly. "It's all relative, don't you see? Incidentally, why are you interested in ouabain?"

"Because," answered Torrent smoothly, "we have reason to suspect that Alicia Howe, of whose death you have doubtless heard, was poisoned by a dose of ouabain introduced into her acne lotion. Of course, the fact that there was actually ouabain on the premises—didn't I understand you to say?"

"Oh yes, yes," Winogradow assured him earnestly, as if wishing nothing better than to implicate himself completely. "Yes, indeed, I have some of that in the laboratory. Why, as a matter of fact, I have quite a collection of toxic drugs evolved from various plants. I am interested in that aspect of herbology."

"Dr. Winogradow, does anybody besides yourself have access to these poisons?"

"Not while I am around. I don't permit anybody to come into my laboratory." Moran began to get his handcuff-getting look. But patient examination by Torrent showed that as a matter of fact, since all these drugs, in carefully labeled capsules, were not locked away but were kept in showcases around the plants from which they were derived, they were easily accessible to anyone really anxious to get hold of them. He also admitted, after prodding, that he had discussed his experiments with several people, among them the Kyria and Dr. Berchtold.

Moran was gloomy when they left the hotel. "That guy fixed me," he complained. "I won't be able to look at any dame's complexion without thinking of some of the things he told me. And how do you like his attitude about poisons? By him it's all relative like Einstein. A fine thing. Say, chief, whyn't we grab this bird? He's screwy enough to have done this. He fills the bill, all right, don't he? Why couldn't he have killed both those dames?"

Torrent shook his head sourly and assured his lieutenant that things weren't as easy as all that. He also told Moran one reason why Winogradow couldn't, on the face of things, have killed Lili Michaud, although he had a motive, farfetched as it was. The gaunt chemist had gone out to lunch at 12:15, that is, before the Michaud-Howe scrap, and when he returned from lunch at about 1:15 he went straight up. He had no way of knowing that Lili had taken possession of Alicia Howe's room. Therefore he couldn't get to her and kill her no matter how much her likeness to his late wife bothered him.

"Not unless he has bloodhound blood in him. Now if you really fancy him as a suspect, you had better go ahead and prove that he had overheard a conversation telling him where the Michaud woman was having her facial."

Moran groaned dismally and conversation lagged.

CHAPTER 14

THURSDAY AFTERNOON found Torrent poring gloomily over his desk, on which was spread the entire history of the Lais case. He knew everything there was to know about all the people involved, down to the last unsavory secret, all their hopes, fears, ambitions, dislikes—everything, in short, except which one of them was the murderer. All of the people he had so tenderly groomed for the role of the murderer bore up bravely only to let him down at the last minute. Winogradow was a fine example of that. Torrent, loath to relinquish him, had sent Moran out to find out if there was some way for him to have found out about Lili's whereabouts. It was possible that Winogradow might have lunched at the same place as some of the girls and had heard it discussed. Nevertheless, it was a slim chance and here was Torrent faced with the prospect of a perfectly good suspect ruled out because some of the crucial details didn't fit.

Or take Dr. Berchtold. Torrent would have liked nothing better than to do just that. As a matter of fact, he had spent the whole morning trying to break down the fine unbreakable alibi the doctor and Hortense had cooked up between them. Hortense, whom he questioned again, hung on to it like grim death. Nor did he fare better with the doctor, who came to see him at his invitation early in the afternoon. The doctor was for some reason not quite his usual suave self. Torrent, who had no way of knowing about his encounter with Toni and Skeets, fondly ascribed it to guilty nervousness. He faced him with the business of the folder and watched anxiously for results. The doctor came back with a glib answer. Yes, it was true he had changed that entry. That was because while in the beginning he was sure that Alicia Howe had only false angina, he later changed his mind about it.

"Apparently," Torrent told him dryly, "you were right the first time. The autopsy showed that Howe's heart was all right. Do men in your profession often make mistakes like that?"

"Often," said Berchtold and showed his teeth.

Torrent asked him when he had changed the entry and, upon being told that it was long ago, pointed out that the folder was missing on the night after Alicia Howe died. Berchtold denied taking it home with him. "Your—investigators," he said, "must have missed it. I did take it out of the file but I put it back. I must have misfiled it with all the excitement around me because as a matter of fact, I had considerable trouble finding it the next day when you asked for it." His cold eyes challenged Torrent to do anything about it and the latter conceded with irritation that he couldn't. There *was* a possibility that the kids had missed the folder. He himself was perfectly sure Berchtold had known that there was nothing wrong with Alicia Howe's heart and that her death must have been due to other than natural causes. An inquiry would have been inconvenient to him, and so he avoided as much as he could by issuing the certificate of death from natural causes and changing the entry in the medical record which, he knew, might be called for. If Toni had not been attacked that night, indicating that the murderer was still at large, there would have been no autopsy. There were two possible reasons for the doctor's reluctance: he might have been afraid that an inquiry into the death of Howe, with whom he had been connected, would have thrown an undesired light on his own activities; and, of course, it might have been simply that he had killed her. Torrent had a feeling that an examination into the doctor's private affairs might prove very fruitful. There was nothing to do except go on with it, and, above all, to keep on digging at that alibi. For no matter how deeply the doctor was shown to be involved in unorthodox medical practices and even blackmail, it would all come to nothing if he wasn't on the spot when Michaud was killed.

The trouble was that while almost anybody could be fitted in as the murderer of Alicia Howe, you invariably came up against a blank wall when you tried to think of why that same person should want to kill Michaud. The motives for the latter were so thin that they wouldn't stand up to plain reasoning, let alone in court. And in the case of the two people who had even a semblance of a motive—Dr. Winogradow and Henri Barrat—you would have difficulty proving how they got at their victim.

It was late when Torrent finally moved the reports to one side and decided to call it a day. He told himself that he was now too close to the elaborate mass of detail he had collected. What he needed was perspective. Pleasant relaxation, namely ballet, was indicated. He would think no more of the Lais murders that night.

That he did was not a fault of his. During the intermission he spied a pair of fellow balletomanes, and when after the ballet he and Eric Skeets walked Toni home, the talk turned almost automatically from *entrechats* to murder.

Toni said that she had been trying to figure out what sort of person the murderer was. "You can't help but get some feel of a person when you've been in contact with him or her, as I," she added rubbing her head gingerly, "have certainly been."

Torrent wanted to hear her ideas. He sounded frankly anxious. The truth was, and he admitted it somewhat sheepishly, he was somewhat superstitious about Toni. There was something uncanny about the way he got ideas from just talking to her. It was almost as if she were a very sensitive medium. Sometimes even her most trivial remark would jolt the collection of unconnected facts into a pattern.

"There are certain things we do know about—shall I say M? That'll save me the trouble of saying him or her in every sentence. Isn't it funny," she said, digressing, "you always think of a murderer as him, the way you think of ships in the feminine gender."

"Never mind these aspersions," said Skeets. "As a matter of fact, this particular murder could very easily have been done by a woman. Isn't poisoning a typically feminine crime, Captain Torrent? But to come back to M. Of course we know that M knows jujitsu."

"And a bit of chemistry. That ought to narrow the field down to people we really don't like."

Torrent wondered if Toni knew that Jeanne used to work as a chemistry lab assistant in Germany. In spite of everything the girl was far from being cleared. Her virulent hatred for Alicia Howe kept her under suspicion, although there was nothing that connected her with Lili Michaud's murder.

"It must be someone with more than a casual acquaintance with Lais," Toni pursued, "because he seems to know his way around, there. And—you talk about Winogradow's being crazy—well, I don't think M is crazy. I mean M might have a mania on one point or another but certainly is not a lad with straw in his hair thinking he's Gandhi. And from personal experience I can tell you that M, if it was M who went for me that night, walks lightly and has very strong hands."

They walked faster, their shadows deep violet against the bluish snow. They all looked pinheaded and that was rather discouraging. Toni sighed and said apologetically, "I guess we don't know much about M, do we?"

"No," said Torrent. "M isn't the only person we know very little about. We don't know enough about the Michaud gal. That's so damned provoking, don't you know," he burst out as if his grievance was suddenly too much for him. "There probably were many good reasons and fine opportunities for bumping her off in France. Instead—"

"You sound like one of our foremost isolationists, Captain. The oceans are getting too narrow," said Skeets.

Toni shivered a little. "It's nasty, all the same. Imagine that girl leaving France and coming here to her death."

"Kismet and that sort of thing," Skeets agreed. "Don't be too impressed by it, though. It happens every day."

Toni said thoughtfully, "Look, isn't it possible, perhaps, that Lili's and Alicia's murders weren't done by the same person? I am all for Aristotle's three unities but is life like that?"

"You always did have a soft spot for weak lame theories that haven't a leg to stand on, poor things," Skeets gibed gently. "The idea of two murderers buzzing around Lais, both equally well acquainted with the beauty business and possessing similar characteristics, simply charms me. Strange they haven't bumped into each other yet."

"Well," said Toni defiantly, "what's the use of hanging on to a theory that won't work? We've been proceeding all the time on the assumption that Alicia was killed because she knew who did away with Lili. We've thought that if we knew what Alicia knew we'd have the murderer. Well, now we do know and it doesn't get us anywhere. She thought Winogradow the mad chemist was the one, and I don't see you clapping any irons on him. Why not try another theory?"

"Anything as long as it's new," Skeets tut-tutted. "This younger generation, eh, Torrent?"

"Maybe M is a madman. Think of all the fun we'd have guessing at his mania. Perhaps he's sworn to exterminate all the blondes, or, even better, all the blondes who take treatments in Alicia Howe's room. Of course! That would give you the common denominator in the two murders!"

"How do you figure that out, my fanciful fay?"

"Yes, that's it! The minute a blonde steps into Alicia Howe's room something explodes in M's brain. It doesn't matter who it is, as long as the hair is blond. To his diseased mind all blondes look alike, particularly when taking a treatment. In a way it's a compliment to dear deceased Alicia because I am sure this is the first time anybody has thought of her as just a blonde."

"Talking about explosions in the brain," Skeets began pityingly. He got no further, because Torrent, who had been listening to all this nonsense in peaceful silence, suddenly let out a whoop, snapped his fingers rapidly several times, grabbed Toni by the shoulders and imprinted an enthusiastic kiss upon her cold glowing cheek.

"By George," said Torrent, "damned if you didn't do it again."

"But what did I say?" Toni pleaded for the fifth unavailing time. She and Skeets had shanghaied the grinning Torrent into her apartment, where he was plied with hot buttered rum and doughnuts and watched narrowly for any sign of relenting. Torrent sipped his drink, ate the doughnuts, and beamed beatifically at his interrogators.

"Can't be," said Skeets, "that Toni's unspeakable idea really found favor with you? I don't believe it!"

Torrent shook his head in high good humor.

"You were both talking a lot of nonsense," he admitted amiably. "But in the midst of it Toni made two remarks that placed things in an entirely new light." He beamed at her fondly. "Does it every time!"

"But what did I say?" Toni moaned. "This is inhuman. You can't do this to us!"

"You'd better tell us, or we won't let you have the use of Toni's prophetic gift in the future," Skeets threatened. Torrent yielded with a laugh.

"Two things," he said. "Toni's saying that we should discard the theory of Howe's being killed because she knew who the murderer was. And her remark about the blondes in Howe's room."

Gray eyes and green met each other in a gaze of pure bewilderment and slowly, accusingly turned back on Torrent.

"I don't get it," said Skeets baldly. Torrent shrugged his shoulders elaborately, knocking off Tom Jones who had come up on the arm of his chair to pay his respects.

"Why does this cat like you?" Skeets asked idly. "He has nothing but bitterness toward me."

"Damned if I know," said Torrent. He snapped his fingers and the cat came back, demonstratively making a detour around Skeets' chair. Torrent nudged him gently with the toe of his shoe and Tom Jones groveled before him, purring loudly.

"I don't want a sickening demonstration like that," said Skeets, "Just a little friendliness."

"How do you expect him to feel friendly," said Toni, "after you kick him?"

"I didn't!"

"You did."

They wrangled mildly. In the midst of it Skeets said, "Got it!" He leaped up from his chair, "I think I know… Are you going home now?" As Torrent rose, Skeets added, "I'll come along and you can tell me if I'm right."

"What about me?" Toni demanded, outraged. The two men, locked in insufferable masculine solidarity, exchanged pitying looks.

"You figure out for yourself, dear. The funny part about it is that you said it yourself once, the first time we went out together. It's lucky for you that you are as long on intuition as you are short on logic."

"It's lucky for *you,*" said Toni in a marked manner, "that you remember my every casual remark. Good *night!*"

Torrent went home feeling that the log jam of his ideas was finally blasted into motion. He was moving, and presumably in the right direction. The next morning he plunged into work with a vigor that delighted his colleagues who confided to each other that it looked like "Limey" was going to break the case.

It was noticed particularly by Moran that Torrent's attention was again turned to Winogradow. But apparently from a different angle, because Moran was, to his great relief, instructed to drop the line he was following, which was lucky, since the possibility of Winogradow's having overheard any discussion about Michaud was a slim one. Among other things Torrent proceeded to disrupt the life of Lais by rechecking the testimony about the times. Toni, burning up with curiosity at the other end, was further mystified by the sudden summons of several girls to be interviewed. She relieved her feelings by calling up Skeets and being nasty to him. Skeets merely laughed.

"So the old boy is getting busy," he commented.

"He certainly is. Moran interviewed all the girls from the third floor. Illona tried to stop him, and he just looked at her patiently and said, 'Lady, stop fluttering them long sleeves at me like a damned spook. It makes me nervous.' And now Brigitte has been taken to headquarters to talk to the heap big chief himself. I hope he chokes on her."

Brigitte came back at about noon and the story she told Toni, who had been lying in wait for her, seemed to indicate that Torrent had indeed found her an unpalatable morsel. Toni gleefully dragged her off to lunch and pumped her.

Brigitte, known to fellow employees as Bridgie, a snub-nosed redhead with freckles showing plainly under the Baiser d'Ange powder, gladly shared her information. She was the one who had been stationed at the exit on the day of Lili Michaud's death, and Torrent wanted to check over the list of times with her himself. According to her everything went on nicely at first, then Winogradow's name came up and she told Torrent, as she did before, that he went up right after Alicia Howe had breezed out of the building. "As a matter of fact," Brigitte had added, "I remember now that they bumped into each other in the doorway." Torrent had nodded his head at that and put it down and then something seemed to hit him. Did she mean Winogradow and Alicia Howe had *seen* each other? They certainly had. Torrent had grilled her about it feverishly, obviously hoping that she would take her statement back.

"And honestly I would have loved to, on account of he was so broke up about it, but with him questioning me I kept on remembering it more and more clearly and being more and more sure about it. That Winogradow guy came out of the salon door just as Miss Howe was passing it and ran into her. They sort of glared at each other. So that's what I told Captain Torrent. And he looked as if his mother died or something and said, 'That's torn it.' "

"Didn't care for it, did he?"

"No, ma'am! He checked on all the other times with me but you could see his heart wasn't in it. I'm sorry." Brigitte looked genuinely regretful. "He's so nice with that cute mustache. I kinda like little mustaches on older men, don't you?"

Toni allowed absentmindedly as how she did. Her thoughts were elsewhere.

"Bridgie," she said, "can you remember that list of times?"

"Can I?" said Bridgie. "My Gawd, I've been through it so often now I can see it in my sleep."

Half an hour later Toni was poring over a rough time-schedule she had devised with Bridgie's assistance and from the facts she herself remembered. Little by little the puzzled frown left her brow to be replaced by an expression of enlightenment.

"So that's what he meant," she muttered, and a little later added, "So that's what's bothering him."

After this cryptic remark she called Skeets again and, after having briefly conveyed to him Torrent's mysterious discomfiture, indicated that she was ready to do some fancy gloating. Skeets laughed.

"So you've caught on? I'll be down in a while to take you down a peg."

In fifteen minutes he appeared on the second floor and gravely asked Toni to grant him a few moments' interview about some publicity releases. They sedately repaired to Toni's room, where Skeets tossed aside his notebook and regarded Toni with the waggish expectancy of a puppy about to receive a biscuit.

"Well," he said, "there's still another suspect. Or could we be wrong? I am assuming you know what I am talking about."

"Indeed, I do," Toni reassured him brightly. "I'll even make a little prediction. In a little while you will hear a rending crashing sound. That will be our friend Torrent trying to break the alibi of a certain alien party. If he's successful, you have your murderer. If not, well, it was a nice theory and we were very fond of it. Something tells me that he's going to have trouble. Eric. Are you listening?

Eric, who was staring intently at Toni's schedule, started and said in a faraway voice, "That's an idea." He grinned at Toni and got up. "May I take this along with me? Thanks. I'll pick you up for dinner today." He drifted out, dreamily.

Toni went on with her work. Her current cross was an extremely prudish matron who scornfully discarded the usual habiliments Lais offered for exercising and insisted on wearing a shapeless baggy creation of her own. She made Toni's life miserable by adjuring her to assume a more modest costume, one that wouldn't inflame men.

"But there are no men here, Mrs. Smythe," Toni protested sweetly. "There is just you."

Mrs. Smythe disregarded this and remarked that her husband had never seen her naked. Toni volunteered nothing to this interesting piece of information. She did not see any point in telling Mrs. Smythe that her next appointment after one was with an extremely curvaceous blonde, who suffered from no form of inhibition and whose bills, probably by pure coincidence, were paid by a Mr. Smythe.

Skeets, in the meanwhile, went up to the fifth floor in a very thoughtful mood. He sat at his desk figuring things out and completely disregarding the printer's proofs of a new Lais booklet that had just been put on his desk. Presently he called up Torrent and got him at the psychological moment when the latter dropped all reasonable theories and began to consider improbabilities. Skeets tackled him in sweet and persuasive tones.

The printer's messenger, who was waiting to pick up the proofs of the *Harper's Bazaar* ad and who was of a curious disposition, couldn't make anything out of the conversation.

"Of course," said Skeets after listening to Torrent, "I thought of that, too, and it does make things difficult. But it could be done without leaving traces. I personally have climbed out of worse spots. I'm going to try, anyhow. Oh, I see. You are going to try, too? Well, I'm staying late. I'll watch the fun."

At quarter to six Toni, who had just polished off her last client, got a call from Skeets to tell her that he wasn't meeting her at six but would be over at her place later. He sounded elaborately casual, but Toni, who sensed an undercurrent of excitement, immediately wanted to know what he was hiding from her. After a little sparring Skeets admitted that it had something to do with the case.

"Now don't be reproachful," he said uneasily. "It's an idea I've had and if it doesn't work out, I don't want to be gloated at."

"As if I—" said Toni indignantly..

"Yes, as if you... Baby, it's a very difficult thing to keep two jumps ahead of you. Give me my brief moment of glory. Keep the latch open for me, will you?"

Toni hung up and went home in high dudgeon.

Skeets showed up at eight o'clock and one look at his too expressive face showed Toni that the experiment, whatever it was, was far from successful. A second and closer look caused her to gasp. Skeets was very grimy indeed. There was a black streak running along his cheek, his hands were grimy, and when he took his coat off his clothes had greasy spots on them.

"My, but you're dirty," said Toni. "What have you been doing?"

"Trying to prove who the murderer was," Skeets responded glumly.

"Well, for goodness sake. Did you have to get so filthy to prove it?"

"On the contrary." Skeets' grin was wry. "I could only have proved it by staying immaculately clean."

"Riddles, eh? Well, we'd better get you clean."

"You can't do it. Soap doesn't seem to get this stuff off. I'll probably have to stay that way all my life."

"I have some stuff that'll clean you," Toni said. "It's so powerful it'll take your skin off." She darted into the bathroom and came back carrying a large yellow bottle. "Another of Dr. Winogradow's little gifts to womankind. Officially it's supposed to bleach mustaches but everybody at Lais uses it to clean off spots that ordinary soap won't get off."

As the pungent smell of lemon verbena filled the room, a dim recollection stirred in Toni's head. She groped for it and almost had it, but not quite. The mocking ghost whisked its shadowy skirts around the corner and fled out of reach.

It'll come back, she said to herself. Those things always do if you don't try to think of them. Probably nothing important.

But all the rest of that evening the uncompleted recollection tugged at the corner of her mind, vaguely irritating like an itch that you can't get at. So that Skeets, his sensibilities already wounded by his failure, which he obstinately refused to discuss, complained that Toni was too distrait to do him any good and left early and in a mild huff.

CHAPTER 15

THE IMPRESSION of something undone, a terribly important thing not quite remembered, stayed with Toni the next day. It seemed a part of a confusing dream with which she had been hagridden that night. She had been wandering through a Daliesque landscape, lunar and desolate, and finally approached a skeleton ship precariously perched on a barren cliff, and then somebody, somebody whom she knew very well and yet couldn't see clearly, smashed a bottle on the ship's crumbling stern, and the ship soared up into the air as if wafted upward by the unbearably powerful odor of lemon verbena.

The odd part was that she had a definite sensation during the dream that she was getting a terrific revelation of some sort, and of course, like most dreams it turned out to be complete nonsense, with most of it pretty vague anyhow.

It haunted her all the way to the salon, which by that time had achieved a nightmarish quality all its own. The Keep Young Club of East Orange, New Jersey, consisting of twenty-odd matrons of assorted ages and shapes, was having its yearly outing and they were to be shown through carefully selected portions of Lais. This invasion by the New Jersey matrons was by the way of being some what of a nuisance, and Toni, during one of her trips downstairs to the salon, came upon M. Maurice giving Illona hell because of it.

"Has it occurred to you that the reason why all those plump harpies have picked this particular time to descend on us is because of what has been happening here? You think you'll be able to keep them out of what the *News* has been calling the murder room? They'll be asking for their money back!"

"But—"

"My dear Illona, I don't expect you to have any feeling of delicacy about this, but you might have consulted me."

"I know," said Illona, in choked tones, "that the Kyria would want us to carry on as usual. Of course, you—These women are all prospective customers."

"Are you trying to imply that my mother is as mercenary and devoid of any proper feelings as you are?"

Illona burst into genteel tears, and M. Maurice said maliciously, "Your mascara is running," and walked away. Illona's discomfiture had obviously put him into a very good mood and he was strutting a little when he got into the elevator with Toni. Toni asked him when they were going to get the Toulouse Lautrecs he had promised them for the second floor and he positively beamed upon her.

"What a greedy young woman." He smiled. "Aren't you content with my vases for the time being?"

"They are quite marvelous," Toni said and couldn't help adding slyly, "I applaud your choice of subject matter." She was referring to the fact that the vases belonged to the Amazonomachy series and were full of warring and wrangling Amazons, an impertinent commentary, she thought, on the disagreeable and quarrelsome atmosphere reigning in the salon.

M. Maurice gave her a quick sharp glance, then he grinned. "You are very intelligent, Toni." There was a little note of mockery in his voice. "Much too intelligent. The exhibit will be unveiled today. I want your opinion of it." He grew confidential. "It's very important for me to have this be a success. I would have liked mother to see it."

He stopped, his face contorted by a sudden grimace of grief.

Poor little man, Toni thought, with that terrific mother complex. As they went out of the elevator, he gave her arm a little squeeze, a singularly confiding, inoffensive little gesture.

Mrs. Sterling was Toni's next appointment. It was her last visit for some time. She was going to Palm Beach.

"Chester decided he was going to take me away from it all. After all, I've been through a great deal. Do you know what?" She giggled. "I really do believe that detective suspected me of killing Lili Michaud. It just dawned on me the other day. I told him so today and he laughed."

Toni wondered if the prospective trip to Palm Beach meant that Mrs. Sterling was definitely rejected as a suspect. A little gentle pumping elicited the fact that Torrent didn't know about the trip. He had been questioning her again about the day Lili Michaud was murdered. And she hadn't told him that she was going away, because after all, my dear, is it any of his business and besides Mrs. Sterling was bored with being questioned about the same thing over and over again and had decided that she wasn't going to talk about it any more.

"My psychiatrist thinks it's very bad for me. I've been having anxiety dreams instead of the nice Freudian ones I like so much. And after all, there's a limit to what you can do for the police. That's what Chester says too about Washington. He says there's a limit to what you can do for your company for one dollar a year."

Toni emerged from this lesson with the usual feeling of dizziness. A telephone call from downstairs warned her that the members of the Keep Young Club, East Orange chapter, were on their way up. M. Maurice was pottering around his exhibition. Only a skeleton of the scaffolding was still left, with a few men working on it, and M. Maurice with infinite caution was getting ready to put the vases into the nests prepared for them in the glass spiral going around the column. Near him was Dr. Berchtold, who was being jovial. She wondered why Berchtold, who had never paid attention to M. Maurice before, was doing so now and realized that of course it was the natural thing to do, with the Kyria sick. Even if he didn't know the extent of her sickness it was in character for him not to overlook any bets.

Then the East Orange ladies poured out of the elevator. They trooped after Toni with subdued oohs and ahs of admiration. The largest one, who was apparently delegated to get information, had her little pad and pencil ready and kept firing questions at Toni.

"For my report on Wednesday, you know," she told Toni. Usually it was possible to get a group off a floor in a comparatively brief time. But the lady with the pad and pencil made that impossible. She kept on delivering lectures. She delivered one on the Greek character of the solarium— it was laid out like an atrium, with a fountain in the middle and cool blue-glass-tiled walls—and another rather stern one on the *baigne* where her companions showed a tendency to linger with a wistful eye on the fluffy masses of soap in the tiled baths. On this occasion she held forth at length on the softening qualities of the baths as compared with the hardening powers of exercise.

"And we want to be hard, not soft, don't we, girls?" she inquired and got a rather doubtful chorus of wistful yeses.

The catastrophe happened on their way back to the elevator. By that time M. Maurice had got up on the ladder and was putting the fifth vase on the highest level of the glass spiral. Jeanne—this was her first day back—was standing below with a trayful of tiny amphorae, ready to hand them to M. Maurice whenever he wanted. Berchtold was still there, standing next to Jeanne, and Toni noticed with relief that there was no expression of any kind on the girl's face except a sort of stony contempt, and that when he brushed against her she moved away with a genuine little shiver of revulsion. "The stomach pump," Toni thought and smiled.

The note-taker whooped with delight. "Girls, look! Greek vases. How simply divine! I really think I'll take a little time to sketch this." She whipped out the inevitable notebook and loped toward the edifice. The next moment a shriek of anguish and fury had rent the still air. She had knocked the props from under M. Maurice.

Toni stared fascinated at the ensuing events, which seemed to unfold with the deliberateness of a slow action film. The ladder was falling forward. Inevitably it would crash into the lucite structure, with M. Maurice and all. It was the latter's agility that saved the situation. He had caught hold of the crossbar of the scaffolding that was still standing there and had swung himself clear of the impending ruin. Not only that, but with a well-placed kick he sent the ladder in the opposite direction. It crashed into a showcase full of bottles, and the floor was immediately full of glass splinters and fumes of heavy and varied perfumes. Somebody laughed hysterically—Mrs. Sterling, who had just emerged from her room. M. Maurice looked at the mess under him, lifted himself up to the crossbars, where he seated himself with unexpected agility, and began to curse out the East Orange chapter of the Keep Young Club. His falsetto tenor rose easily above the hubbub. He looked like a malignant monkey perched precariously near the ceiling. But he kept his place easily until Berchtold brought the ladder to him.

Toni went dazedly through the motions of untangling the chaos. Her head was spinning and she wanted badly to get away. For during the commotion suddenly something had clicked in her head. The elusive memory had come back and she had looked into the murderer's cold eyes and knew how the thing was done.

She was badly frightened. It was only a glance, a swift lightning-like interchange of silent exclamations. But her eyes had said, "So that's it !" and the murderer's had replied with a cold deadly affirmation. It was a frightening, unexpected contact and Toni felt herself shivering in small convulsive shivers from the shock.

She didn't know what to do. You don't suddenly stand up and announce melodramatically, "Here's your killer." This favorite pronounce-ment in detective fiction was usually made with the announcer safely ensconced amid a group of Scotland Yard detectives or some other pro-tective agency. Yet she knew she must move fast because that one mur-derous glance had suddenly transformed what she now wryly admitted had been a fascinating guessing game into menacing reality.

The thing to do was to get on the telephone and get Skeets down as soon as possible. She looked around and saw that the two telephones available on this floor were being frantically used. Taking the elevator was impossible. The murderer would see her going and try to forestall her and, everything taken into consideration, she disliked the idea of sharing the elevator with the murderer.

At that moment Dr. Berchtold, who had been bending down over the pouter-chested lady who had fainted, asked Toni to bring him some water. She sped toward the water fountain, which was in the direction of the solarium. But she didn't stop there. Instead, she went on into the solarium where she knew there was a telephone.

Nobody was in the solarium, as she knew from having just visited it with the Keep Young Club. Only the little fountain murmured musically in the silence. Toni's hand trembled as she lifted the receiver out of the absurd shell-like contraption in which it rested.

Skeets wasn't on his floor, she was told. Nobody knew where he went. As a matter of fact, the voice that answered her was a little irritated over his absence. Toni told him to tell Skeets to come down to the second floor where he was urgently needed, and hung up. She sat for a moment thinking furiously. Then she lifted the receiver again and gave the opera-tor the number of the homicide bureau.

A hand fell lightly on her shoulder and a voice said, "I think you had better cancel that call, my dear." Toni sat quite still while the hand tight-ened, reminding her of the grip she once had felt in the dark. Then she said evenly into the receiver, "Never mind that call," and turned to face the person who had come in so softly after her.

M. Maurice took his hand from her shoulder, put it into his pocket and moved away. He looked quite the same, very gentle and dapper. Only there was a steely blankness in his eyes and in his smile.

"I told you," he said gently, "that you were much too intelligent. For a moment this morning when you spoke about the vases I thought you knew. I was so very relieved when you didn't. What made you finally decide about me?"

Toni said, "The lemon verbena. When all the bottles broke, I remembered." Her voice, she thought, sounded all right. She found that after the first rabbit-like sinking of her heart when that hand lighted on her shoulder, she wasn't really afraid. She kept on thinking incongruously, after all, this is only M. Maurice. Only occasionally her heart pulsated painfully in a great hollow space in her chest, like a captured bird fluttering as the hand of the captor approaches. "And when you swung up on the crossbars."

M. Maurice nodded a little. "That's what I thought. Too bad. Well, darling, what shall we do about it now?" He seemed honestly worried. "I could kill you, you know," he said quite casually. "It would be quite easy. Nobody would look for you here because that's not where you are supposed to be, and nobody noticed my slipping away, because I'm such a nobody, you see. And there are some good places here where I could hide you after you are dead. Not even your friend Torrent would find you for a while."

Toni thought incredulously, It's my body he is talking about. It's me, Toni Ney, who is going to be killed and hidden where not even my friend Torrent— Why, this is ridiculous.

"But," M. Maurice continued, and the fountain played a plaintive obbligato to his incredible words, "I don't want to kill you. I've always liked you, Toni. You aren't like the rest of those women. My God, how I've always hated them with their wobbly flesh and their squabbles and their loose tongues. You're different. You're like a very young Greek boy on one of my vases, clean and straight and slim and quiet. I wasn't sorry about killing those two women, not that little French tart, whom I killed by mistake, and certainly not that other blackmailing snake, but I would hate to have to kill you. I could have, you know. That night—I didn't want to hurt you, I just had to fix it so that you couldn't see me."

Toni stared at him. He really seemed to mean it. A sentimental murderer. Somehow when he spoke about liking her it was with difficulty that she suppressed a shudder. And that was odd because she was at the same time obscurely sorry for him. Next thing I know I'll start consoling him for the necessity of killing me.

"You were always in the way," said M. Maurice reproachfully. "That active intelligence of yours was constantly making you a peril to me."

"I am sorry I was a nuisance," Toni said irrepressibly. M. Maurice gave her a long penetrating look.

"So bright," he said, sighing, "so young. If I could only trust you. Look here, Toni, if I only knew that you wouldn't go to the police with what you have guessed, I could make it pleasant for you. My mother—she's dying, you know. In a year I'll be master here. Without Alicia here trying to worm in her way I'm set. I know I'll inherit. And oh, how I've wished to get my hands on this place. I won't mind your running it with me. It would be nice, because your ideas are so much like mine. We'll throw out all those females, and it'll be fun building the place the way we want to. How about it, Toni?"

"S—sounds nice," Toni said weakly. To herself she said: Now I know that it's one of those senseless dreams. The thing to do is wake up before things get too weird.

"But how to be sure?" M. Maurice struck his brow with his hand. "That's the problem. I think I have it. I'll marry you. Oh, don't be alarmed. It would be just a precautionary measure. You could live your own life. I wouldn't interfere, but it would be nice to have someone around to whom I could talk."

Toni felt her eyes growing rounder and rounder in her spinning head. She covered her mouth with her hand to hold back a spurt of hysterical laughter. Meanwhile Maurice was going on happily making plans and beaming at her.

"The perfect solution. In that way I can be quite sure of you. You won't be able to testify against me. And I'll have you constantly under observation. If the worst comes to worst, I will be able to—control you."

Suddenly Toni couldn't stand it any more. It was with a mixture of exasperation and pity that she cried out, "Oh, stop talking this nonsense. It's no good. Really it isn't. Because I'm not the only one who knows. The police do. They know all the things I do."

She knew immediately that that was the last thing she should have said.

That outburst stopped M. Maurice in his tracks, like a bullet. His eyes went mad and pale with a small slit of pupil like an enraged cat's. The next moment he flung himself at Toni without another word.

There were voices and sounds of running steps in the corridor outside of the solarium. M. Maurice apparently was too busy choking Toni to notice. Torrent and Skeets had to pull him off by main force, and to duck him in the fountain before he returned to normal and saw that he was caught.

CHAPTER 16

"YOU LITTLE FOOL, whatever possessed you to tell him all instead of stalling him along? Do you realize what might have happened if we hadn't been along? I get cold chills down my spine when I think of it." Eric Skeets shuddered demonstratively as he tenderly applied a cold compress to Toni's slender neck, splotched with purplish bruises. Toni smiled at him. Her voice was still husky.

"Well, I've been taught not to accept proposals made under a false impression. I guess men just don't appreciate honesty." Her grin wavered. "Do you know what? I'd rather not talk about it, please." Her eyes shifted to where Captain Andrew Torrent, still in his overcoat, was poking at the dying fire. "Captain Torrent, take your coat off. You'll catch your death of cold."

"I've just dropped in for a minute," said Torrent. But he eased out of the coat and applied himself industriously to the fire. "Do you think you can tell me something about this, Miss Ney? What brought on the attack, I mean. Or is your throat too sore?"

Toni cleared it experimentally and dragged off the compress. "No, I'm really all right, though I probably won't be able to manage that debut at the Met. About Maurice, now. You see," Toni explained, "I knew, and he saw that I knew. Even yesterday when Eric came in with his hands all dirty and I helped him to clean them with lemon verbena, the smell of the damn thing was bothering me terribly. And then when all those bottles fell, I placed it. When they released Maurice from the elevator on the day that Michaud died, that was the smell that pervaded the whole car because the bottle of lemon verbena and several others were broken. And then when I saw him clambering up that scaffolding, I thought, of course! We have always thought of Maurice as rather dainty and effeminate, but as a matter of fact, he's damn strong and agile. I suddenly knew what Eric had been trying to prove. Maurice had climbed out of that stalled elevator just as Eric did last night when he got so dirty. But Maurice wasn't dirty. He was immaculately clean. And why shouldn't he be? After having killed Lili Michaud and climbed back into the elevator, he had twenty more minutes in which to clean himself up with the best cleaner-uppers in the world. Why, besides that infernal bleacher, lemon verbena, he had all the creams and lotions to take off any traces of disorder. And of course, he had to break all those bottles after using them so that nobody would see that they had been used. And it all came back to me."

"But how did he know that?" Skeets asked. "If he read anything from the expression of your poker-face, he's a better man than I am, Gunga Din."

Torrent nodded, "Yes, but he was watching her very carefully for days. You see, when I'd figured that whole business out yesterday, I realized what a danger you've been in, Toni. As a matter of fact, he himself admitted that he tried to get hold of you for three nights and you were out every time. So I thought I'd take measures."

"Yes, that's what I want to know! How did you happen to come there so opportunely, to say the least?"

"Well," said Torrent smiling, "not to put too fine a point on it, one of the men working on that exhibit was one of my men. When he saw you fade and your pal Maurice follow you in an unobtrusive manner, he called me downstairs where I was talking to one of the girls. I came up fast, with Skeets, who also happened to be there."

Toni remembered M. Maurice's face bent over hers, a pallid grinning mask, and the feel of his iron hands on her throat, and shivered.

"For a moment there I thought I was a dead pigeon."

"You are not to think of it any more," said Skeets authoritatively. He sat down on the couch, put Toni's small feet in his lap and began to stroke them gently. "Do you mind? It relaxes me. Look here, Torrent, you said you knew yesterday. How come, even after our experiment failed?"

"We went on working after you went home," said Torrent and grinned. "You see, it had to be he. There simply was nobody else.

"The reason why we never even thought of him in the beginning is the screwy way that case panned out. There were plenty of people who had the opportunity to kill Michaud. The trouble was that we could find no motive. There was just no good reason why anybody should kill that dame. Nobody except her husband knew her. Alicia seemed a logical suspect, but even then it seemed peculiar to me that a dame with her dislike for exercise should know jujitsu. Then, of course, when Howe was killed that possibility also expired.

"We sweated blood trying to find out why anybody should want to kill that blonde. And no results whatsoever.

"The motives were so damned thin. The only one who conceivably might have had some reason was Henri Barrat, Michaud's impresario-husband, who came over from France with her. And the idea of his waiting to kill her until he came to the United States was quite ludicrous.

"Now when Alicia Howe died, we had an entirely different situation. Everybody had a motive there. We sort of restricted ourselves by taking it for granted that she was killed because she knew who the murderer was. As a matter of fact, any one of the principals had a reason for doing away with her even without that!

"The fact was, Alicia was the logical murderee!

"And things began moving as soon as I realized that, after a remark that you let fall by chance—something about blondes all looking alike under the mask."

"Remember," said Skeets, "the first time we went out together you said, 'Alicia should have been the one who was killed. It's all a hideous mistake.' Well, apparently that's just what it was."

"Just so. That theory explained many things. Especially it told us why Michaud, a perfect stranger, was killed in a room which belonged exclusively to Alicia Howe. And it narrowed down the ring of suspects. Because everybody in the salon knew about the scrap between Alicia Howe and Lili Michaud, and the fact that Michaud was left victorious in Howe's room, a victory that cost her her life.

"Everybody who was in the salon during the crucial period knew about it except three persons."

Toni counted them off on her fingers. "Let's see. Dr. Winogradow who was out for lunch; Henri Barrat, who was also out during that time; and of course Maurice, who stalled the elevator just at that time and didn't know about the quarrel until much later."

"Precisely. Well, for a while I thought that Winogradow, the mad chemist, was our dish. He was going upstairs at about that time. Why shouldn't he have paused for a moment on the third floor to do away with what he thought was Alicia Howe and arrive upstairs in time to look at that damnable dye or what have you? And then that little girl blew it sky high."

"That's right," Toni lifted herself to her elbow. "I couldn't imagine why Bridgie's remark should have upset you so. And then I realized if Winogradow bumped into Alicia going out he couldn't possibly have thought that she was in her room getting a Winogradow pack."

"Precisely. Maurice seemed an impossibility and I tried hard to break Barrat's alibi. But I couldn't get around the fact that to get to the third floor he would have had to pass this Bridgie and she swore he didn't.

"Well, that left Maurice. And now that my attention was forcibly directed to him, so to speak, I began to see how he might have done it.

"You see, there was another thing pointing to him. We knew that the murderer, whom we, more appropriately than we knew, called M, was in the room next to Howe's at about one-ten. At one-twenty he was gone. Now where did he go? If he had gone downstairs he would have met Winogradow coming up, and according to Bridgie nobody came down after Winogradow went up except Mrs. Sterling, who couldn't possibly be M. Nor could M have gone up, that is, to the fourth floor (the doors at fifth and sixth, remember, were closed) and not have been seen by the receptionist. Where did he go then? The answer, back to the elevator where he came from.

"The business of his keeping his hands clean floored me, too. But after I went asking around and found out about all the stuff he had with him I began to see how it could have been done. And when you, Skeets, told me today how you had to use that skin bleach to get the stuff off your hands, that clinched it."

Torrent looked at their fascinated faces and grinned.

"I admit that I didn't expect to get him on just that. I figured that he'd break down after a long grueling questioning and that meanwhile I would get other incriminating evidence. Like the fact that he had taken jujitsu lessons on the sly. It's easy, after you know who the guy is, because then you know what to look for. But as a matter of cold fact, he made it unnecessary for me." Torrent turned a frankly awestricken look on Toni. "You know, you've been my good angel through this, practically at a peril to your life and limb. Everything you said and did helped me. I even sort of grew to expect that sort of thing from you. But when you throw in my lap a confession by the murderer and help me to catch him in the act of perpetrating another murder—well, I—"

Toni managed a wry grin and moved her head gingerly. "I assure you that my services were entirely involuntary on that occasion. But tell us more. Why did that poor little—"

"Poor little, hell. I think that's one of the reasons for the whole thing, the fact that everybody underestimated that guy. His mother always kept him down and everybody followed suit. In reality, he is a cold ambitious little guy whose ideas were always suppressed. And he had plenty of ideas. But as long as his mother ruled the roost he just had to content himself with the prospect of inheriting the salon in the sweet by and by when his old lady would finally kick the bucket. That this pleasant prospect became reality too late to do him any good is just one of those things.

"Now then. You remember a few months ago the Kyria started thinking seriously of selling Lais. I think she began to realize subconsciously that she wasn't getting any younger and that she was a pretty sick woman, although she refused to admit that to anybody. The thing that inclined her to do so among other things was a severe case of sabotage in publicity and promotion. The competitor was always one step ahead of Lais. If Lais was coming out with a gland cream, the competitor would beat her to it with something very similar."

"Why yes, I remember Eric telling me this in confidence."

"It was quite bad," Eric said. "We thought there was a leak in the promotion department. But even some of Winogradow's formulas were stolen. The Kyria was wild."

"Did M. Maurice do that? But why?"

"Well, he saw an opportunity to get out from under his mother's domination, don't you know. He made a deal with the competitor who was trying to get the salon from his mother. This transaction if successful would have landed him a sizable bonus, which would have come in handy, the Kyria being pretty close with money, and a position of importance under the new management. His sabotage was an attempt to persuade his mother to sell the establishment which was beginning to give her so much trouble. Last night, we got hold of the man who was paying Maurice and of course, that was part of our case.

"This activity of Maurice's came to an end exactly a month ago, and that coincided with the time when Dr. Manning told him that his mother was incurably ill and had not more than another year to live. There was no point in his struggling to get on his own. In another year he would inherit all the money. And that's where Alicia Howe came in. She had found out about Maurice's little scheme and threatened to tell all to the Kyria. That would have been disastrous. The Kyria would have never forgiven him and he would have been immediately cut out of the will."

Skeets had drifted to the kitchen and was quietly making a cocktail. Toni was watching Torrent, her green eyes growing as round as Tom Jones's yellow peepers. Both the girl and the cat were silent and taut, as if mesmerized.

"That Alicia Howe was a stinker of the first order," said Torrent reminiscently. "Yes, she certainly was that. You see, besides the rather profitable profession as a gossip writer she had an even more profitable sideline."

"Don't tell me, let me guess," Toni intervened. "Blackmail, wasn't it?"

Torrent nodded and sipped thoughtfully at a cocktail which Skeets handed to him. "That's what it was. She had something on everybody—on Mrs. Sterling, whose husband had to pay for her indiscretion by buying Alicia a share of Lais; on Winogradow, about whose wife she knew, not that he gave a good goddamn about it; even, I suspect, on the Kyria herself, who was much too relieved about the death of her best client. And I suspect that she got a lot of her information in the salon through the doctor and Hortense, who were the natural confidants of the screwy dames who came here."

Toni said, "I remember how Hortense got her wind up when I suggested something of the sort. And I think that's why Dr. Berchtold was trying to date me up. He wanted to find out how much I knew. Hortense must have told him about my perfectly innocent crack."

Skeets sat down on the couch and went back to stroking Toni's feet. "I went over Alicia's column for the last year and it became sort of obvious how she worked it. For example there was an item like 'Mr. and Mrs. Astorbilt expect a blessed event.' Then there would come a correction. 'Your correspondent is all wrong. The Astorbilts do not expect any events, blessed or otherwise, particularly since Mr. A. has been off on a world cruise for the past year.' You see what happened? Miss Howe has meanwhile been paid a neat sum for changing her information, and so probably has the doctor, from whom she got it in the first place. Lovely people!"

"Anyhow," Torrent pursued, "the Howe woman got to work on Maurice. He had to pay her much more than he could afford, particularly since she knew about the Kyria's state of health from the doctor. And there was another angle. There was always the possibility that she would betray him anyhow, because with him out of the way she might wangle a share in the will for herself or for the doctor, for whom the Kyria had sort of a soft spot. So that after a while it became clear to Maurice that he just naturally had to do away with the woman.

"He had it all worked out very nicely. Winogradow's experiments with the poison gave him the idea. He swiped some ouabain and a bottle of that acne lotion and bided his time. The trouble was that the Howe woman just perversely seemed to be cured of acne for the time being until the nervous upset due to our investigation brought it back. All he could do was wait around until she began complaining of it again and then sneak in the poisoned bottle. And Alicia was getting more and more demanding and driving him nuts.

"And now we come to the day when Lili Michaud came for her day at Lais."

Torrent paused impressively and tried to outstare Tom Jones, whose fixed gaze was beginning to discomfit him. He stretched his hand out and pulled a silky ear. The gray cat's purring became an obbligato to his businesslike recital.

"One of the great mistakes I made was to think that the murder was planned and that a stage was set. The beauty of that particular murder was that it was so impromptu. When Maurice took that elevator at twelve-thirty and stalled it, he was as innocent as a babe unborn. After sitting there for what must have seemed an eternity to him, he got fidgety and decided to see if he could get out. One can get out of stalled elevators, you know, if one is agile and strong enough. There is a stool for the operator to sit on and that made it even easier for him to reach the roof. He opened the lid and lifted himself up, just as you saw him do with the scaffolding. He had taken off the artist's smock which he always wore, because it hampered his movements. He stood up on the roof of the elevator, with the elevator door to the third floor at the level of his chin. He released the bottom catch, slid the door open and hoisted himself up again. He found himself on the third floor, from which the receptionist was gone, and the L-lamp on the door of Howe's room was on. Now, he tells me, he had been trying to get hold of Howe and talk to her for some time and she had been avoiding him. So he went into the room and saw what he thought was she.

"There was no reason for him to think that it was anybody else. Nobody used this room but Howe. In front of him was a blonde with goo on her face and a large cape over the rest of her. She was obviously asleep, quite helpless and entirely at his mercy.

"And as he hesitated there, he saw that the door to the elevator was still open a crack, and that he could get back there if he wanted to. And there was nobody in the hall."

There was a brief rustle as the glowing embers scattered on the hearth, and everybody started. Torrent poked at the fire and went on talking.

"The little blighter explained it all to me. He stood at the threshold of Alicia Howe's room for ten seconds while the whole wild plan whirled through his head. Then it was like a fever coming to a boil and he grew deadly cool. He stepped into the room and hit the girl lying there, one short powerful blow across the throat with the heel of his hand. He says he felt the larynx give under his hand and then he was out of the room.

"And just then he saw the door to Mrs. Sterling's room open. He did the only thing possible. He ducked into the next room. He thought he'd die when she almost blundered into it. She went on into Howe's room and he almost died again. But she was out directly and he heard her close the door behind her and then go back to her room. The minute she was safely in her room, he moved. But even then he didn't forget to wipe his fingerprints off the doorknob. He was across the loggia in a second and had let himself down into the elevator within the next two minutes, still careful to close the elevator door and wipe off fingerprints. He replaced the lid, then he sat down on the chair, picked out the bottles he needed and worked furiously. There were smudges on his suit which he partially removed. But they could be covered by the smock which he had so providentially left behind him. Of course, the main thing was to keep his hands and face clean, and he scrubbed them with lemon verbena and then used cream to get off the traces of the rubbing. By the time the elevator was fixed he was ready to face his audience. The smell of the broken bottles covered up the fact that he himself was reeking to high heaven of all the stuff he used. And it was perfectly natural for him to throw a tantrum and go home, where he quickly got rid of the suit together with the handkerchief he used by throwing it down the incinerator."

Skeets stirred and muttered, "Gosh!" in an awed manner.

Torrent continued, "After the smoke had cleared, what did he have? He had committed a perfectly useless murder. True, it didn't look as if they would get him for it. There was absolutely nothing to connect him with Michaud and therefore no question of suspecting him. But the situation as far as Alicia Howe was concerned remained the same. He still had to get her, and that before she turned her slightly distracted attention back to him.

"This time fortune favored him. Alicia Howe's acne came back. So on Sunday he sneaked into Lais and put the poisoned lotion on her shelf of cosmetics, secure in the knowledge that she would use it. If not for you, Toni, and your inexcusable sleuthing around, he would have gotten away nicely. Everybody thought that Alicia had a bad heart except Jeanne, who always insisted that she was shamming. He was fairly sure that Dr. Berchtold would let it go by, because he wasn't any too eager to have any investigation about Alicia. And that was exactly what did happen. Of course, your running into him when he was taking the poisoned bottle away and replacing it with the harmless one fixed it.

"The rest of the story you know."

They sat in silence watching the firelight shifting redly among the shadows. Then Torrent stirred. "I've got to go now. I'd just dropped in to see how Toni was. Incidentally, you know, you'll probably have to testify."

Toni shivered a little. She could see in the fire a tiny figure of Maurice, dapper and pallid as ever, with just that dreadful backward snarl of a smile as they took him away. He looked so little somehow.

"You mustn't feel badly about it," said Torrent gently. "You aren't going to be the one to convict him. As a matter of fact he has convicted himself ten times over by now. He keeps on talking about how clever he was and he gets a great kick out of the fact that the whole country is going to know about it. Those giant headlines make him particularly happy. He says he's glad he got those two women anyhow."

"He never did like women," said Toni.

"Isn't that a bit of an understatement, dear?" asked Skeets. Toni laughed a little.

"I was thinking of something else. You know, Captain Torrent, he actually gave us a deliberate clue, which he put right under our noses. You remember the vases for his exhibit? Well, all of them showed Amazons being killed by the Greeks!"

"Nerve," said Torrent appreciatively. "Yes, he told me that for a minute today he thought you'd guessed that. You were pretty smart, he said." He looked at her with a peculiar expression in his shrewd blue eyes. "I can see that you are being bothered by his apparently being so decent to you and so reluctant to kill you. As a matter of fact, that was all hogwash, don't you know. He couldn't have killed you in the salon just then and remained undiscovered. What he hoped was that you'd pretend to humor him and stall him off, kind of. You know, pretend to fall for his offer. That would have given him a better chance to get rid of you later."

"My vanity should be hurt, I suppose," said Toni, laughing. "But I assure you, I am greatly relieved."

"You see," gibed Skeets, "you are too intelligent for your own good. Men never propose to girls like you, unless they are dopes like me." He tweaked her toe gently. Torrent cleared his throat and tactfully pretended to ignore the look of utter and humorous understanding that flashed between them.

"At least," he said, "I will no longer need to haunt beauty salons and boudoirs." Skeets grinned.

"That goes for us too, Captain. That is, I don't know about boudoirs, but we have seen the last of Lais. Toni and I have walked out of that establishment, into the dark night, hand in hand, just as we said we would."

"Yes," Toni affirmed. "It suddenly got too much. We just couldn't stick it another minute. Just as well, under the circumstances, don't you think?"

"Good," Torrent applauded heartily. "I'm glad to hear it. It always seemed sort of a wrong place for you. Well…" He shrugged into his overcoat and extended a cordial hand. "This has been a pleasant association. I hope I shall see you again. At a ballet, say?"

As the door closed behind him, Toni sighed and burrowed deeper into the cushions. The cat crept closer to her, purring loudly, and she pillowed her face on its pale fur. Her dark eyelashes made quivering, shadowy half-moons on her cheek. To Skeets she suddenly seemed to grow smaller and softer, as if all the tension had finally flowed out of her. She smiled at him sleepily.

"Darling," he breathed and moved to gather her in his arms. The purring in her vicinity stopped promptly and a low menacing growl issued from Tom Jones' furry throat. His paw semaphored threateningly.

"Bad mean-tempered cat," said Toni. "Go away." She pushed him to the floor and stretched her arms to Skeets. "He's just jealous." Her words were smothered against Skeets' shoulder and she made a funny contented half-yawning sound.

After a while Skeets said, "Jealous, eh?" His eyes met his rival's resentful yellow ones across the tangle of Toni's dark curls and he stretched a magnanimous hand toward him. Tom Jones regarded it morosely, like a Trojan eyeing gifts from Greeks, while he visibly debated the advisability of a coldly dignified exit. The embers glowed warmly and he sighed. He allowed Skeets' hand to descend gingerly on his silvery pate, then his flat mustachioed face showed an expression of pleased surprise as the latter's fingers found the right spot behind the ear, an expression that plainly said, "Maybe I've misjudged the guy after all." The next minute he was back on the couch, draped across Toni's ankles. His purring shook the couch and his eyes were narrowed benignantly.

Tom Jones was nothing if not a realist.

THE END

Toni Ney's second and final case, *Corpse de Ballet*
(0-915230-67-4, $14.95) is also available.

Notes on Dell's unacknowledged abridgement

Painted for the Kill was first published in 1943 in hardcover by Duell, Sloan & Pearce. Dell issued a paperback edition of it a year or so later in its famous and very collectible Mapback series. Each book contained a diagram or map on the back cover. The back of *Painted for the Kill* showed the layout of each floor of The House of Lais.

Although a notice in the front of the book states that this edition was produced under wartime conditions, it does not mention that the book was severely abridged. Perhaps as many as 10,000 to 15,000 words were cut to make the book conform to the 240-page format used by Dell for other books in this series. So far we have not run across another Dell Mapback that was abridged.

Often the cuts only involve removing an adjective or an adverb. Sometimes a phrase or a whole sentence is left out. To show how these cuts were made we've put the excised words in italics.

The cuts begin with the opening paragraph. The hardcover (and this reprint) begins: "How about lunch with me? *After all, you've just had breakfast with me.* After a girl has had breakfast with a man, *it's more or less indicated that* she should have lunch with him."

Sometimes the changes are very slight, the kind of routine deletions any copyeditor might make to speed the action of the narrative along, as in the following passage: Hortense, a facial operator from the third floor, poked her thin, foxlike face around the door. "May I come in?" She whisked in without waiting for permission. Her sharp eyes darted around the room and she grinned. "Ah, I see. You have taken the map down. Listen, I'm going to smoke *a cigarette. I need one.*" She sat down and lit a cigarette swiftly. "You won't squawk *on me*, will you, Toni? I know you aren't the sort." Or: Her first acquaintance with Skeets was during one of her demonstrations *for the clients* when he had taken the place of Illona.

Some changes are a bit more drastic: In a very short time she had sampled all that the second floor had to offer. A streamlined naiad, she lolled coyly in a bubble bath blowing iridescent bubbles at the delighted

188

photographers who invaded the sacred confines of the baigne. She posed in the sunroom lying on her stomach in a sand bed, clad chiefly in sun glasses, with a towel flung carelessly over her pretty rump. *This was after a brief discussion about the exact amount of bosom to be exhibited. Mlle. Michaud was fairly generous about this but willing to listen to advice, as she didn't know how much breast it was permissible to show in the United States.* After the photographers withdrew reluctantly, she sprang up to put on her robe, which her young man with the eyelashes (addressed as Henri) had whipped out of a dressing case he carried around.

Or: The *enormity of the* catastrophe was brought home to the employees when they were dismissed an hour earlier than usual. Making a day at Lais shorter was a phenomenon comparable to Joshua's stopping the sun *in heaven. It could only come as a result of flood, fire, or similar act of God.* So they filed out with many a grateful and awe-stricken glance at the blue uniforms posted in strategic places.

Sometimes the changes don't alter the length of the sentence but reflect the copy editor's theories on grammar and word usage. In the hardcover edition a passage reads: there was a naive helplessness about the little Viennese that aroused <u>a feeling of maternal protectiveness</u> in Toni. The paperback copy editor obviously thought one modifier needed to be put elsewhere: there was a naive helplessness about the little Viennese that aroused <u>a maternal feeling of protectiveness</u> in Toni.

The hundreds of little and not so little changes made in the Dell edition don't affect the outcome of the story but they do take something away from the flavor of the book. The version you hold in your hands now retains every word found in the original edition. We did, however, change the author's punctuation. Lucy Cores was apparently as fond of colons as a proctologist, often using two in one sentence. We also added one word, putting "German" before "invasion." When *Painted for the Kill* was published in 1943, people quite naturally thought of the German invasion of France in 1939 as *the* invasion. The events on June 6, 1944, would, of course, alter forever change our opinion as to what constitutes *the* invasion..

About The Rue Morgue Press

The Rue Morgue vintage mystery line is designed to bring back into print those books that were favorites of readers between the turn of the century and the 1960s. The editors welcome suggests for reprints. To receive our catalog or make suggestions, write The Rue Morgue Press, P.O. Box 4119, Boulder, Colorado (1-800-699-6214).

Catalog of Rue Morgue Press titles as of April 2004

Titles are listed by author. All books are quality trade paperbacks measuring 6 by 9 inches, usually with full-color covers and printed on paper designed not to yellow or deteriorate. These are permanent books.

Joanna Cannan. This English writer's books are among our most popular titles. Modern reviewers have compared them favorably with the best books of the Golden Age of detective fiction. "Worthy of being discussed in the same breath with an Agatha Christie or a Josephine Tey."—Sally Fellows, *Mystery News*. Set in the late 1930s in a village that was a fictionalized version of Oxfordshire, both titles feature young Scotland Yard inspector Guy Northeast. *They Rang Up the Police* (0-915230-27-5, $14.00) and *Death at The Dog* (0-915230-23-2, $14.00).

Glyn Carr. The 15 books featuring Shakespearean actor Abercrombie "Filthy" Lewker are set on peaks scattered around the globe, although the author returned again and again to his favorite climbs in Wales, where his first mystery, published in 1951, *Death on Milestone Buttress* (0-915230-29-1, $14.00), is set.

Torrey Chanslor. Sixty-five-year-old Amanda Beagle employs good old East Biddicut common sense to run the agency, while her younger sister Lutie prowls the streets and nightclubs of 1940 Manhattan looking for clues. The two inherited the Beagle Private Detective Agency from their older brother, but you'd never know the sisters had spent all of their lives knitting and tending to their garden in a small, sleepy upstate New York town. *Our First Murder* (0-915230-50-X, $14.95) and *Our Second Murder* (0-915230-64-X, $14.95) are charming hybrids of the private eye, traditional, and cozy mystery, published in 1940 and 1941 respectively.

Clyde B. Clason. *The Man from Tibet* (0-915230-17-8, $14.00) is one of his best (selected in 2001 in *The History of Mystery* as one of the 25 great amateur detective novels of all time) and highly recommended by the dean of locked room mystery scholars, Robert Adey, as "highly original." It's also one of the first novels to make use of Tibetan culture. *Murder Gone Minoan* (0-915230-60-7, $14.95) is set on a channel island off the California coast where a Greek department store magnate has recreated a Minoan palace.

Joan Coggin. Meet Lady Lupin Lorrimer Hastings, the young, lovely, scatter-brained and kindhearted daughter of an earl, now the newlywed wife of the vicar of St. Marks Parish in Glanville, Sussex. You might not understand her logic but she always gets her man. *Who Killed the Curate?* (0-915230-44-5, $14.00), *The Mystery at Orchard House* (0-915230-54-2, $14.95), *Penelope Passes or Why Did She Die?* (0-915230-61-5, $14.95), and *Dancing with Death* (0-915230-62-3, $14.95).

Manning Coles. The two English writers who collaborated as Coles are best known for those witty spy novels featuring Tommy Hambledon, but they also wrote four delightful—and funny—ghost novels. *The Far Traveller* (0-915230-35-6, $14.00) , *Brief Candles* (0-915230-24-0, 156 pages, $14.00), *Happy Returns* (0-915230-31-3, $14.00) and *Come and Go* (0-915230-34-8, $14.00).

Norbert Davis. There have been a lot of dogs in mystery fiction, from Baynard Kendrick's guide dog to Virginia Lanier's bloodhounds, but there's never been one quite like Carstairs. Doan, a short, chubby Los Angeles private eye, won Carstairs in a crap game, but there never is any question as to who the boss is in this relationship. *The Mouse in the Mountain* (0-915230-41-0, $14.00), was first published in 1943 and followed by two other Doan and Carstairs novels, *Sally's in the Alley* (0-915230-46-1, $14.00), and *Oh, Murderer Mine* (0-915230-57-7, $14.00).

Elizabeth Dean. In Emma Marsh Dean created one of the first independent female sleuths in the genre. Written in the screwball style of the 1930s, *Murder is a Serious Business* (0-915230-28-3, $14.95), is set in a Boston antique store just as the Great Depression is drawing to a close. *Murder a Mile High* (0-915230-39-9, $14.00) moves to the Central City Opera House in the Colorado mountains.

Constance & Gwenyth Little. These two Australian-born sisters from New Jersey have developed almost a cult following among mystery readers. Each book, published between 1938 and 1953, was a stand-alone. The Rue Morgue Press intends to reprint all of their books. Currently available are: *The Black Thumb* (0-915230-48-8, $14.00), *The Black Coat* (0-915230-40-2, $14.00), *Black Corridors* (0-915230-33-X, $14.00), *The Black Gloves* (0-915230-20-8, $14.00), *Black-Headed Pins* (0-915230-25-9, $14.00), *The Black Honeymoon* (0-915230-21-6, $14.00), *The Black Paw* (0-915230-37-2, $14.00), *The Black Stocking* (0-915230-30-5, $14.00), *Great Black Kanba* (0-915230-22-4, $14.00), *The Grey Mist Murders* (0-915230-26-7, $14.00), *The Black Eye* (0-915230-45-3, $14.00), *The Black Shrouds* (0-915230-52-6, $14.00), *The Black Rustle* (0-915230-58-5, $14.00), *The Black Goatee* (0-915230-63-1, $14.00), and *The Black Piano* (0-915230-65-8).

Marlys Millhiser. Our only non-vintage mystery, *The Mirror* (0-915230-15-1, $17.95) is our all-time bestselling book, now in a seventh printing. How could you not be intrigued by a novel in which "you find the main character marrying her own grandfather and giving birth to her own mother."

James Norman. The marvelously titled *Murder, Chop Chop* (0-915230-16-X,

$13.00) is a wonderful example of the eccentric detective novel. Meet Gimiendo Hernandez Quinto, a gigantic Mexican who once rode with Pancho Villa and who now trains *guerrilleros* for the Nationalist Chinese government when he isn't solving murders. At his side is a beautiful Eurasian known as Mountain of Virtue, a woman as dangerous to men as she is irresistible. First published in 1942.

Sheila Pim. *Ellery Queen's Mystery Magazine* said of these wonderful Irish village mysteries that Pim "depicts with style and humor everyday life." *Booklist* said they were in "the best tradition of Agatha Christie." Beekeeper Edward Gildea uses his knowledge of bees and plants to good use in *A Hive of Suspects* (0-915230-38-0, $14.00). *Creeping Venom* (0-915230-42-9, $14.00) blends politics, gardening and religion into a deadly mixture. *A Brush with Death* (0-915230-49-6, $14.00) grafts a clever art scam onto the stem of a gardening mystery.

Craig Rice. *Home Sweet Homicide* (0-915230-53-4, $14.95) is a marvelously funny and utterly charming tale (set in 1942 and first published in 1944) of three children who "help" their widowed mystery writer mother solve a real-life murder and nab a handsome cop boyfriend along the way. It made just about every list of the best mysteries for the first half of the 20th century, including the Haycraft-Queen Cornerstone list.

Charlotte Murray Russell. Spinster sleuth Jane Amanda Edwards tangles with a murderer and Nazi spies in *The Message of the Mute Dog* (0-915230-43-7, $14.00), a culinary cozy set just before Pearl Harbor. "Perhaps the mother of today's cozy."—*The Mystery Reader*.

Sarsfield, Maureen. These two mysteries featuring Inspector Lane Parry of Scotland Yard are among our most popular books. Both are set in Sussex. *Murder at Shots Hall* (0-915230-55-8, $14.95) features Flikka Ashley, a thirtyish sculptor with a past she would prefer remain hidden. It was originally published as *Green December Fills the Graveyard* in 1945. Parry is back in Sussex, trapped by a blizzard at a country hotel where a war hero has been pushed out of a window to his death, in *Murder at Beechlands* (0-915230-56-9, $14.95). First published in 1948 in England as *A Party for None* and in the U.S. as *A Party for Lawty*.

Juanita Sheridan. Sheridan's books feature a young Chinese American sleuth Lily Wu and her Watson, Janice Cameron, a first-time novelist. The first book (*The Chinese Chop* (0-915230-32-1, 155 pages, $14.00) is set in Greenwich Village but the other three are set in Hawaii in the years immediately after World War II: *The Kahuna Killer* (0-915230-47-X, $14.00), *The Mamo Murders* (0-915230-51-8, $14.00), and *The Waikiki Widow* (0-915230-59-3, $14.00) .